EPISODES I–V

STAR VOYAGERS

ADVENTURES OF THE
SS STARGAZER

JONBLAIR

Edited by Kristen Corrects, Inc.
Cover art design by Shutterstock.com
Typesetting by Kingsman Editing Services

ISBN: 979-8-9895376-1-7 (paperback)
ISBN: 979-8-9895376-4-8 (e-book)

Fiction>Science Fiction>Action & Adventure
Fiction>Science Fiction>Alien Contact

First edition published 2024

CONTENTS

Stargazer Specifications

Commissioned in 2090, *SS Stargazer* (NC-X1) is a Galactic Fleet class 1 battle cruiser which has been fitted with a fusion drive propulsion system for interplanetary/interstellar travel. Additionally, impulse engines and thrusters are used for sub-light speed, battle, maneuvering, orbital insertion, resupply, and docking, respectively. The *Stargazer* can land on a planet where conditions meet requirements for a safe landing. Warp engine research is in its infancy and is expected to continue over several decades.

Current missions are designed for discovery and exploration of celestial bodies and other life forms by means of developing and expanding technology, and are limited to two years for the safety and morale of crew members along with maintenance requirements longer voyages would impose.

The *Stargazer* can maintain orbit and ferry its one shuttle to a planet's surface and back. The shuttle is equipped with a two-person mini-rover as well as an array of scientific equipment to facilitate research and specimen collection. Maximum shuttle capacity is eight crew members. The *Stargazer* has a larger, pressurized all-terrain rover that can cover greater distances with a maximum capacity of eight and can be rolled out and used only when the *Stargazer* sets down on a planetary surface. Transporter research and development is in its infancy and is expected to continue over several decades.

Tactical systems consist of directed energy laser cannons and torpedoes with a maximum range of fifty thousand kilometers, adjustable in power increments to disable or blast apart targets in space or on a planet's surface. Phaser/photon research and development is in its infancy and is expected to continue over several decades. All Galactic-class starships are fitted with a rudimentary cloaking system linked to the fusion reactor drive. This cloaking device exhorts an enormous energy drain on the starship's reactor and is only capable of concealing the ship for limited periods. Protective energy shield research and development is in its infancy and is expected to continue over several decades.

All Galactic-class starships are designed with comfortable crew quarters, a galley for meals, medical department, administrative offices, recreational facilities, entertainment lounge, gym and spa, ship's stores, hair salons, shuttle, and cargo bay.

Galactic Fleet Historical File:

Foxwell, Jon L.

Mid-level Biography

Rank: Captain
Current Assignment: Commanding Officer
Full Name: Jon Leonidas Foxwell
Date of Birth: July 20, 2059
Place of Birth: Tecumseh, Nebraska, Earth
Ancestry: Lineage traced back to 18th-century Cape Verde
Education: Galactic Fleet Academy, 2076–2080
Marital Status: Single

Galactic Fleet Career Summary:

2080 – First-year academy graduate with the rank of ensign, assigned to *SS Explorer*.

2085 – Promoted to lieutenant and transferred to *SS Constellation* as engineering officer, distinguished by saving the ship from an energy fusion anomaly that left Foxwell with serious internal injuries.

2089 – Promoted to lieutenant commander and assigned to *SS Centurion* as weapons officer; developed a reputation as an independent, take-charge leader during enemy engagements in space or on a planet's surface.

2095 – Promoted to commander and assigned to *SS Parthia* as first officer; took command when Captain Miles Everett was killed during the battle of Alpha Centauri B when, without provocation, certain rogue elements of the Alpha Centauri high command initiated an attack on the *Parthia*.

Commander Foxwell assumed immediate command and ordered a counterattack, destroying two of their attack warbirds in what was later recognized as an innovative counteroffensive strategy.

2096 – Promoted to captain and assigned to *SS Stargazer* as commanding officer.

Foxwell was thirty-seven at the time of his promotion to captain of the *Stargazer*. His career and new command are reflected in his fitness reports and the many awards and accommodations earned during his career with Galactic Fleet, culminating with his assignment to the battle cruiser.

On a personal level, he enjoys the emotional and physical intimacy of a woman, but never forms a lasting relationship as a result of dedication to his career. He understands friendships and intimate relationships occasionally occur among crew members, particularly during long voyages, but Foxwell is resolute never to cross that line with any member of the crew. For Foxwell personally and professionally, he believes it to be improper fraternization, detrimental to good order, morale, and discipline.

Galactic Fleet Historical File:

Beta

Mid-level Biography

Rank: Commander
Current Assignment: First Officer/Science Officer
Birth Name: Ghislaine Vangelos
Date of Birth: April 8, 2063
Place of Birth: Marseille, France
Ancestry: Lineage traced to 18th-century France
Education: Galactic Fleet Academy, 2081–2085
Marital Status: Single

Galactic Fleet Career Summary:

2085 – First-year academy graduate with the rank of ensign, assigned to Galactic Fleet Shuttle Command Center in Houston, Texas.

2087 – Promoted to lieutenant and reassigned to *SS Apollo* as engineering officer.

2092 – Promoted to lieutenant commander and transferred to *SS Orion* as weapons officer; distinguished by use of "superior reasoning" counteroffensive tactics during the battle of the Epsilon Eridani star system in which cloaked Eridani "warbirds" initiated a surprise attack on the *Orion* and *Perseus*.

2096 – Promoted to commander and assigned to *SS Stargazer* as first officer/science officer.

Beta was thirty-three at the time of her promotion to first officer/ science officer of the *SS Stargazer*. Her career and current assignment is reflected in the many awards and accommodations earned during her tenure with Galactic Fleet, culminating with assignment to the battle cruiser. Ensign Vangelos was critically injured during her first assignment with Shuttle Fleet Command when a refitted shuttle she was piloting lost power and crashed just after liftoff. She sustained severe head and limb injuries and was taken directly into surgery. Damage to her brain's frontal lobe and limbic system rendered her incapable of reasoning and emotions. The damaged half was replaced with a beta neutronic labyrinth emulator model AI with advanced state-of-the-art reasoning circuitry. She was subsequently fitted with bionic arms and legs which has endowed her with incredible physical strength. The name "Beta" was assigned with her approval to confirm her uniqueness as the only "cyborg" in Galactic Fleet with "superior reasoning" capability. Although her relationship with Captain Foxwell is relatively new, she is fiercely loyal to him and the mission of the *Stargazer*.

Galactic Fleet Historical File:

O'Donovan, Peter M.

Mid-level Biography

Rank: Lieutenant Commander
Current Assignment: Chief Engineering Officer
Full Name: Peter Malcolm O'Donovan
Date of Birth: February 16, 2054
Place of Birth: Killarney, Ireland
Ancestry: Back to 16th-century Ireland
Education: Galactic Fleet Academy, 2072–2076
Marital Status: Single

Galactic Fleet Career Summary:

2076 – First-year academy graduate with the rank of ensign, assigned to Galactic Fusion Propulsion School, Glasgow, Scotland.

2078 – Promoted to Lieutenant Junior Grade and assigned to *SS Essex* as assistant engineering division officer.

2086 – Promoted to lieutenant and reassigned to Galactic Fusion Propulsion School in Glasgow, Scotland as an instructor. Promoted to lieutenant commander and named chief instructor.

2092 – Refused promotion to commander to accept position as chief engineer of the newly commissioned *SS Stargazer* under the starship's first commanding officer, Captain William J. Hunter. Commended and decorated for successfully training the *Stargazer*'s pre-commissioning crew and supervising the numerous civilian engineers, designers, and technicians during the *Stargazer's* month-long "shakedown cruise" and initial performance trials.

2096 – Remained aboard as chief engineer at the request of Captain Jon L. Foxwell subsequent to Foxwell assuming command.

Lieutenant Commander Peter O'Donovan was forty-two when Captain Foxwell assumed command of the *Stargazer*. Commander O'Donovan was honored that Captain Foxwell requested he remain aboard as the chief engineer, not surprising considering the superb reputation he garnered during his twenty-year career with Galactic Fleet Command.

Loyal to his Irish ancestry, he enjoys Irish music, dancing, whiskey, and the many varieties of dark beer brewed throughout the country. "It's so thick you can chew it," he often enjoys saying in the company of crewmates and friends. He's a huge fan of Irish sports, his favorites being Gaelic football, hurling, handball, and rounders. He enjoys Irish folklore, music, and literature, and is a collector of many Irish relics, some of which he displays in his stateroom.

Although never married, he became involved with a civilian employee of Galactic Fleet Command while previously an instructor, but it fizzled out after his transfer to the *Stargazer*. Captain Foxwell oftentimes addresses his chief engineer by the nickname, "POD."

Galactic Fleet Historical File:

Warwick, James M.
Mid-level Biography

Rank: Lieutenant
Current Assignment: Weapons Officer/Chief Security Officer
Full Name: James Michael Warwick
Date of Birth: July 4, 2068
Place of Birth: Birmingham, United Kingdom
Ancestry: Anglo-Saxon and Danish origin.
Education: Galactic Fleet Academy, 2086–2092
Marital Status: Single

Galactic Fleet Career Summary:

2092 – First-year academy graduate with the rank of ensign, assigned to Galactic Fleet Tactical Weapons Electronics School in Sheffield, United Kingdom.

2094 – Promoted to lieutenant junior grade and assigned to *SS Reprisal* as assistant tactical/security officer.

2096 – Promoted to lieutenant and transferred to *SS Stargazer* as weapons and chief security officer.

Lieutenant Warwick reported aboard *SS Stargazer* subsequent to reassignment of the previous weapons officer, the result of normal career rotation. Warwick easily breezed through two years of advanced weapons electronics school, following the military footsteps of his family on his father's side, all career pilots and bombardiers dating back to the Royal Flying Corps and later the Royal Air Force. As a youngster, and later a teenager, he was always tinkering with "electronic and robotic projects" of some fashion in his parents' garage, designing and building power cells, battery- and solar-propelled miniature flying cars, model-size cyborgs and robots, and a prototype low-power handheld "phaser." He is a rabid "football" fan of the Sheffield "Wednesday" Football (soccer) Club based in Dronfield, Derbyshire. Lieutenant Warwick enjoys viewing current or recorded matches streamed in on his viewer in his stateroom or the crews' lounge when off duty, inviting others to join him whenever possible.

Warwick is gregarious and a known charmer; he occasionally enjoys romantic relationships, but his *over exuberance* has landed him in hot water on more than one occasion. Captain Foxwell approved and implemented Warwick's recommendation for the use of "CONDITION RED" as more appropriate terminology in lieu of "battle stations."

Galactic Fleet Historical File:

Rivera, Jorge M.
Mid-level Biography

Rank: Lieutenant
Current Assignment: Chief Medical Officer, *SS Stargazer*
Full Name: Jorge Manuel Rivera
Date of Birth: October 16, 2062
Place of Birth: Mexico City, Mexico
Ancestry: Traced back to 16th-century Spain
Education: Galactic Fleet Academy & School of Medicine, 2080–2088
Interned: Galactic Fleet Medical Center San Francisco and Stockholm, Sweden
Marital Status: Single

Galactic Fleet Career Summary:

2090 – Promoted to ensign and assigned to Flagship *SS Galactica* as assistant chief medical officer.

2093 – Promoted to lieutenant junior grade and transferred to *SS Conquistador* as assistant surgical officer.

2096 – Promoted to lieutenant and reassigned to *SS Stargazer* as chief medical officer.

Lieutenant Rivera was twenty-eight when assigned to the newly commissioned *SS Stargazer* as chief medical officer. Lieutenant Rivera distinguished himself as an excellent physician and trauma surgeon, helping create new emergency triage protocols during his service aboard the *SS Conquistador*. The battle cruiser sustained serious damage and multiple casualties during a supply replenishment operation alongside a Galactic Fleet freighter after the docking clamps failed, resulting in explosive decompression. Lieutenant Rivera is credited with not losing a single patient during that serious incident. He is a dedicated physician and career Galactic Fleet medical officer. He's known to be amiable, well liked, and respected by the ship's crew. He does not believe in specific "medical hours" but has an open-door policy of encouraging all crew members to contact him should they have any questions or concerns, and to seek his immediate help should they become injured or ill.

Lieutenant Rivera is very close to his immediate and extended family in Mexico City, and has many friends in San Francisco and Stockholm, a result of his time in both cities before assignment to the fleet.

Galactic Fleet Historical File:

Xuriya, Lovisa
Mid-level Biography

Rank: Lieutenant
Current Assignment: Chief Communications Officer
Full Name: Lovisa Xuriya
Date of Birth: February 14, 2061
Place of Birth: Helsinborg, Sweden
Ancestry: Dates back to 18th-century Sweden
Education: Galactic Fleet Academy 2079–2083
Marital Status: Single

Galactic Fleet Career Summary:

2083 – First-year academy graduate with the rank of ensign, assigned to *SS Rimkus* as a junior communications officer.

2087 – Promoted to lieutenant junior grade and reassigned to *SS Tribune* as assistant communications officer.

2091 – Promoted to lieutenant and transferred to the Galactic Fleet Academy in San Francisco as a starship communications instructor.

2096 – Reassigned to *SS Stargazer* as chief communications officer.

Xuriya was thirty-five at the time of her transfer to the *SS Stargazer* as chief communications officer. Her story begins as she finishes her second year at Galactic Fleet Academy, where she meets future Captain Jon Foxwell shortly before his graduation. Senior Cadet Foxwell asks her to his pre-graduating class prom as his date where they begin a short courtship before he graduates and is assigned to his first starship, *SS Explorer*.

Over the years, both focused on their careers as she attempts to suppress her memories and feelings toward Cadet Foxwell, whom she had fallen in love with during their brief relationship. She didn't blame him for his career ambitions, but her feelings were reignited when, years later, he personally recommended her very qualified younger brother for an appointment to the academy. Xuriya subsequently turned down a promotion to lieutenant commander for the opportunity to be assigned to the *SS Stargazer* as the chief communications officer, with the trepidatious approval of Captain Foxwell.

Episode I

Target Earth

Prologue

Welcome to my new series *Star Voyagers*, a story of space exploration and adventure. Please read the introduction to the story's main characters, beginning with the *SS Stargazer* as you journey faster than light speed on its most critical mission: the salvation of planet Earth from ruthless extraterrestrial warriors bent on conquest and enslavement of the human race.

PART I

Stardate: Sept. 01, 2096

Commander Beta sensed Captain Foxwell and his surveillance party were anxious to begin exploration of planet Vorcia, the only class M and previously thought uninhabited planet of the Vorcian star system. Following a successful landing the previous day aboard their starship, the *SS Stargazer*'s First Officer and Science Officer Beta informed the captain that atmospheric conditions were suitable for human life. Strangely beautiful, non-familiar vegetation and plant life were visible on the surface from the *Stargazer*'s observation panes. Spacesuits would not be necessary outside the ship, and the surveying party—fusion laser pistols holstered to their service belts and led by their new captain—were soon surveying the landscape and thick vegetation.

"Down! Get down!" Foxwell shouted in a whisper as he motioned for the trail of crewmembers behind him to drop. Beta fell to one knee, the others immediately following suit. The captain's expression was cool, almost impassive while he visually scanned a metropolis of gargantuan and futuristic design as far as the eye could see.

"Hand me the vortex field viewer," Foxwell ordered,

extending his arm to receive the 3D laser telescope carried by a member of the surveying party. *Odd, very odd*, he thought to himself as the viewer automatically adjusted the zoom and focus for optimal viewing. Buildings, infrastructure, industry all appeared intact, with no humanoid, other mortal, or mechanical movement of any kind. Captain Foxwell handed the binary telescope to Beta. She raised the viewer to her eyes, beginning a sweeping view of the enormous city below the elevated mountain ridge where the surveying party waited for their commanding officer's next order, their presence shielded by the heavy vegetation.

"It's enormous, Captain. More like a conurbation. Even with the viewer I can't see it all, nor do I see any evidence of activity, as if the entire region has been abandoned," she reported.

"My thoughts exactly," Foxwell replied. "Let's get back to the *Stargazer*. I want a new reconnaissance team comprised of you, myself, and five security officers as well as a driver. Prepare the larger rover and supplies for a possible twenty-four-hour excursion into that metropolis . . . or whatever it is. Let's find out what's going on down there."

"Acknowledged, Captain," Beta replied.

Several hours later, a reconnaissance team to include the rover's driver/navigator, Ensign Roberts, was slowly making its way down a rocky, fifteen-degree pitted slope from the elevated vegetative terrain.

"Distance to the outskirts of the city, Ensign?" Foxwell inquired.

"Approximately thirty kilometers, sir."

"Time to get there?" the captain continued.

"Taking into consideration we don't stop or reduce our current speed, time of arrival to the mountain's base and level ground is approximately three hours, forty-three minutes."

"Captain, recommend we stop prior to arrival at the city's outskirts," Beta quietly interjected. "We can undertake further reconnaissance and allow for a short break before continuing into the city."

Foxwell slowly nodded in agreement. "Have one of the security officers relieve Roberts at the fifteen-kilometer mark; everyone else get some rest until we reach our stopping point," the captain ordered.

"Acknowledged," Beta replied.

Three and a half hours later the rover stopped approximately one hundred yards shy of the mountain's downward slope, which had incrementally leveled to less than five degrees.

"Captain, we're just short of a football field from the end of the tree line," the relief driver reported.

"Recommend we initiate a brief area reconnaissance before revealing ourselves and continuing into the city," Beta repeated.

"Agreed," Foxwell replied. He now directed his remarks to all members of the reconnaissance party. "Ensign Roberts will remain with the rover along with a security officer. The remaining crew will divide into two teams to scout the immediate area around our current position; we're attempting to determine if there's any evidence of activity before breaching the tree line and heading into open terrain leading to the city. Any questions?"

There was no response.

"All right," the captain continued. "Two security personnel will accompany Beta and conduct a sweep approximately one hundred yards left of our current position; the other two security officers will accompany me to sweep the right quadrant. Everyone, check your laser pistols and communicators. We'll meet back here in fifteen minutes. Let's roll."

Ensign Roberts and security officer Sarah Lindsey waited uneasily inside the rover for word or return of the reconnaissance party. They didn't know each other well, occasionally catching a glimpse of one another in the corridors of the *Stargazer* during official duty or personal time. Silence permeated the inside of the vehicle as they both impatiently glanced through the thick windowpanes for any sign of the scouting crew members. Roberts decided to break the tension with a little humor, fidgeting nervously as he finally asked, "Hey, uh, have you heard the latest space joke?"

"No, can't say I have," Lindsey replied in a perfunctory tone, continuing to focus on the status of the reconnaissance personnel, occasionally scanning the terrain through the vortex field viewer.

Roberts hesitated for a moment, then decided to tell the joke. "Two astronauts were in a spaceship circling high above the earth. One had to go on a spacewalk while the other stayed inside. When the space walker tried to get back inside the spaceship, he discovered the cabin door was locked, so he knocked. There was no answer. He knocked again, louder this time. There was still no answer. Finally, he hammered at the door as hard as he could and heard a voice from inside the spaceship asking, 'Who's there?'"

Security Officer Lindsey turned around slowly, staring at Ensign Roberts before rolling her eyes and replying dismissively, "Oh puh-leeze." She shook her head and turned back in the direction of the windowpane. The embarrassed young ensign now wished he had kept his mouth shut.

Fifteen minutes later, both groups returned to the rover with no evidence of activity or unusual sightings. After reboarding, they continued onward into the open terrain, the ground underneath the rover now level.

"Distance to the city?" Foxwell asked.

"Just over three kilometers per the range finder—smooth terrain ahead," Roberts replied.

"Ensign, set the scanner for evidence of movement or activity; increase the rover's speed and prepare to stop on my order," Foxwell directed.

"Aye, sir."

Five minutes later, the rover entered the city. A series of linked streets contrasted with the gold-colored, smooth metallic surfaces of structures resembling buildings that enveloped the *Stargazer*'s crew and vehicle. Unfamiliar writing and symbols were visible on most of the structures as the rover passed one configuration after another.

"Captain, scanner readings indicate no movement, no evidence of humanoid or alien life forms," Beta reported.

"Stop the rover," the captain ordered.

"Aye, sir," Ensign Roberts responded, bringing the vehicle to a stop.

"Ensign, you and Lindsey will again remain here with the rover; everybody else outside. Same three-party teams as before, armed with laser rifles. Select three structures—use the rifles to cut openings if there are no visible means of entry; let's see if we can figure out what's going on. We'll meet back at the rover no later than 1800 hours."

Foxwell and two security officers walked one side of the street, Beta and her two officers patrolling the opposite side, both parties selecting three structures at random. Using their laser rifles, they cut through what was thought to be possible access points. After each entry, a luminescent array of rectangular holographic screens presented themselves within twenty-five feet of entry, levitated vertically approximately ten feet and tilted forward fifteen degrees as they slowly rotated, depicting what appeared to be the same celestial display with indecipherable writing and symbols running along the bottom. Scanner recordings were taken of each screen. Both parties completed their sweeps and returned to the rover to begin the journey back to the *Stargazer*.

"Any idea what those displays are?" Foxwell inquired, directing the question to Beta.

"Working on it, Captain. All screens depict the same image; they appear to be a map—interstellar of some kind," Beta replied. She focused on the scanner's playback of the displays, reviewing the star map and using the scanner's database to assist in deciphering the unfamiliar language.

Moments before the rover returned to the ship, Captain Foxwell received a signal from the *Stargazer*'s communications officer.

"Foxwell here."

"Captain, you have a priority-one message from Galactic Fleet Command."

"Put it on speaker."

"This is Admiral Perry, Galactic Fleet Command. Earth is under attack from intergalactic vessels and beings of unknown origin; planetary damage and casualties extensive. Global defenses have been insufficient to repel invaders. All fleet combat vessels are to cease and desist current operations and set a course for immediate return to Earth. Maintain open communications on secure channels for updates and briefings regarding Galactic Fleet and starship offensive strategies—end of message."

The crew was stunned into silence by the content of the report. Before the captain had a chance to respond to their overwhelming shock, Beta turned quickly toward Foxwell.

"Captain, I've completed my analysis of the data

collected from the Vorcian displays," she said hurriedly.

"What is it?" Foxwell asked, the tension now palpable.

She turned her head in Foxwell's direction. "It's a map, Captain, with an invasion plan. Target is . . . EARTH."

PART II

Stardate: Sept. 02, 2096

Captain Foxwell and Beta exited the turbo lift after reaching the bridge. The senior conning officer vacated the captain's chair and confirmed successful liftoff into orbit around Vorcia as Foxwell prepared to issue new mission orders. Beta took her station at the science console and began an immediate search for all data regarding the Vorcians, particularly that of their military vessels and weapons capabilities.

"Navigator, set a course for return to Earth."

"Acknowledged, Captain; new heading 265 mark 20, entered and ready to execute."

"Helmsman, prepare to take us out of orbit; enable fusion drive."

"Understood, Captain. Impulse engines disengaged, fusion drive enabled; awaiting order to engage."

"Engage fusion drive—ahead light factor 9," Foxwell ordered.

"Aye, Captain, light factor 9," the helmsman acknowledged. With an almost imperceptible nudge, the *Stargazer* confirmed immediate acceleration to greater-than-light speed. The main viewing screen and observation panes captured entire star systems streaking by in the blink of an eye.

"Navigator, what is our estimated time of arrival to Earth?"

"Three days, eight hours, Captain."

"Helmsman, increase speed to light factor 9.5."

"Aye, sir, light factor 9.5."

"Captain, the chief engineer is hailing you," Communications Officer Xuriya announced.

"POD! How's the temperature down there?" Foxwell asked.

"A rhetorical question, Captain. Can I trouble you to pay a visit?" Chief Engineer Peter O'Donovan requested, a hint of frustration obvious by his heightened Irish accent.

"On my way. Beta, you have the conn," Foxwell directed, exiting the captain's chair and walking toward the turbo lift before uttering voice command: "Engineering."

"Navigator, recalculate time of arrival to Earth," Beta ordered as she assumed command of the bridge.

"One day, six hours, Commander," the navigator replied.

Beta relayed the new arrival time to the captain. "Maintain current course, steady as she goes," Beta said, returning to her science station and continuing her database scan regarding the Vorcians.

"Aye, Commander," the helmsman and navigator replied in unison.

* * *

"What's up, POD?" Foxwell asked after arriving in engineering.

O'Donovan hovered over a control panel with the

assistant chief engineer, an expression of concern embedded on his face. "Captain, just thought you might be interested to know the plasma diffuser temperatures are rising. Anything over light factor 9.5 and we risk a possible catastrophic heat transfer to conduits that feed directly into the rilidium reactor circuitry."

Foxwell needed no further explanation; he knew the risks involved by pushing the fusion drives to their limits.

"Thanks, Chief. I understand what you're telling me, but understand this as well: We're dealing with malevolent beings we know little about. As I explained to the crew via shipboard announcement after returning from the reconnaissance mission, Earth is currently under attack by the Vorcians; the news so far is not good. The additional half light factor will get us there in a little over twenty-four hours. Beta is researching and creating a profile regarding this advanced and apparently hostile species. She will brief senior officers shortly. I expect you there."

"Aye, sir, understood," the chief engineer acknowledged, his Irish accent accentuated by a crisp reply. A cheeky grin now replaced his previous expression of doubt as he added, "You know I love the *Stargazer*, Captain. She's giving all she can give, but I'm sure if I treat her real nice, I can manage to coax light factor 10 out of her . . . if you need it."

"You always do." Foxwell smiled, giving a reassuring pat on the chief engineer's shoulder.

"Captain to the bridge," Xuriya announced through the *Stargazer*'s PA system.

Foxwell walked to the nearest companel. "On my way."

* * *

The Bridge

"Status?" Foxwell asked, exiting the turbo lift.

Xuriya swiveled her chair in the direction of the captain. "Sir, you have a recorded priority-one secure message from Galactic Fleet Command."

"Transfer it to my ready room," he replied, glancing at his first officer. "Beta, please join me."

Foxwell and Beta walked to his desk, where he reached down and pressed the play button on the viewer screen.

"This is Admiral Perry, Galactic Fleet Command. Tactical situation deteriorating globally. Attacks are ongoing and relentless. Conventional weaponry including our newest directed energy weapons have been ineffective. Alien vessels are deploying energy shielding of unknown composition that is impenetrable. *SS Constellation* will execute a high-tonnage, high-yield neutron bomb attack at 1400 hours today on a fleet of Vorcian raptors spotted just outside the middle Rocky Mountains of Wyoming, Utah, and southeastern Idaho. It is theorized high-yield neutron radiation will penetrate the alien vessel energy shields and destroy said vessels and enemy combatants. Civilian populations have been evacuated. All Galactic Fleet combat vessels en route to Earth are to rendezvous on the far side of Jupiter after reaching the Orion Arm of the Milky Way Galaxy. Captain Foxwell of the *SS Stargazer* will assume overall command and await further orders subsequent to the bomb drop—end of message."

Captain Foxwell glanced at Beta. "Are you prepared to conduct your briefing regarding the Vorcians?"

"Affirmative . . . but my research has been curtailed due to limited information in the database."

"Nevertheless, schedule a meeting of department

heads from engineering, weapons, and medical to be held in my ready room in half an hour."

"Aye, Captain," Beta replied, following him out of the ready room onto the bridge.

"Navigator . . . time of arrival to planet Jupiter at light factor 10?" Foxwell inquired.

"Six hours, fifteen minutes," the navigator responded, exchanging an anxious look with the helmsman.

"Ahead light factor 10," the captain ordered.

Aye, Captain, light factor 10."

* * *

Captain's Ready Room

"I've called this meeting to bring everyone up to date regarding the situation on Earth," Captain Foxwell began. "Beta will first provide a briefing in reference to this newly encountered species, the Vorcians, their characteristics, ships, and weapons systems. Commander Beta, you have the floor."

Beta rose from her seat at the conference table as she began her briefing. "My research has revealed the Vorcians are a humanoid species characterized by prideful ruthlessness and brutality. They apparently have a genetic predisposition for hostility and an absolute distrust of anyone non-Vorcian. Their warrior ethic is generational; it's their nature to conquer and expand, to include the destruction of civilizations and worlds if it facilitates their goal of expanding a growing empire. They will fight to the death before dishonoring themselves, and they take no prisoners. Their combat vessels are equivalent to ours in terms of speed and maneuverability, with the added advantage of invisible deflector shielding for defense, and offensive disrupter weaponry which can dematerialize any matter targeted that is not protected by appropriate counter-shielding. Galactic Fleet Command has assigned a designated name: Raptor."

Captain Foxwell stood and continued the briefing. "As you're all aware, Earth is under attack by the Vorcians. Their weaponry and shielding are overwhelming Earth's defensives; we have a limited period in which to search out weaknesses in the Vorcians' capabilities and to coordinate a counteroffensive strategy with other Galactic Fleet combat battle cruisers we're scheduled to rendezvous with shortly. *SS Constellation* will soon attack a nest of Vorcian raptors with a high-yield neutron bomb in an attempt to penetrate their shields. Weapons Officer, make sure all energy weapons and laser canons are ready for combat. Medical Officer, make triage preparations in sick bay and inspect first aid stations for readiness throughout the ship. Engineer, continue to keep close tabs on the fusion drives; we're at light factor 10 now, but only until we arrive at our rendezvous point. Any offensive operations will be conducted at sub-light speed, reserving fusion light drive as a defensive strategy if needed. Any questions?"

There were no questions and the captain ended the meeting. "Report back to your departments, complete your preparations, and brief your subordinates regarding this meeting. Beta, you'll accompany me back to the—"

The captain was interrupted by the hailing sound of the ship's interior communications system.

"Captain, Xuriya here. Sir, ship's sensors have picked up two unidentified vessels traveling at sub-light speed moving perpendicular to our heading."

"Distance?"

"One hundred twenty thousand kilometers and closing."

"Go to **CONDITION RED**. On my way to the bridge."

PART III

Stardate: Sept 02, 2096

"Status," Foxwell shouted as he hurried onto the bridge. Beta exited behind him then made a beeline for her science station.

"Unidentified vessels still closing at sub-light speed," the navigator reported.

"Distance?"

"Seventy thousand kilometers, Captain," Beta replied as she viewed sensors. "Their current course will allow for intercept in six minutes."

"Helmsman, disengage fusion light drive; prepare to engage impulse engines."

"Aye, Captain, decelerating to sub-light. Impulse engines enabled; awaiting your order to engage."

"Xuriya, hail the weapons officer and instruct him to report to the bridge," Foxwell directed.

"Aye, sir."

"Helmsman, engage impulse engines, ahead one-quarter impulse power."

"Aye, Captain, one-quarter impulse power," the helmsman acknowledged.

"Navigator, enter new heading, bearing 355 mark 0.

Since they appear so eager to meet, let's accommodate them head-on," Foxwell asserted confidently.

"Aye, sir, heading 355 mark 0."

"Beta—sensor update?"

"Four minutes to intercept; vessel ID and origin still unknown, Captain."

"Captain, I have the weapons officer on the companel; he's asking to speak with you," Xuriya said.

"Put him through."

"Captain, confirming you want me to change my **CONDITION RED** station from weapons control central to the bridge?"

"That's affirmative, Lieutenant. I want you on the bridge for this one."

"Aye, sir, on my way."

"Captain, unidentified vessels have come to a dead stop; distance forty-five thousand kilometers," Beta called out, reconfirming her findings as she reviewed the scanner results a second time.

Lieutenant Warwick exited the turbo lift and immediately assumed his duties at the tactical weapons console.

"Helmsman, disengage impulse engines; engage reverse thrusters. Bring us to a dead stop," Foxwell ordered.

"Aye, Captain—all stop."

"Captain, sensors confirm unidentified vessels have not deployed shielding or charged weapons," Lieutenant Warwick announced.

"Put them on screen—extreme magnification."

Foxwell and Beta both stood, staring intensely at the magnified images of the two unidentified vessels appearing before them. Together they studied the peculiarities of the starships that now filled the main viewing screen.

"They appear familiar," Beta noted.

"Captain, we're being hailed by the lead vessel," Xuriya announced.

"On screen," Foxwell replied. The viewing screen shifted from the exterior of the unidentified ships to what now appeared to be a familiar humanoid species. "This is Captain Jon Foxwell of the *SS Stargazer* representing Galactic Fleet Command of planet Earth. Please identify yourselves and explain the reason for your intercept trajectory."

"I am Captain Sorak from the planet Vulcan," the eloquently dressed speaker answered. "Our intentions are peaceful. We are aware of the situation occurring on Earth regarding current hostilities initiated by the Vorcians. We have deliberately intercepted your vessel in order to offer assistance. As your data search will confirm, first contact between Vulcans and humans occurred in your year 2063, although we have studied and researched your planet, star system, and species beginning with the launch of Sputnik I in 1957. We are monitoring communications with our envoys on your planet and request approval to proceed alongside your ship to the rendezvous point on the far side of Jupiter."

"Standby, Captain," Foxwell answered, craning his head in the direction of his watchful communications officer, simultaneously motioning his hand to cut the viewing screen's audio. Xuriya rendered a slight nod confirming she had muted the signal.

Foxwell turned toward Beta. "We both knew moments after Sorak appeared on screen he is Vulcan. As science officer, what's your initial evaluation regarding his sincerity and offer of assistance?"

"He is correct in reference to his assertion regarding first contact," she explained. "Low level, informal meetings and discussions between Galactic Fleet Command and several other governments have continued in an effort to conclude and ratify a more formal scientific, cultural, and amicable treaty between our worlds. It would be the first in the history of our planet. Vulcan is at least a century ahead of Earth in reference to science and technology. On a personal and professional level, Vulcans are characterized by their desire to conduct themselves by suppressing emotions and substituting the discipline of logic, yet they are sometimes seen to be arrogant and cold in their dealings with humans. They're uncomfortable being untruthful. Based on my knowledge of the Vulcans, I have no reason to suspect insincerity regarding Captain Sorak's offer of assistance. It *could* be the other half of the reason for the rendezvous at Jupiter, with that information purposely withheld to further maintain security."

Foxwell smirked. "Talk about the other shoe that dropped," he mumbled to himself, shaking his head slightly.

"Say again, Captain?" Beta asked, a puzzled expression on her face.

"Never mind," Foxwell replied as he turned again in the direction of Xuriya. "Cancel CONDITION RED, re-engage audio."

"Aye, sir," Xuriya replied.

"Captain Sorak," Foxwell resumed, "my first officer and I accept your offer and invite you and your starships to accompany us to our rendezvous point with designated Galactic Fleet combat vessels."

"Estimated time of arrival is four hours, thirty minutes," the navigator chimed in.

"Very well, Captain. Our combat cruisers can easily match your light speed," Sorak responded ingenuously.

The Vulcan's unpretentious response reminded Foxwell of their technical superiority. "Uh, yeah, okay," he replied in an awkward tone.

"They employ warp drive technology, Captain," Beta clarified.

"I'm aware of that," Foxwell retorted. "I'm also aware of their history of reluctance to share their knowledge regarding our own warp drive research and development," he continued, forgetting for a moment he and Beta were still on screen with the Vulcan.

"Perhaps we can reserve that conversation for another time," the Vulcan captain suggested.

"Perhaps," Foxwell replied, a hint of uncomfortable cynicism in his voice. "Navigator, resume course for Jupiter. Helmsman, ahead, light factor 10."

"Aye, Captain," both replied.

Foxwell used the time to securely update all Galactic Fleet battle cruisers on the Vulcans' involvement as their two cruisers flanked the *Stargazer*. The Vulcans used their transporter technology to beam all Galactic Ship captains aboard their larger starship for a briefing regarding their offer of assistance.

Sorak, accompanied by several of his staff, greeted the convened Galactic Fleet officers impassively during the briefing. "As discussed with Captain Foxwell, we are aware of the attack by Vorcia on your planet. They are a savage and hostile species. We have engaged in hostilities with the Vorcians over the last several decades regarding repeated encroachments into our territory. Unfortunately, there is no formal treaty of any kind between Earth and Vulcan which would allow us to directly intervene on behalf of your planet, but to allow the Vorcians to conquer Earth while our two worlds engage in peaceful discussions would be . . . *illogical*.

"We do, however, possess the technology to neutralize their shielding. Once that is accomplished, their attack vessels will be vulnerable to your weapons. Although their weaponry is superior to yours, you still have cloaking technology which can be incorporated with tactical and operational strategies of which you and Captain Foxwell will decide. Regretfully, I must inform you I was made aware just a short time ago the neutron bomb attack against the Vorcians carried out by Earth Defense Command was unsuccessful." Captain Sorak paused briefly, scanning his audience impassively before continuing: "As they say on your planet . . . good luck." The Vulcan captain ended the briefing as stone faced as he began.

The strategic plan involved both Vulcan combat cruisers proceeding ahead of the cloaked Galactic Fleet starships. Assuming high-altitude geosynchronous orbits over Earth and out of sensor range of the Vorcians, the Vulcan cruisers would then neutralize all Vorcian attack vessel shielding followed by offensive operations initiated by Galactic Fleet battle cruisers as they de-cloaked. Captain Foxwell and *Stargazer* would then lead the attack against lower-orbiting Vorcian raptors while simultaneously notifying Galactic Fleet and Earth Defense Command the Vorcian shielding was no longer effective, allowing Earth to redirect counteroffensive operations as necessary to search out and destroy Vorcian vessels within Earth's atmosphere.

The Vulcans beamed Captain Foxwell and all senior officers back to their respective battle cruisers, but not before Captain Sorak informed Foxwell of one additional tactical advantage. "Your engineers will be provided specifications that will allow reconfiguration of the electromagnetic field of each Galactic Fleet combat vessel. This change will make it possible to alter the polarization matrix in the armored hull. Your battle cruisers will then have the ability to polarize the hull plating, which in turn will result in a hull several magnitudes of strength harder than its non-polarized state.

Bear in mind, however, repeated attacks will weaken and eventually depolarize the matrix, but you will have that added protection against their disrupter weaponry."

"Understood—and thanks, Captain, for everything," Foxwell acknowledged. The Vulcan captain responded with the same impassive expression.

Beta stood at her science console on the bridge and turned in the direction of Foxwell. "Captain, all Galactic Fleet battle cruisers have confirmed polarization shielding successfully configured; all starships are combat ready and awaiting your orders. The Vulcans are proceeding ahead at one-quarter impulse power."

"Very well," Foxwell answered, turning his attention to his communications officer. "Xuriya, open a secure channel to all Galactic Fleet and Vulcan vessels. Tie-in communications with the public address system on all starships."

"Aye, Captain, secure channel established—PA systems linked."

"This is Captain Jon L. Foxwell of the *SS Stargazer*," he began, addressing the entire ship's company. "We will proceed behind the Vulcan starships at a predetermined sub-light speed which will result in our arrival to Earth in one hour, fifteen minutes. In exactly one hour all Galactic Fleet combat vessels will engage their cloaking device and go to CONDITION RED. Exactly fifteen minutes afterward, the Vulcan ships will disable the Vorcian shielding; *Stargazer* will initiate and lead the attack on Vorcian raptors in Earth orbit. Each Galactic Fleet Starship captain will seek out and engage enemy vessels at their discretion. All channels are to remain open to provide updates, report damage and casualties, and provide requests for assistance. Good luck, and may the solar winds be with you all—Foxwell out."

The Vulcan starships proceeded at sub-light speed to

time their arrival and placement in geosynchronous Earth orbit ahead of the Galactic Fleet battle cruisers who followed. Cloaking was engaged followed by setting CONDITION RED. Sorak transmitted a secure code confirming the Vorcian shielding was neutralized.

Weapons Officer Warwick turned in Foxwell's direction. "Captain, all battle stations manned and ready. Weapons systems fully charged. Hull plating polarized at one hundred percent."

Foxwell managed a smile. "Xuriya, put those Vorcian devils onscreen."

"Aye, sir . . . onscreen."

"Navigator, plot an intercept course for the closest Vorcian raptor."

"Aye, Captain, intercept course entered."

"Helmsman, ahead one-half impulse power."

"Aye, Captain, one-half impulse power."

"Xuriya, open a secure channel to all starships."

"Aye, sir, secure channel open."

"This is Captain Foxwell to all Galactic Fleet starships. Concealment successful—disengage cloaking devices—commence attack on all Vorcian vessels."

"Captain, distance to the raptor is ten thousand kilometers and closing," Beta reported.

Foxwell swiveled his command chair back toward his weapons officer. "Lieutenant, lock starboard laser cannons onto the Vorcian raptor . . . *maximum power*."

"Aye, sir, starboard cannons locked."

Foxwell stood, then turned and faced the main viewer. "FIRE!"

PART IV

Stardate: Sept. 02, 2096

The Vorcian ship sustained repeated hits to its tubular-shaped hull, weapon ports, and engines before finally breaking apart and exploding, debris scattering in the same direction as the ship. It's likely the Vorcian crew never knew their shielding was neutralized, with the maximum power setting of the *Stargazer*'s laser canons destroying the enemy vessel after half a dozen volleys of cannon fire. The element of surprise achieved by the cloaked Galactic Fleet starships caught the Vorcians completely off guard; other Galactic Fleet battle cruisers attained similar results as they destroyed more than a dozen enemy ships before the remaining raptors finally realized their shielding was inoperative. Vorcian vessels still capable of operating ultimately responded by taking evasive action and initiating counterattacks, two immediately challenging the *Stargazer* as they turned, heading directly for the bow of the battle cruiser.

"Navigator/helmsman—hard about, bearing 340 mark 15," Foxwell ordered.

"Aye, sir, heading 340 mark 15."

"Lieutenant Warwick—make ready starboard energy torpedoes. Target both vessels; prepare to fire on my command," Foxwell directed, leaning forward in his command chair and focused on the main viewing screen.

"Energy torpedoes locked onto the Vorcian raptors," the weapons officer confirmed.

"FIRE!" the captain shouted.

Both Vorcian ships were destroyed.

"Two enemy vessels approaching our stern," Beta announced, swiveling her chair in the direction of the captain. Foxwell turned his chair around and stood in response to his first officer's announcement. Before he had a chance to reply, the *Stargazer* was violently rocked by repeated shockwaves, the aft-approaching Vorcian raptors firing disrupter blasts and striking the top of the *Stargazer* near the bridge.

"Everyone—grab on to something and hang on!" the captain yelled out.

Additional disrupter fire was deflected by the polarized hull plating, the Vorcian ships firing at random.

"Forward hull polarization down to sixty percent," Warwick hollered, his voice breaking from the brutal vibration of the starship.

Two large metallic supports broke loose from the bridge ceiling. One struck Foxwell, driving him to the floor and rendering him unconscious. The other support fell on top of the first one.

"Medical team to the bridge!" Beta shouted, hailing the *Stargazer*'s medical department for assistance. Xuriya immediately exited her station to attend to the captain.

Beta stood and locked eyes with the weapons officer. "Target their disrupter cannons, Lieutenant."

"Raptor cannons targeted, Commander."

"Aft laser canons—FIRE!"

"Disrupter cannons neutralized," Warwick reported.

"Lock aft energy torpedoes on their hulls," she further ordered. "Continue repeated volleys until both vessels are destroyed."

Beta moved toward the captain; using her bionic legs to brace and her bionic arms to lift, she removed the first mangled support, then the next. Emergency medical personnel exited the turbo lift and rushed to aid the injured captain. "He needs to be moved to sick bay," the lead medic yelled out. The others prepared Foxwell for transport to the medical department.

"Both raptors destroyed," Warwick shouted.

Beta realized she was now in command of the *Stargazer*. She quickly surveyed the bridge crew. "Xuriya—damage report." Her order jolted the communications officer to regain her composure as she returned to her station.

"All departments report minimal shockwave damage; several crew members treated for minor injuries. Engineering reports hull intact; propulsion units online and functional," Xuriya reported.

"Warwick—weapons and polarization status?"

"All weapons systems intact and operational; ship's hull polarization re-initialized—current level forty-eight percent and rising."

"Acknowledged," Beta replied, craning her head toward the communications station. "Lieutenant, activate the *Stargazer*'s public address system."

"PA system enabled."

Beta walked to the captain's command chair and sat. "Attention all hands. This is Commander Beta. We have destroyed five enemy vessels. We have sustained minimal damage and several minor crew injuries," she announced, followed by a pause, "with the exception of Captain Foxwell, who has been moved to sickbay. I have assumed command pending the captain's status. We will remain at **CONDITION RED** until further notice."

Xuriya swiveled her chair toward Beta. "Commander, Earth Defense Command and Galactic Fleet combat vessels report more than one hundred Vorcian raptors destroyed or damaged. All enemy offensive operations within Earth's atmosphere and Earth orbit have ceased; eleven remaining enemy vessels appear to be fleeing."

Beta stood. "Lieutenant, open a secure channel to Galactic Fleet Command, the Vulcan ships, and all Galactic Fleet combat vessels."

"Secure channel opened."

"This is Commander Beta of the *SS Stargazer*. I have assumed command. Captain Foxwell has been injured and is currently incapacitated. Request permission to pursue enemy ships and engage."

Following a short pause, Xuriya turned again in Beta's direction. "Secure message received from Admiral Perry as follows," Xuriya said. The message began.

"Authorization granted to pursue and engage remaining enemy vessels. The following Galactic Fleet battle cruisers are ordered to accompany the *Stargazer* as a task force: *Parthia, Centurion, Orion, Reprisal, Valiant,* and *Yorktown*. Commander Beta of the *Stargazer* will assume overall command—all remaining Galactic Fleet and Vulcan starships will remain in Earth orbit until further notice—end of message."

With the channel still open, Beta wasted no time. She directed navigational and speed telemetry to be transmitted to the assigned task force. As soon as data transmission and receipt was confirmed, she stood in front of the main viewing screen in reciprocal view of the assigned task force battle cruisers. "Execute," she ordered. Separately, one after the other, each Galactic Fleet battlecruiser accelerated at light factor 6.5 in the direction of the fleeing Vorcian raptors.

Beta glanced at the bridge crew. "I'm on my way to sick bay to check on the captain's condition," she announced. "Change our alert status to CONDITION YELLOW. Lieutenant Xuriya, you have the bridge," she directed, walking to the turbo lift.

"Commander, may I please accompany you?" Xuriya requested.

Beta turned and gazed at the distraught communications officer.

"Commander . . . I'll take the conn," Lieutenant Warwick volunteered.

Beta nodded her approval. "Navigator, fill in for communications until we return."

"Aye, Commander," he replied.

The turbo elevator proceeded in the direction of sick bay in response to Beta's voice command. She and Lieutenant Xuriya exited, walking through a short corridor before arriving at the medical facility. A medical assistant escorted Beta and Xuriya to Foxwell's assigned cubicle. A medic was busy checking IV lines and reviewing overhead monitors above the front of the captain's diagnostic bed, his head wrapped with capeline bandaging.

"The captain's condition is stable," the chief medical officer reassured Beta and Xuriya. "He sustained a severe concussion and a very badly bruised right neck and shoulder, as well as a laceration that required thermal suturing. He's currently sedated, but we'll start him on neural wave therapy tomorrow to help reduce swelling and inflammation; that and bed rest should see him back on his feet in about three days, complications notwithstanding."

"Thank goodness it wasn't any more serious than it

was," Xuriya commented. "Those supports that fell him were enormous. If it were not for Commander Beta, he might not have—"

"Thank you, Doctor," Beta interrupted, purposely raising the volume of her voice. "Are any other crew members being treated?"

"Just one—Ensign Weber from engineering. He's in another cubicle—back pain—we're treating him with analgesics and heat therapy."

"Can you take me to him?" Beta requested.

"Certainly," Rivera replied.

"May I stay with the captain for a few minutes?" Xuriya pleaded.

"If the doctor has no objections," Beta answered, deferring the answer to Rivera.

The doctor nodded, displaying a sympathetic half-smile. "It's okay—just don't disturb him," he instructed.

Beta and Rivera proceeded in the direction of Ensign Weber. Xuriya stood next to the captain for several minutes, gently slipping her hand into his, her eyes moistening. "I still love you, Jon Foxwell," she whispered. Leaning over his bed, she gently kissed him. She removed her hand from his, then turned and slowly walked away from the captain's bedside, rejoining the doctor and Beta as they exited Ensign Weber's cubicle.

"Commander, Lieutenant Warwick is hailing you," a medical assistant informed her. Beta walked to the companel and keyed the speaker. "Beta here."

"Commander, sensors indicate the fleeing Vorcian raptors have detected our pursuit and are incrementally reducing their light speed. Accompanying task force ships have confirmed the same. They may be preparing to turn and fight."

"Acknowledged. Respond and instruct all task force battle cruisers to implement phased speed reductions— prepare for possible engagement. Xuriya and I are returning to the bridge. Reset alert status to **CONDITION RED**."

GALACTIC
FLEET
COMMAND

PART V

Stardate: Sept. 03, 2096

"Status, Lieutenant?" Beta bellowed at the weapons officer. The turbo lift elevator doors closed behind Xuriya.

"The raptors have reduced speed to sub-light," Warwick said. "*Stargazer* and accompanying task force ships have adjusted speed accordingly. We remain in pursuit."

"Distance?"

"Eighty thousand kilometers—holding steady," the navigator replied, having returned to his station.

Beta stared at the main viewing screen, thinking. *Why have the Vorcians abruptly reduced speed, knowing we can now overtake them and attack?* Her eyes remained focused on the main viewing screen, staring intensely at the magnified view of the Vorcian raptors when the reason for their change to sub-light speed became startlingly obvious. "Xuriya, open a secure channel to all task force ships." She hurried toward the communications officer's station.

"Secure channel open, Commander."

"This is Commander Beta to all task force ships," she began. "Polarize hull plating and make ready all weapons. The Vorcians have—"

"Commander," the weapons officer interrupted,

swiveling his chair. "Sensors indicate enemy shield power fluctuations; they're charging weapons."

"They've outdistanced the range of the Vulcan dampening telemetry; they're attempting to re-activate their shields," Beta conjectured.

"Commander, the raptors are executing course changes; it appears they are regrouping," the navigator reported.

"The Vorcians have engaged impulse engines; moving ahead at one-quarter impulse power," the helmsman added.

"Helmsman, reduce speed to one-quarter impulse power—maintain stationary velocity."

"Aye, Commander."

Beta wheeled around and walked to the main viewing screen. "They're turning, maneuvering for an attack. If their shields become fully operational, we'll be outgunned," she voiced sternly, turning again and walking toward the weapons officer. "What's their current shield strength, Lieutenant?"

"Thirty percent and rising. *Stargazer* hull plating polarized at one hundred percent . . . all weapons charged."

"Is the secure channel still open?" Beta asked, turning her attention to Xuriya.

"Aye, Commander. Task force ships confirm your secure message and discussion with Lieutenant Warwick was received and understood. All task force battle cruisers have polarized their hull plating and have charged weapons—awaiting further orders. Secure channel still open."

"This is Commander Beta to all task force ships. On my command to cloak and proceed, Group Two battle cruisers *Orion, Reprisal, Valiant*, and *Yorktown* will engage cloaking and set a course to reposition at a distance of ten thousand kilometers behind the Vorcian raptors. Group One battle cruisers *Stargazer, Parthia,* and *Centurion* will remain uncloaked and initiate a frontal assault on the enemy vessels after confirmation Group Two is in position. Group Two cruisers will decloak and engage the enemy ships with all weapons at maximum power on my further command—end of message."

"Group One battle cruisers responded with acknowledgment of your transmission, Commander," Xuriya confirmed.

"Keep this secure channel open, Lieutenant."

"Aye, Commander."

"Status on the raptors?" Beta asked, directing her attention to the weapons officer.

"Sensors indicate regrouping will be complete in three minutes."

"Group Two battlecruisers—execute cloaking and proceed," Beta ordered. The Group Two starships engaged their cloaking devices and moved undetected in a wide arc as they maneuvered behind the Vorcian raptors.

"Commander, the Vorcians are bound to take notice that half our starships are now cloaked," Lieutenant Warwick pointed out.

"If they successfully activate their deflector shields, it will be a moot issue, Lieutenant. Provide a status on their shielding's current strength."

"Forty percent and rising."

"Time remaining to regroup?"

"One minute, thirty seconds."

"My neutronic brain has *reasoned* they have timed completion of their regrouping with deflector shield strength reaching fifty percent or greater. They feel confident they can successfully attack and destroy the pursuing task force with minimal damage. What's their shield status, Lieutenant?"

"Forty-five percent and still rising."

"Commander, Group Two battlecruisers confirm they're in position behind the enemy vessels; they remain undetected," Xuriya reported.

"Time remaining to regroup, Lieutenant?"

"Thirty seconds—Vorcian shielding at forty-eight percent," Warwick replied.

"Group One battlecruisers," Beta shouted out to the open channel, "prepare to go to full impulse power. Fire laser cannons at maximum power on my command."

"Less than ten seconds remaining to regroup, Commander."

"Full impulse power—NOW. FIRE!" Beta shouted.

The Group One battlecruisers closed the distance with the Vorcians within seconds, firing and scoring multiple hits on several enemy ships. Beta's decision to attack succeeded in creating confusion, with the enemy raptors scattering like dust after a meteor strike on a dead moon.

"Group Two battlecruisers—decloak and engage," Beta ordered.

Orion, Reprisal, Valiant, and *Yorktown* decloaked and immediately attacked the scattered raptors, firing their laser canons at will, the continuing barrage of both Galactic Fleet Battle Groups weakening the half-strength shielding of the enemy vessels. A few of the Vorcian ships managed to counterattack with their disrupter cannons, their power so enormous each hit resulted in a ten percent or greater reduction in hull polarization.

"Commander—polarization at sixty percent," Warwick reported. The *Stargazer* rocked violently by two more shock-waves, both impacting the hull section of the ship near engineering.

Xuriya turned toward Beta. "Commander, the chief engineer is hailing you."

"Go ahead, Chief."

"Commander, the plasma coils are beginning to buckle. I don't know how much more they can take. If we lose the coils, we'll lose both fusion drive and impulse engines."

"Acknowledged, Chief. Lieutenant Warwick, can you strengthen polarization adjacent to engineering?"

"I can, but it will reduce overall hull polarization to forty percent," he yelled.

"Do it," Beta ordered.

Another disputer blast struck the top of the *Stargazer* behind the bridge; sparks and smoke filled the enclosed compartment as exhaust fans worked overtime to facilitate ventilation. As soon as the shockwave dissipated, Beta stood and hurried toward the communications officer.

"Xuriya—damage report."

"*Reprisal* and *Reliant* report two Vorcian raptors have sustained damage and appear to be fleeing. *Orion* has lost forward laser cannons; the *Yorktown*'s targeting array has been damaged; they're firing weapons visually. Group One and Two battle cruisers report ship-wide minor to severe shockwave damage with seventeen injured, five fatalities. Hull polarization averaging less than thirty percent."

"Lieutenant Warwick, status on enemy vessel shielding?" Beta requested.

"Overall, less than twenty percent."

"Commander, the *Parthia* and *Centurion* report a third Vorcian vessel is fleeing," Xuriya yelled out.

"This is Commander Beta to all Galactic Fleet starships; on my command all battle cruisers will follow *Stargazer* into a closed elliptical orbit around the remaining enemy fleet to prevent any further escapes. Maintain distance of no greater than fifty thousand kilometers—confirm when in position. Helmsman, enter the required coordinates," Beta ordered.

"Coordinates entered, Commander."

"Engage."

The inertial navigation system quickly placed the *Stargazer* into a tight circle around the Vorcian raptors, with the remaining Galactic Fleet vessels following suit. Beta paced back and forth between the command chair, communications and weapons stations, and the main viewing screen.

"This is Commander Beta to all Galactic Fleet ships. It is imperative you target and neutralize the shielding of the remaining enemy raptors before their disrupters depolarize our hulls. Now is the time to hit them with all weapons—maximum power. Loss of enemy vessel shielding is to be immediately followed by total destruction. All battle cruisers will tighten their orbit proportionately in unison with canon and torpedo fire. On my command, all ships will FIRE FOR EFFECT. Hit them with everything we've got."

"All battle cruisers report they're in elliptical orbit around the Vorcian vessels. They're trapped," Xuriya reported.

"Standby, weapons," Beta directed, exchanging glances with Warwick.

"Ready when you are, Commander."

Beta turned and stared directly into the main viewing screen. "FIRE!"

The elliptical orbit confined the Vorcian raptors as they reeled from massive cannon and torpedo hits. The enemy vessels returned fire, the accuracy of their disrupter weapons diminishing. Galactic Fleet battle cruisers tightened their orbits.

"Their shields are beginning to buckle, Commander," the weapons officer reported.

"Continue the attack," Beta shouted, the secure channel

still open and transmitting to the task force ships.

One by one, the remaining Vorcian raptors broke apart, disintegrating into enormous fireballs. Debris scattered in random patterns, each exploding ship creating its own spectacular mini supernova.

"Task force ships report Vorcian raptors destroyed, Commander," Xuriya reported.

Beta craned her head. "Lieutenant, can you confirm?"

"Aye, Commander, the trapped Vorcian vessels have been destroyed," the weapons officer responded.

"Commander, shall I set a pursuit course for the Vorcian ships that escaped?" the navigator asked.

Beta looked around, noting the physical and emotional exhaustion of her bridge officers. Smoke billowed from overloaded circuits, damaged equipment and displays.

"No," she answered somberly, directing her answer to the entire bridge crew. "The return of three heavily damaged warships out of their original total will send a clear message. We've destroyed their ability, and hopefully their will to continue. It's a diplomacy issue now."

* * *

The Galactic Fleet task force set a course for return home. It was decided the battle cruisers would remain in Earth orbit, civilian technicians ferrying back and forth while they worked in tandem with crew members to affect repairs. All orbiting repair stations sustained damage and required repair as well. None would be available for docking until rebuilding was complete. Repairs would be a massive undertaking—a mixture of refitting, reconstruction, and rebuilding. It was anticipated several more seriously damaged starships would require "shakedown" cruises after they were deemed ready to reenter service. Similar planning was underway for repair of damage incurred to infrastructure on the planet, which was worldwide in scope and complexity.

* * *

Foxwell pushed the portable monitor to the side in response to Beta's visit. He was sitting up, his head bandages removed earlier. Several medical staff personnel were gathered around his bed, moving aside to make room for Beta.

"Dr. Rivera tells me you'll be cleared to return to duty tomorrow, Captain."

"Thanks to you," Foxwell replied. "I've read your report; to say you did one helluva job is an understatement. I'm putting you in for a commendation. I'm also recommending you for command of your own starship."

"Thank you, Captain," Beta replied. "With all due respect, however, I would prefer to remain aboard the *Stargazer*."

"Why?" Foxwell asked, puzzled. "You proved again you're the best first officer in the fleet."

"Let's just say I've developed an affinity for the *Stargazer*, its crew—and its captain," Beta replied, her face deadpan.

Foxwell was hard-pressed for a response; he was obviously moved by his first officer's dedication and loyalty. "Tell you what," he responded whimsically. "As difficult as it is, I'll belay my recommendation regarding your own command—*if* you can manage to crack even the slightest smile."

Beta appeared befuddled by the captain's request. She

furrowed her dark eyebrows, a baffled look replacing her normal stalwart appearance. She looked around the cubicle, glancing at staff gathered around her and the captain in an attempt to gauge their reaction. It was obvious they were having difficulty containing themselves, some with their hands over their mouths, others deliberately staring at the floor, trying to hide their expressions.

Finally, Beta gave in, managing to crack the faintest smile, although with noted effort, but it *was* a smile.

"There," she said, "I smiled."

The room exploded in laughter, the captain falling back on his bed, howling as the medical staff joined in.

Beta glanced bewilderingly at the combined laughter. *"Totally unreasonable,"* she scoffed.

THE END

Episode II

Journey to Paradise

PROLOGUE

New orders received from Galactic Fleet Command: the *Stargazer* is tasked with embarking a team of geologists and mining engineers before breaking orbit around Earth's solar system and proceeding to Luyten b, a known exoplanet in the Milky Way galaxy. Their mission: to locate and confirm known deposits of rilidium ore, vital for starship propulsion and the continued exploration of new solar systems, celestial bodies, and other life forms. Join the captain and crew on their new adventure, until sabotage, murder, and madness threaten to cripple the *Stargazer* and derail the mission. Welcome to "Journey to Paradise."

GALACTIC
FLEET
COMMAND

PART I

Stardate: Nov. 26, 2096

For weeks *Stargazer* and three accompanying starships maintained concentric orbits around the outer edge of the Earth's solar system, each battle cruiser linked in a ninety-degree circular arc. It was a routine early morning, the bridge crew leisurely focused on their duties as Captain Foxwell slowly swiveled his command chair away from the main viewing screen. Science Officer Beta was now the object of his attention, bringing the chair to a stop after aligning it with her station on the bridge.

"Beta, please join me in my ready room," Foxwell requested. "Xuriya, you have the conn."

"Aye, Captain," Xuriya replied.

Beta turned in acknowledgment, rendering an impassive glance as she stood then quietly followed the captain into the small briefing chamber.

"Please take a seat." Foxwell motioned with his hand, and Beta sat opposite the captain at the oval-shaped table just large enough to accommodate the *Stargazer*'s department heads. Foxwell reached toward the overhead and pulled down one of two movable monitors, adjusting the angle to make it ready for viewing. "We've received new orders from Galactic Fleet," he continued. "I want to disclose and obtain your opinion regarding this new mission assignment before breaking the news to the senior officers."

"Understood, Captain," Beta replied, her explorative curiosity aroused.

Foxwell pressed the play button and moved the screen in the direction of his first officer, then walked around the table, pulling out a seat next to Beta as the video began.

"Captain Foxwell—priority-one secure message from Admiral Perry of Galactic Fleet Command now streaming directly to your personal channel," the computer-generated voice announced, and a uniformed figure appeared on screen.

"Greetings, Captain. On behalf of Galactic Fleet Command, we extend our appreciation and thanks to you and the crew of the *Stargazer* for your time in orbit around our solar system. This was a necessary precaution to guard against any further intrusion or malevolent actions by the Vorcians in response to their failed invasion just over two months ago," he continued. "Galactic Fleet is announcing new mission orders: At 1400 hours today, your time, the *Constellation* will rendezvous and dock with the *Stargazer* for the purpose of transferring a team of geologists and mining engineers. The *Stargazer* will leave orbit no later than 1600 hours and set a course for Luyten b, a confirmed exoplanet in our galaxy. The purpose of this new mission is to confirm the presence of—and subsequent logistical extraction of—rilidium ore, which is theorized to be abundant on the planet. You will assist and work with the arriving geologists and engineers to successfully complete the mission. This particular group of professionals is comprised of experts regarding rilidium ore, its properties, usage, and dangers. Galactic Fleet Command has assigned the highest priority on nothing less than the successful outcome of this mission. It is classified TOP PRIORITY. The *Constellation* will assume your present orbit and continue the mission you were previously assigned."

The admiral appeared to relax, grinning as he finished his message. "Captain Foxwell—as always, I have the utmost confidence in your leadership and ability to successfully complete this mission. I wish you and your crew fair winds and following seas. End of message."

"Interesting," Beta responded as she turned and gazed at Foxwell. "Rilidium is a radioactive chemical element used in starship fusion reactors to facilitate fission of rilidium atoms for release of energy by the light speed drive assembly. It can be dangerous if not properly handled."

"That's why I want you, O'Donovan, Xuriya, Warwick, and Dr. Rivera back here at 1300 hours for a briefing. Access the database and research what information we have regarding Luyten b, to include its location and distance, time required to get there, atmosphere and environmental conditions, and so on. As science officer, you will be responsible for coordination of your department as well as engineering in order to facilitate and provide whatever assistance and support the geologists and mining officials require."

"Acknowledged, Captain. I will complete the research and schedule the meeting with our senior officers for 1300 hours. Just to confirm, will you be in attendance at this meeting?"

Foxwell responded with a nod.

* * *

Having been locked in a circular orbit around the Earth's solar system, it was obvious the crew's level of boredom was increasing—not that they didn't understand and appreciate the importance of the current mission, but a new journey to a terrestrial, Earthlike planet theorized by Galactic Fleet astronomers and geologists to be rich in rilidium ore would be right up their "new mission" alley.

A geological mission and assistive survey of this magnitude and importance would serve not only as much-needed relief from the boredom of a continuous, no-frills circular orbit, but a welcome reminder of the *Stargazer*'s primary mission: the discovery and exploration of new solar systems, celestial bodies, and other life forms.

Privately the captain was pleased, even thankful at this unexpected but welcome turn of events.

* * *

Captain's Ready Room, 1300 hours

"All department heads present," Beta announced, the *Stargazer*'s senior officers taking their seats in the captain's ready room.

Foxwell briefly glanced around the oval table, a collective feeling of anticipation enveloping the small room as he began the meeting. "I've called you here because we've received new mission orders from Galactic Fleet. Please observe the screen in front of you." Foxwell pressed the restart button on a small control panel, repeating the video message he and Beta had previously viewed.

The viewing concluded with the senior officers looking pleased, even excited about the new assignment. Foxwell switched off the monitors, then rose from his seat. "As you have just seen, we have been ordered to embark a team of geologists and mining engineers, break orbit, and proceed to planet Luyten b. I have asked Beta to research and bring us all up to speed regarding this known exoplanet, to include our involvement regarding our soon-to-be *guests* . . ." He gave a quick glance to his first officer, his signal that she now had the floor.

Beta stood and continued the briefing; her neutronic brain allowed her to proceed without files or notes, all information committed to memory after initially consulting the *Stargazer*'s database. "As the video message stated," she began, "we have new mission orders to planet Luyten b. Discovered in June 2017, Luyten b is considered a super-Earth, approximately three times the mass of planet Earth, and receives only six percent more starlight than our home planet, making it one of the best candidates for habitability. Luyten b is a confirmed exoplanet located in the Constellation of Canis Minor in the Milky Way Galaxy, orbiting within the habitable zone of the nearby Red Dwarf Luyten's Star. It is one of the most Earthlike planets ever found and is currently the fourth closest potentially habitable exoplanet known, at a distance of 12.2 light years. Our current estimated time of arrival is one day, three hours, forty-seven minutes at light factor 2."

The senior officers looked around the captain's ready room, smiling and exchanging glances.

"As a reminder," Beta continued, "all of you are aware of the dangers of mishandling rilidium, even non-processed rilidium ore. That will be discussed further with our guests in due time. Upon arrival to Luyten b and confirmation of class M status, the *Stargazer*'s science and engineering departments will render all requested and available assistance to our Galactic Fleet geologists and engineers."

Captain Foxwell moved toward the table, resuming the meeting. "The Galactic Fleet geologists and engineers will be assigned quarters upon arrival, along with sufficient time to securely stow their equipment and personal effects. Beta will make arrangements for assignment of quarters for our guests. Chief Engineer O'Donovan will lead the entire group on a familiarization tour of the *Stargazer*. Make sure our guests are thoroughly familiar with our starship and its basic control functions, safety features, and location of critical departments such as sickbay, triage, and emergency evacuation stations. I have made arrangements for a formal dinner in the wardroom for our guests and senior officers at 1800 hours. I expect all of you to be there—attire will be the class A formal uniform. Any questions?"

There were none as the department heads grinned, shook their heads, and looked around, all seemingly pleased about the new mission.

"It is now 1345 hours. Report back to your departments, brief your subordinates regarding this meeting, and make preparations to dock with the *Constellation* at 1400 hours." Captain Foxwell hailed the bridge through the companel. "Navigator, what's the status on arrival of the *Constellation*?"

"Arrival scheduled for 1400 hours is confirmed, Captain. They are approaching our port side on a parallel course at one-quarter impulse power. Distance is twenty thousand kilometers. The *Constellation* is preparing to disengage impulse engines and activate thrusters for final approach; docking crews are standing by."

"On our way," Foxwell replied, glancing at his first officer as she accompanied him to the turbo elevator. The captain and Beta returned to the bridge and remained there until docking was completed. "Beta, you and Dr. Rivera will accompany me to the docking port on C deck. Xuriya, you have the conn," Foxwell directed.

"Aye, Captain," Xuriya replied.

* * *

Foxwell, his first officer, and Dr. Rivera greeted the new passengers as the Galactic Fleet geologists and engineers began their transfer through the pressurized airlocks between the two connected starships. The mooring crews were busy observing numerous pressure gauges, monitors, and docking clamps for any possible sign of trouble or failure. The transfer of personnel and equipment proceeded smoothly; engineers and geologists carried equipment and personal belongings as they boarded the Stargazer. Security officers confirmed the passenger manifest via photo IDs attached to the working uniform of every person boarding.

"All Galactic Fleet civilians are safely aboard and accounted for," Chief Security Officer Warwick reported.

It was at that moment Captain Foxwell locked eyes with her, the last member of the exploration and surveillance team to report aboard.

GALACTIC
FLEET
COMMAND

PART II

Stardate: Nov. 26, 2096

"Welcome aboard the *Stargazer*," Captain Foxwell warmly acknowledged, smiling as he discreetly glimpsed at the photo ID clipped to her collared shirt. The name on her ID was strangely captivating: *Leia Athena, Asst. Chief Geologist.*

"Thank you, Captain," she eagerly replied. Her constellation-blue eyes accentuated her heart-shaped lips, and he found her smile curiously inviting. She was affable and friendly, exchanging pleasantries with Beta, Chief of Security Warwick, and other security officers assigned to individually escort the newly embarked guests to their quarters.

"Oh, Captain, before I become too caught up in the moment, can you confirm my father reported aboard?" Leia remembered, having flitted from person to person, starting and ending with the *Stargazer*'s commanding officer. She gave another enticing smile.

"Your father?" Foxwell asked, a puzzled look confirming he didn't make the connection, at least to begin with.

"Yes, Professor Nikolas Adana, Chief Geologist and

head of the surveying mission. He was with the initial group of five to ten personnel that reported aboard," she clarified.

It was then Foxwell remembered speaking with Leia's father after he boarded. They introduced themselves, but he didn't recall the professor mentioning his daughter was a member of the surveying party, or that she would be the last member of the surveying team to report aboard.

"You are correct, Professor Athena," the captain replied with a half-smile. "He was actually the first member of the surveying party I spoke with. You and your father will be assigned individual staterooms. A member of our security team is escorting him to his assigned quarters as we speak." Foxwell paused as he bent forward and looked at her photo ID again, this time not bothering to be discreet.

She smiled again in response to Foxwell's obvious second glance. "Please—call me *Leia*," she requested in a sugary voice, returning the captain's glance. A security team member gathered her personal effects, requesting she follow him to the *Stargazer*'s turbo elevator.

"I'll accompany you to your stateroom," the captain cut in, catching the attention of Beta and Dr. Rivera as he turned to leave with Leia and the security officer. It was apparent there was an attraction of some kind, an observation not lost on his first officer.

"Captain, should I expect you on the bridge at 1500 hours?" Beta chimed in, a subtle reminder the *Stargazer* was due to disengage from the *Constellation*, break orbit, and depart for the exoplanet no later than 1600 hours.

Foxwell pivoted in response to Beta's question. "That would be an affirmative," he replied, appearing irritated by the question.

Rivera and Beta exchanged a puzzled glance as the captain departed with his guest and the security officer.

"She has a vivacious personality, I'll give her that," Rivera noted.

"I'm not so sure, Doctor," Beta countered, staring pensively at the captain and assistant chief geologist, who both followed the security officer toward the turbo elevator.

"What do you mean, not so sure? Not so sure about what?" Rivera pointedly asked.

"If you noticed, Doctor, Leia Athena and her father reported aboard separately. There was no acknowledgment of her by Professor Adana when he initially reported aboard. He was the first person of the surveying party to embark. The chief geologist and his daughter were at opposite ends of the procession of personnel reporting aboard. She's the assistant chief geologist as well as his daughter," Beta reminded the *Stargazer*'s chief medical officer. "Why would they *not* report aboard together—or in tandem? Does that appear *reasonable* to you?"

Rivera threw his hands up. "*Reasonable?*" he repeated, emphasizing the word. "Why does everything have to be *reasonable*? Perhaps it was coincidental. Did you ever consider that?"

"There was nothing coincidental about it, Doctor," Beta answered indifferently.

"What are you saying?" Rivera asked in frustration. "The chief geologist and his daughter boarded the *Stargazer* separately; what is so unusual about that?"

Looking back at Rivera, Beta unfolded her arms, the blank expression on her face as persuasive as any serious expression could convey. "I'm on my way to the bridge in preparation for departure, Doctor. I suggest you ponder our conversation," she urged, turning and walking to the turbo elevator.

Rivera remained where he was, paying scant attention

to the docking crew as they began preparations for the two starships to separate. *I'm not a detective—or a psychiatrist,* he thought to himself, mulling over his talk with Beta. He threw his hands up again as he exited the docking port.

* * *

The Bridge, 1600 hours

Foxwell glanced around the bridge, confirming all stations were occupied. The *Stargazer's* crew had been briefed by the department heads regarding their new mission. "Beta—status report," he requested.

The first officer swiveled her chair in Foxwell's direction. "All departments report ready for departure, Captain. Docking crews report the *Constellation* and *Stargazer* have successfully separated to a distance of five thousand kilometers. Docking port is secure."

Xuriya turned in Foxwell's direction. "Sir, personal message received from Captain Mayberry of the *Constellation.*"

"Read it out loud," Foxwell responded.

"Aye, sir. Per Captain Mayberry: 'Apologies extended for not visiting a deserving friend while docked. As you're aware, time constraints would not allow for said visit. Wishing you and the crew of the *Stargazer* calm winds and following seas.' End of message."

Foxwell chuckled. "Captain Mayberry and I attended the academy together," he replied. "He's a good friend," he continued with a half-smile, electing not to elaborate. "Send a reply: 'Class of '88 alumnus—catch you at the next reunion. Best regards, Jon Foxwell.'"

"Aye, sir," Xuriya acknowledged.

The bridge crew looked around and smiled. Beta furrowed her eyebrows, swiveled her chair again, and resumed monitoring the sensors at her station.

Foxwell issued orders to break orbit. "Helmsman, navigator . . . prepare to take us out of orbit. Set a course for Luyten b, light factor 2."

"Acknowledged, Captain," the navigator replied. "New course heading 014 mark 17, entered and ready to execute."

"Helmsman—enable fusion light drive."

"Aye, Captain. Fusion light drive enabled, awaiting your order."

"Engage."

"Aye, sir, ahead light factor 2," the helmsman replied.

Foxwell exited the command chair and walked toward the main viewing screen, then turned and gazed at his navigator. "Confirm revised time of arrival to Luyten b, Ensign."

"One day, one hour, forty-three minutes, Captain."

"Very well—maintain present course and speed."

"Aye, sir," the navigator and helmsman acknowledged in sequence.

Returning to the captain's chair, Foxwell reminded Beta and Xuriya of the formal dinner scheduled for 1800 hours. "Xuriya, contact Chief of Security Warwick and let him know Lieutenant Baker from the weapons department is to report to the bridge immediately to take the conn. Make arrangements for someone from communications to monitor your station."

"Aye sir," Xuriya acknowledged.

The captain continued in the direction of the turbo lift, stopping as he glanced at his first officer. "I'll be in my quarters. You have the bridge. The moment Lieutenant Baker arrives, you and Xuriya are relieved so you can prepare for the formal dinner."

"Aye, Captain," Beta replied, noting Foxwell appeared restless as he continued into the elevator.

"Captain's quarters," Foxwell uttered, and the turbo lift moved in response to his voice command. Exiting the elevator, he walked around a corner, the pneumatic doors to his dimly lit stateroom opening in response to the microchip embedded in the Galactic Fleet logo on his uniformed shirt. He walked toward his desk to check for messages on his monitor, then stopped and turned, the door chiming as soon as it closed behind him. "Enter," he said. The pneumatic door opened again. The unfamiliar silhouette of a woman appeared at his door.

"Hello again, Captain," she uttered softly, her hands resting against the delicate fabric of her flowing evening gown.

"Leia?"

She smiled and nodded, deftly inviting herself into Foxwell's quarters. The door closed behind her.

"I was expecting to see you at the formal gathering at 1800 hours," the captain continued, surprised by her unexpected appearance. He gazed at her nebulous blue eyes, then walked closer to her. She was esoteric . . . different . . . beautiful.

She reached up and seductively brushed Foxwell's shoulder. "Maybe I prefer to be escorted by the captain," she whispered in a soothingly sweet voice, then paused, looking up into his eyes. ". . . if the captain has no objections?"

Foxwell placed his arms around her tapered waist and pulled her close, kissing her passionately. Her calamine-pink lips tasted like rose petals. Her burnished complexion emitted an aroma of fragrant perfume that was as jolting as an electric current. She nuzzled his neck in a teasingly seductive way, her evening gown flowing like a rippled waterfall as it dropped to the floor.

GALACTIC
FLEET
COMMAND

PART III

Stardate: Nov. 26–27, 2096

No one paid particular attention as Captain Foxwell and Leia Athena made their appearance together in the *Stargazer*'s spacious wardroom. No one, that is, except Xuriya. It wasn't unusual for starship captains to accompany invited guests at such events. Foxwell had issued previous orders no announcement was to be made upon his arrival, anticipating a possible last-minute diversion or unforeseen situation resulting in a delay, his unexpected rendezvous with Leia notwithstanding.

"Good evening, Captain," Xuriya said, a warm smile accompanying her greeting.

Foxwell returned the smile.

"Good evening," he responded, forgetting for a moment it was customary to assign a senior officer to act as simultaneous host and greeter. "Well, this is a surprise," he continued. "I had no idea you were the assigned host."

"Neither did I," Xuriya answered. "I was informed by Commander Beta of the assignment after my replacement assumed my duties on the bridge."

"Couldn't have selected a better host," the captain confirmed with a smile. Turning his attention to Leia, he formally introduced her to his communications officer. As Foxwell proceeded with the introduction, he noticed Xuriya appeared less than enthusiastic. There was no smile, no return greeting, not even the offer of a handshake. Foxwell took notice but was interrupted before he could speculate on it further.

"Captain, so nice of you to accompany my daughter to the welcome aboard dinner," Professor Adana stated, catching Foxwell off guard. "I was just speaking with your chief engineer across the room when I caught a glimpse of you and Leia. Will you be sitting at our table?"

"We will, Father," Leia replied, answering before the captain could respond, surprising everyone with her unexpected reply. She placed her hands around Foxwell's arm, moving closer to him.

Xuriya stared in disbelief at her brazenness. *Who the hell does she think she is answering for the captain?*

Foxwell smirked in response to Leia's announcement. He had given no thought to seating arrangements. It was his usual practice at such events to 'work the room,' enjoying a cocktail while greeting and making small talk with guests and ship's company, choosing where to sit only when the culinary staff began service.

"May I speak with you, Captain?" a familiar voice said outside the circle Foxwell, Xuriya, and the *Stargazer*'s two guests had formed. It was Beta. She was projecting her usual unreadable expression.

"If you will excuse me," the captain politely announced, stepping away from his guests to confer privately with his second-in-command.

"What is it, Beta?" Foxwell quietly asked.

"Captain, Chief O'Donovan was just informed by the assistant chief engineer of a problem with the fusion drive.

Apparently, it's more than a minor issue; it's quite serious. Chief O'Donovan excused himself and is on his way to engineering. He noticed you were busy with our guests, so he alerted me, but did not go into any detail. He simply stated he needed to return to engineering."

Foxwell was concerned, but no more than usual at receipt of such information. Engineering problems and other departmental issues were a normal part of a starship's modus operandi during the course of daily operations. Standard operating procedure was to assess, identify, correct and/or repair, up to and including setting CONDITION RED if necessary for survival of the starship.

"Did POD tell you *anything* before he left for engineering?" the captain asked.

"Something about the rilidium reactor circuits. He didn't elaborate further."

"Which is where we're headed," Foxwell decided.

Foxwell and Beta exited the wardroom and walked into the nearest turbo lift. "Engineering," Foxwell voiced into the companel, and the starship's elevator began its descent to engineering. He tapped the bridge icon on the companel's screen, the hailing chime audible at the captain's chair.

"Bridge, Lieutenant Baker," the conning officer answered.

"Lieutenant, this is the captain. Provide a bridge instrumentation status."

"Aye, sir. Within the last thirty minutes, monitors registered a slight variation in the fusion drive electromagnetic field. According to the assistant chief engineer, the disparity has something to do with the rilidium reactor circuitry. He told me Chief O'Donovan is on his way to engineering; all other monitor and instrumentation readings are unremarkable."

"Any sensor or viewer screen anomalies?" the captain asked.

"Negative, sir."

"Very well, maintain present course and speed. Beta and I will be in engineering."

Moments later, the turbo lift arrived. Foxwell and Beta exited and found the assistant chief engineer studying the main fusion control panels and monitors. Chief O'Donovan was examining and comparing what appeared to be individual circuit boards. The captain sensed his chief engineer was more than a little concerned. "So, POD," he reluctantly interrupted, "what kind of problem are we dealing with?"

Chief O'Donovan took in a deep breath before answering. "Captain, we've discovered several rilidium circuit boards that have developed fissures, like safety glass that initially cracks and then spreads. This has resulted in reflective cracking in the gold conductive tracing on the opposite side of the boards."

"In short, Captain, it's no different than cutting an electrical cord in half," Beta chimed in.

Foxwell sighed. "So the affected boards are no longer functioning; is that what you're telling me?"

"Aye, Captain," the chief engineer replied, his Irish accent accentuated by the unexpected discovery. "There are a total of 120 rilidium circuit boards in six control panels, three panels on each side of the light speed drive assembly."

"How many boards have been affected, and what's causing the problem?"

"So far twelve boards have stopped functioning. I'm not sure what's causing it, but we'll figure it out," O'Donovan assured the captain.

"What effect is it having on the fusion drive?" Foxwell asked.

"None yet, Captain. Just a slight variation in the eddy currents generated by the rilidium contained in the boards, noticeable per instrumentation on the bridge and in engineering. That's what alerted us to the problem. The fusion drive assembly was purposely designed with a ten-percent safety factor to allow for replacement of boards that normally go bad over time. In this particular case, twelve boards have gone bad over a course of approximately two hours, which is not normal. The loss of any additional boards will affect rilidium fission parameters, our ability to maintain light speed, weapons availability, and eventually life support. We've currently reached our safety threshold," the chief engineer explained.

"How many spare boards do we have?" Beta inquired.

"We began this mission by replacing all the boards in the control panels and stockpiled 120 spares. I believed that to be prudent considering our previous engagement with the Vorcians, which pushed the fusion drive and its support systems to their limits. Weapons fire and use of the cloaking system further taxed the entire fusion drive power grid."

"My understanding is we didn't lose a single circuit board as a result of our battle with the Vorcians. Am I correct?"

"Aye, Captain," O'Donovan replied. I replaced them only as a precautionary measure while undergoing repairs in space dock."

"Could the new boards be defective? A manufacturing or quality control issue?" the captain asked.

"Possibly," O'Donovan replied.

Beta glanced at Foxwell, then the chief engineer. "Is it possible the rilidium is decaying, similar perhaps to uranium decay, in which depleting electrons transform the rilidium into a different decaying atom?"

Chief O'Donovan thought for a few moments before replying. "Aye, it's a plausible theory. That would mean the decay process continues until the rilidium ore reaches a stable state and no longer emits ionizing particles. The fusion drive will ultimately begin to shut down."

"Your theory appears *reasonable*," Beta added.

"However," O'Donovan continued, "if the decaying rilidium is causing the boards to crack, I have no idea as to the *why* of it. That will require further investigation."

Foxwell nodded, then walked to the closet companel, hailing the bridge.

"Bridge, Lieutenant Baker," the conning officer responded.

"Lieutenant, this is the captain. Dispatch a security officer to the wardroom and escort Professor Adana and his daughter to engineering. Do this immediately."

"Aye, sir."

Foxwell walked back to the chief engineer and Beta. "Professor Adana and his daughter are on their way. They are Galactic Fleet's premier specialists regarding rilidium." Foxwell turned and looked directly at O'Donovan. "POD, provide our two guests with a thorough briefing; make the engineering lab available and work with these two experts to get to the bottom of this. Beta and I will return to the wardroom and resume mingling with our guests and crew. The formal dinner will end in less than two hours. We will return at that time. I want answers."

"Aye, Captain."

* * *

2230 hours

Captain Foxwell and Beta returned to engineering, having closed out the formal dinner and thanking guests and crew members for attending. Foxwell was hoping the two senior geologists could shed some additional light on the problem. As it turned out, that's exactly what happened.

"You're not going to believe it, Captain," O'Donovan blurted out as he and Beta approached the chief engineer. He was holding one of the defective circuit boards.

"Try me, POD. What are we dealing with here?"

O'Donovan raised the board to eye level and pointed to the treated, non-lethal rilidium semi-conductor chips, microcontrollers, sensors, interface, and gateway components that comprised most of a typical board. "Our fusion drive engines work by using fission of rilidium atoms to heat and compress a starship reactor's hydrogen fuel. The fusion of those isotopes of hydrogen combine under extremely high temperatures to form helium in a process known as nuclear fusion."

"You're not telling me anything I don't already know, POD. Get to the point," Foxwell insisted.

"Captain, we know rilidium cannot be replicated or lab grown. With the assistance of the professor and his daughter, we've discovered our circuit boards have been altered with what appears to be some type of near-depleted rilidium. The depleted rilidium is releasing a caustic chemical compound which is corroding and cracking the boards. When a board cracks, conductivity is lost and that board no longer functions."

A wry expression twisted the captain's face. "Any idea as to how we came into possession of 240 defective rilidium circuit boards?" he asked, exchanging glances with

O'Donovan and Beta.

The chief engineer responded with a puzzled expression. "That's the $64,000 question I would like answered, as they used to say back in the mid-twentieth century."

Even Beta appeared perplexed, but not in a technical or scientific sense. She agreed completely with the assessment provided by the *Stargazer*'s engineers and Galactic Fleet's senior geologists. To paraphrase another related idiom, Beta quoted, "The fly in the ointment, as I see it, is one of logistics, going back to our time in space dock for repairs after our battle with the Vorcians. New equipment installation and resupply of supporting inventory made up the majority of our extensive refit."

Foxwell turned and looked at his chief engineer. "Straight question, POD—and I want a straight answer. Will we make it to Luyten b?"

"Aye, Captain, we'll get there, but I can't guarantee we'll make it back without replacement boards," O'Donovan reluctantly answered. "We've notified all departments to minimize their energy requirements in order to reduce power demand on the reactor. We've already noticed a slight improvement in circuit board longevity."

Foxwell nodded. "POD, I want a complete review of all sub-space transmissions regarding the request for new boards, their receipt, and return of old and damaged boards. I want to know the name of the manufacturer, the delivery courier, and every pit stop those boards made before engineering took possession of them. Have Xuriya review the communications log in reference to courier tracking. Keep me advised."

"Aye, Captain," the chief engineer replied.

Foxwell glanced at Leia and her father, huddled and speaking hurriedly behind the large bay window in the engineering lab. Their manner of conversation appeared brusque, exacerbated by an exchange of hand gestures as they argued quietly. Beta and Chief O'Donovan took notice as well. "What's that all about?" the captain quietly asked, staring at the two senior geologists.

"Interesting," Beta responded.

Chief O'Donovan gave a puzzled shrug. Foxwell turned and looked at his chief engineer. "Do you require any further assistance from Leia and her father?"

"Negative, Captain," he replied. "We've identified the problem and it's just a matter of managing energy requirements until we arrive at Luyten b. We'll need to contact Galactic Fleet Command and arrange for a shipment of new circuit boards once we arrive."

"Prepare the appropriate report and request for new boards; send it to my quarters for review and approval. I'll have Xuriya fast-track it as a priority-one subspace transmission. Beta and I are returning to the bridge. Keep me advised," Foxwell ordered.

"Aye, Captain."

Foxwell and Beta were on their way out of engineering when he stopped and turned. "Oh, and when the professor and his daughter are finished with their 'discussion,' or whatever it is they're doing, have them escorted to their quarters. It's been a long day—for everyone."

"Aye, Captain," the chief engineer agreed. "That it has."

* * *

"Captain on the bridge," the PA system announced as Foxwell and his first officer exited the turbo elevator. Beta continued to her science station, Foxwell to his command chair. The conning officer stood and turned in the direction of the captain.

"Status, Lieutenant."

Lieutenant Baker smiled nervously as he briefed the captain. "Maintaining course for Luyten b; new bearing 015 mark 17, light factor 2. Revised time of arrival is fourteen hours, seventeen minutes."

"Instrumentation . . . sensors?"

"Non-engineering instrumentation readings are within normal limits; sensor scans are unremarkable."

Foxwell turned slightly and craned his head in the direction of Beta. She returned his glance while rendering a confirming nod.

"Very well, Lieutenant. Good job. You are relieved," the captain replied.

"Aye, Captain," Lieutenant Baker replied, the young line officer displaying an appreciative smile.

Foxwell and Beta remained on duty until nearly 0100 hours, exiting the bridge for their quarters after thoroughly briefing the newly arrived-on-duty mid-watch crew and conning officer.

* * *

Captain Foxwell lay on his bed, hands clasped tightly behind his head as he contemplated the day's events. He stared at the overhead for several minutes, his eyes growing heavy with fatigue. The cabin's fiber optic lighting slowly faded, facilitating his transition between relaxed wakefulness and the beginning stages of sleep, until the hailing sound of the companel jolted him out of a sound slumber. He reached over and fumbled with the panel on his nightstand. "Foxwell here," he responded, half-asleep.

"Captain, this is Rivera. Sorry for the early reveille," he continued in a hushed tone, "but I need you in sickbay—immediately."

Foxwell sighed, sitting up and swinging his torso around, placing his feet on the deck of his quarters; he understood that contact from the *Stargazer*'s chief medical officer at two in the morning was not a good sign.

"What is it, Doctor?" Foxwell demanded, rubbing the palms of his hands over his closed eyes.

Rivera emitted a long, audible breath before answering. It's Professor Adana, Captain—he's dead."

Part IV

Stardate: Nov. 28, 2096

"What happened?" Foxwell demanded, exchanging glances with the *Stargazer*'s chief medical officer. They both stood over the examining table and the corpse of Professor Adana.

"Unknown, Captain," Rivera replied. "Initial examination revealed no sign of trauma, nor of any sudden onset of illness. We're preparing to conduct a detailed autopsy to see if we can determine the exact cause of death."

Foxwell and Rivera turned in response to the medical department's hermetically sealed doors opening, followed by Chief Security Officer Warwick entering sick bay, two of his officers accompanying him.

"I was just going to tell you, Captain. These are the three who brought the professor here. I happened to drop by after the formal dinner had ended, just to check in with our night staff. Five minutes later, Warwick and his two security officers arrived carrying the professor. My first thought was perhaps he had had too much to drink. He was still breathing and mumbling slightly; that's when he collapsed and went into cardiac arrest. We initiated standard resuscitation protocol; unfortunately, all efforts to revive him were unsuccessful."

Foxwell turned his attention to Lieutenant Warwick. "What's your story, Lieutenant?"

"We were contacted by Ensign Wells shortly after midnight. He reported he was on his way to his quarters after being relieved from duty in the operations department. He stated he found Professor Adana face down on the deck outside his assigned quarters, just around the circular bend of the corridor where the ensign's cabin is located."

"Ensign Wells—isn't he one of the junior relief helmsmen?" Foxwell asked.

"Aye, Captain. He's a new crew member. Wells reported aboard while the *Stargazer* was in space dock undergoing repairs."

"Continue, Lieutenant."

"We arrived approximately three minutes later. Wells was kneeling next to Professor Adana. He was not fully alert and oriented, but he wasn't unconscious, either. He was moaning and incoherent. My first thought was that he might have had too much to drink during the welcome aboard dinner. We didn't call for medical assistance as we were able to assist the professor to his feet, the three of us helping to support him all the way to sickbay, then he collapsed just outside the entrance."

"Any crew members other than yourselves and Ensign Wells involved?"

"No, Captain. Wells remained on the scene until my two officers and I were able to assist the professor to his feet. Wells then continued to his quarters."

Foxwell sighed, then turned in the direction of the chief medical officer. Noting his grim expression, Rivera took it upon himself to suggest both he and the captain personally notify Professor Adana's daughter of the death of her father.

"Shall we proceed to Leia's quarters, Captain?"

Foxwell paused, then took a deep breath. "It's the absolute worse part of being a starship captain."

* * *

Arriving at Leia's quarters, Foxwell pushed a button on the casing covering the wooden framework housing the auto-controlled doors. They could hear the muffled chime inside the cabin—no response. Foxwell and Rivera exchanged glances.

"Something doesn't feel right, Doctor."

"Well, it was a long day. I wouldn't blame her for being sound asleep," Rivera speculated. "Not to mention—who in their right mind would want to hear the news we're about to deliver?"

Foxwell pushed the chime button again, then lightly knocked on the doors. "Leia, it's Captain Foxwell," he announced in a quiet tone. Still no response.

Rivera looked at Foxwell. "I'm beginning to agree with you, Captain. Something is off here."

Foxwell pressed the red security button on the bulkhead companel.

"Security here," the unidentified voice answered, "state the nature of your contact."

"This is the captain—send a security team to E deck, section 2, stateroom 112."

"Aye, sir, on our way."

* * *

Within minutes, two security officers arrived on scene. Using a sensor-controlled device attached to his utility belt, the senior officer triggered the double doors' hydraulic actuator. Both panels separated opposite each other and into their respective doorframe cavity.

The cabin's fiber optic lighting sensor responded in tandem, fully illuminating Leia's assigned stateroom.

"*Leia*?" the captain shouted, entering her quarters, followed by the security officers and Rivera.

"Doctor, she's here, in her bed," Foxwell declared.

Rivera moved hurriedly past the security officers as he made his way to the bedside of the assistant chief geologist. "*Leia—Leia*?" Rivera leaned over her as she lay face up on her bunk. The chief medical officer placed his hand on her shoulder and gently shook. Her eyelids remained tightly closed with no return to any state of wakefulness. Rivera stood, flipped open a diagnostic medical analyzer, then slowly waved the detachable scanner over Leia's head and upper torso.

The security officers discreetly examined her quarters, looking for any evidence of foul play. Rivera flipped the medical analyzer shut, snapping the scanner into its compartment on the back of the unit.

Foxwell remained silent until Rivera concluded his examination. "What is it, Doctor? What's wrong with her?"

"Her vital signs are stable, but she's comatose. We need to move her to sickbay. She needs a more extensive examination, and we'll need to run some tests."

"We've covered the entire stateroom, Captain," the senior security officer chimed in. "There's nothing here that stands out or raises any kind of red flag."

Foxwell looked around, puzzled. "Professor Adana is dead, and now his daughter is in a coma. What the hell is going on? What's the common denominator? There's got to be a connection. These two incidents cannot be purely coincidental."

"On its surface I would tend to agree with you," Rivera opined. But the current priority is to move Leia to medical. And we need to do that immediately."

Foxwell sighed, pursed his lips, then turned and placed a hand on Rivera's shoulder. "Arrange for a medical team to move Leia to sickbay. Security will remain here and seal her cabin. I'm on my way to Beta's quarters. Keep me informed on her condition."

* * *

Beta's Stateroom, 0400 hours

"Most unfortunate," Beta replied, acknowledging Foxwell's brief summary regarding the death of Professor Adana and his daughter Leia's medical condition. "May I speak freely, Captain?"

"Go ahead."

"While I agree with you and Dr. Rivera that these events appear to be related, our first priority continues to be the mission. We'll need someone to assume the duties of the professor and his daughter."

Foxwell locked eyes with Beta. "I don't need a reminder about priorities, Commander. I'm very well aware of our primary mission."

"I only meant to suggest that we refocus our attention to determine which of their scientists would now be the most qualified to lead the geological survey team. I did not mean to infer we terminate the investigation or minimize the serious nature of what has happened."

Foxwell paused, pondering on the suggestion of his first officer. She was right, of course, on both counts. He turned to her. "Beta, before we reach Luyten b, I want you to complete a review of the database personnel files on the Galactic Fleet geologists aboard *Stargazer*; as science officer, I want your recommendation regarding the most qualified to be appointed chief geologist."

"Understood, Captain. May I ask the status of the current investigation regarding the professor and his daughter?"

"Chief Security Officer Warwick will be fully briefed and instructed to conduct the appropriate investigation in unison with Dr. Rivera and his findings," Foxwell replied. He turned again, staring pensively at the bulkhead.

"Would it be *reasonable* to assume something else is bothering you, Captain?"

Foxwell paused, then craned his neck and locked eyes with Beta. "There's a killer aboard the *Stargazer*."

Part V

Stardate: Nov. 28, 2096

"Go ahead, Doctor," Foxwell responded from the command chair, adjusting the volume on the chair's companel. Fatigued after leaving Beta's quarters and managing only a few hours' sleep, he arrived late morning on the bridge. Beta had relieved the on-duty conning officer upon arrival two hours earlier; she exited the command chair and provided the captain with a brief status before returning to her science station. Foxwell glanced at the small digital clock on the chair's armrest. It was approaching noon.

"I have some news for you, Captain," the doctor began.

"Hopefully good," the captain yawned.

Rivera was exhausted. He had not slept since accompanying the captain to Leia's quarters several hours earlier. "Can I trouble you to drop by the medical department? There are more particulars to go over than is appropriate to discuss over the intercom."

"On my way," Foxwell replied. The captain rose from his chair. "Navigator, what is our current time of arrival to Luyten b?"

"Two hours, fourteen minutes, Captain."

"Very well. Continue present course and speed."

"Aye, sir."

Foxwell turned toward the turbo elevator, recessed into the bulkhead between the science and communication stations. "Beta, please accompany me to medical. Xuriya, you have the bridge."

"Aye, Captain."

"Sickbay," Foxwell uttered into the elevator companel, the turbo lift beginning its descent toward the medical department. He turned and gazed at his first officer. "What's our engineering status?"

"The chief engineer reports the loss of several additional circuit boards in the light speed drive assembly control panels; boards are being replaced as they fail; there are sufficient spares to get us to the exoplanet. Bridge and engineering monitors continue to reflect the instability of the defective boards, with no current danger to the fusion drive or life support. We should be in orbit around Luyten b in a little over two hours."

Foxwell nodded.

* * *

"Leia has regained consciousness," Rivera informed the captain and Beta. "She's weak but resting comfortably in a private cubicle in the general patient ward."

"What have you been able to find out?" Foxwell asked.

"Rilidium poisoning—both Leia and her father," the chief medical officer replied.

Foxwell exchanged glances with Beta. "Did we hear you say *rilidium poisoning*, Doctor?"

"Her father's autopsy and laboratory tests confirm enough rilidium in his system to kill five adults," the doctor replied. "Fortunately, all starship medical departments carry the standard protocol medical kits to counter the effects of Leia's level of absorbed radiation dose. She's receiving treatment intravenously and is showing signs of improvement. The how or why it occurred is unknown at this time. I'll provide an update this evening. She's not in any condition to be questioned presently."

"She's very fortunate," Beta affirmed. "The same or even lesser dose would have proven fatal, regardless of treatment. I find it interesting that whoever caused the death of her father failed to sufficiently dose Leia."

Rivera looked at Beta, a condescending smile on his face. "You talk as if you're disappointed she *didn't die*. Perhaps that neutronic *reasoning* brain of yours can shed some light on the mindset of the perpetrator?"

Beta furrowed her eyebrows. It was obvious Rivera was irritated by her dispassionate observations. "I only meant to suggest that a non-fatal dose was administered, perhaps intentionally, Doctor. The how or why it occurred part of it, as you earlier stated, is currently unavailable pending the results of a joint investigation involving—"

"Well," Rivera interrupted, "something we finally agree on. You know, Beta, perhaps you—"

"Ladies, gentlemen," Foxwell snickered. He threw his hands in the air, waving them back and forth. "We'll never get anywhere arguing over what we already know." He pivoted in the direction of his chief medical officer. "Doctor, let me know when Leia is well enough to be questioned."

Before Rivera could acknowledge the captain's request, a medical assistant appeared. "Captain, Chief Engineer O'Donovan is hailing you, said it's urgent."

Foxwell walked several feet to the closet companel and tapped the engineering key. "Foxwell here."

"Captain, I sent the assistant chief engineer to relieve Xuriya on the bridge; she's here with me in engineering. The circuit board logistics review you ordered previously has been completed. We both agree a meeting with you and Beta should take place—as soon as possible," O'Donovan said, urgency permeating every word.

The chief engineer's message registered. Foxwell turned and locked eyes with his first officer before turning back to the companel. "So you're telling me you and Xuriya have solved this circuit board logistics mystery?"

The chief engineer and Xuriya exchanged a quick glance. "We've completed the review as ordered, Captain. We'd like to review those findings with you and Beta," he replied, avoiding the question.

A pause. "We're on our way."

* * *

Foxwell and Beta observed as O'Donovan and Xuriya focused on the oversized monitor. They began by retracing the original shipping route for the circuit boards requested for the *Stargazer*.

"The original shipment of 240 new rilidium circuit boards was received while in space dock following battle with the Vorcians," the chief engineer began. "It's the result of a requisition I previously submitted to Galactic Fleet Logistical Support. The boards were delivered a day later by shuttle courier. Ensign Beth McCollough was the logistical support shuttle pilot. She made the trip alone."

Foxwell nodded as the chief engineer spoke. Beta remained motionless, listening, staring at the monitor, her arms crossed.

Xuriya craned her neck and continued. "Upon arrival,

Ensign McCullough was escorted by security to engineering. She exchanged the new boards for the previously extracted and spare boards with Engineering Technician Jameson. She was escorted back to the shuttle and returned to Galactic Fleet Logistics Center."

"I can confirm that," O'Donovan chimed in. "I was present and observed the exchange. Ensign Jameson and the assistant chief engineer installed the new boards into both control panels. The remaining boards were tagged as spares and left in their mylar pouches, then placed into storage."

"Cyber Boards, Inc., is the circuit board manufacturer," Xuriya continued. "They have an exclusive contract with Galactic Fleet Command to manufacture *all* starship rilidium circuit boards."

O'Donovan swiveled his chair around. "It's standard procedure for Galactic Fleet Logistics to send a courier to the manufacturer to pick up boards ordered or exchanged for use by the fleet. The boards are then delivered to the recipient starship aboard a logistics shuttlecraft if the starship is in Earth orbit. Larger, heavier freight is delivered via freighter while in Earth orbit; *all* shipments are delivered by freighter beyond Earth orbit, then delivered to starships via shuttle transfer."

Foxwell nodded again, then glanced at his first officer. "Anything you would like to add, Beta?"

"The standard requisition protocol as explained is correct," Beta confirmed, "to include our request for and delivery of the *Stargazer*'s replacement rilidium boards."

"Understood," Foxwell responded, nodding. He turned back to O'Donovan and Xuriya. "But that doesn't solve the mystery as to why *our* boards are malfunctioning."

"Aye, Captain," O'Donovan answered. "Following normal requisition protocol," he continued, "there's nothing egregious in the requisition and delivery procedure itself that would result in the transmutation of these boards. Something else caused that to happen."

Xuriya pushed her chair back slightly, then pulled the retractable keyboard out from under the chief engineer's desk. "Captain, I have the security video which reveals a member of Galactic Fleet Logistics departing the facility with our requisitioned boards." Using her index finger, she moved the cursor over the Cyber Board, Inc., video icon and tapped the touchpad, repeated the process a second time for the main door security camera, then tapped the play arrow icon.

Beta unfolded her arms. She and Foxwell leaned closer to the monitor, viewing the video footage recorded during the time frame it occurred. Date and time embedded in the video at activation was *10-16–96 Wed 14:20:01*.

"Xuriya and I agreed it would be prudent to check security camera footage on the day the boards left the facility," O'Donovan whispered.

Less than ten minutes into the playback, the *Stargazer*'s first officer and science officer took a step back. "Pause the video," Beta shouted.

Xuriya immediately moved the cursor over the pause icon and tapped the touchpad.

Beta leaned forward again. "Rewind to timeline 14:20:01 and bookmark."

Foxwell pivoted. "What is it?"

Beta moved forward a step. "The boards ordered by Chief O'Donovan were *not* picked up by anyone from Galactic Fleet Logistics."

The captain exchanged glances with O'Donovan and Xuriya, then gazed at his first officer. "Explain."

Beta nodded. "Pay close attention to the monitor.

Xuriya, play the timeline bookmarked and pause the video when I say."

Xuriya moved the cursor as directed and tapped the touchpad. The video replay confirmed movement of several personnel in and out of the circuit board facility, most of whom were assumed to be civilian employees or authorized Galactic Fleet personnel. The video continued until an unknown party outfitted in a Galactic Fleet Logistics uniform exited the facility's main door. The unidentified party was pulling a small dolly with two identical-size boxes secured on the nose plate.

"Pause," Beta directed. "Enhance frames 189 to 221 — move in — stop — track left and up — stop — enhance — stop." The video paused on the shipment tag attached to the top box. The image was now enlarged and sharpened, identifying the content of the boxes to be rilidium circuit boards bound for the *Stargazer*.

Foxwell turned and locked eyes with Beta. "Okay, so it's a logistics crew member exiting the facility with our shipment of rilidium circuit boards. Where are you going with this?"

"Down the proverbial rabbit hole, Captain, to borrow the well-coined phrase. May I continue?"

Foxwell sighed. "Please do." He smirked, throwing his hands out.

Beta focused again on the monitor. "Resume the video."

Xuriya tapped the touchpad; the video playback resumed.

"Pause," Beta uttered again. "Track right — stop — track up — stop — center and stop — pan right and pullback — stop — enhance frames 241 to 244 — stop."

The video paused, centered directly over the enlarged face of the alleged logistics crew member.

O'Donovan and Xuriya exchanged a startled glance. Both stood and stepped away from the desk. A bewildered Foxwell leaned forward, repositioning O'Donovan's desk chair, his eyes glued to the monitor as he slowly lowered himself into the chair, pulling himself closer to the desk.

A pause. "How did you know, Beta?" the captain asked. He stared at the monitor, his disheartened tone of voice mirroring the expression on his face.

"My cybernetic eye, Captain, replaced after my long-ago shuttle accident. I can initiate a thought command which instructs the bionic eye to further enhance and sharpen video, prints, negatives, et cetera, simultaneously streaming those images to my neutronic brain. Identity was obvious the moment that particular figure became visible in the camera lens *entering* the facility, but only to me, which is why I instructed Xuriya to isolate and enhance the exiting frames."

Foxwell nodded. He looked up, his gaze scrolling over Beta's face.

"This is the rabbit hole I referred to earlier," Beta said, echoing the previous metaphor.

Foxwell pushed the chair back and stood. He took a deep breath, then sighed heavily. "It's her . . . it's *Leia.* Her father is deceased, she's in a coma, and the *Stargazer*'s propulsion support system is failing." He paused again before finally adding: "It appears we have discovered the common denominator."

"That would be a *reasonable* deduction," Beta acknowledged.

PART VI

GALACTIC
FLEET
COMMAND

Stardate: Nov. 28, 2096

The *Stargazer* continued on its journey toward Luyten b, drawing closer by the hour. The on duty conning officer and bridge crew were under orders to remain vigilant regarding the starship's propulsion monitors. Deviation beyond the previous anomalous readings were to be reported to and acknowledged by engineering, followed by a notification alert to the captain and first officer.

Foxwell entered his ready room to a standing audience of his senior officers, a briefing ordered after conclusion of the requisition and logistics review in engineering. The positive atmosphere which characterized the initial mission conference attended by the starship's department heads was now dampened by the dual tragedy befalling Leia and her father, and to a lesser extent the *Stargazer*'s engineering problems.

"Please be seated," the captain directed. He turned toward Beta and nodded. She pushed the power button on the ready room monitors and repositioned the screens.

"This briefing is for the benefit of Dr. Rivera and Chief Security Officer Warwick," Beta began.

After replaying the security video and providing a

short synopsis of the meeting in engineering, Rivera and Warwick both agreed the person in the video was, in fact, Professor Adana's daughter, Leia Athena.

Foxwell continued. "We know Leia took custody of properly requisitioned rilidium circuit boards bound for the *Stargazer* using false identification, posing as an authorized member of Galactic Fleet Logistics. There was no discrepancy regarding later delivery and receipt of those same boards."

The senior officers looked around. They were clearly befuddled to learn Leia was somehow connected with the circuit board failures, and possibly the death of her father.

Beta stood. "Operational Support in San Francisco has confirmed no abnormal rilidium circuit board failures in other starships that requisitioned and replaced boards during repairs or while in space dock." She tapped the appropriate icon on the monitor, the subspace message appearing on screen corroborating her statement.

"Which means *Stargazer* is the only affected starship," Foxwell added.

"But *why*, Captain?" Chief Security Officer Warwick asked, his puzzled look mirroring the thoughts of the other senior officers.

Foxwell looked around his ready room. "That's exactly what I intend to find out," he replied, turning in the direction of his first officer. "Beta, when will we reach Luyten b?"

"At present course and speed—one hour, thirty-six minutes."

Foxwell pivoted toward Rivera. "What is Leia's current medical condition, Doctor?"

"She's no longer comatose, but sedated. She should be well enough for questioning this evening."

Foxwell turned and glanced at his chief security officer.

"Lieutenant Warwick, gather a security team and proceed to A deck. The geologists and mining engineers have set up makeshift labs in the shuttle bay. I want you and your officers to conduct a thorough search of Leia's geological instruments, to include field supplies, lab equipment, and containers. You'll be looking for *anything* that is not consistent with their pending survey."

"Aye, Captain, on my way," Warwick replied as he hurriedly exited the ready room.

Beta locked eyes with Foxwell. "Captain, I have completed my review of geologist personnel files per your previous order. I would strongly advise Dr. Zara Veillon, a geophysicist, accompany the security team."

Foxwell returned an inquisitive look. "Why that particular scientist?"

"Other than Leia and the late Professor Adana, she is the most qualified of three geologists reviewed regarding knowledge and handling of rilidium and rilidium ore," Beta answered.

Foxwell nodded. "Agreed—see to it Dr. Veillon is made aware."

"Captain, with your permission, I will accompany Lieutenant Warwick and the security team to the shuttle bay, and I will inform Zara Veillon of her new duties."

"Make it so, Commander," Foxwell acknowledged, turning toward his assembled senior officers. "This meeting is concluded. Report back to your departments and make preparations for arrival to Luyten b."

Foxwell and Beta were the last to exit the ready room. Rather than return to his command chair, he paced around the circular bridge platform, an observation not lost on his first officer. Just as Beta reached the turbo elevator, she turned and momentarily gazed at the captain. She motioned for the other senior officers to proceed without her, turning and walking back toward Foxwell. He stopped as she approached him.

"May I request that you accompany me back inside the ready room, Captain?"

Foxwell pursed his lips, then sighed. "Of course," he whispered, politely extending his arm.

The automatic doors closing behind them, Foxwell and Beta stood next to the oval conference table.

"What is it, Beta?" Foxwell inquired.

A pause. "Captain, is it your belief Leia—"

The ready room companel emitted an audible hailing signal.

"Foxwell here."

"Captain—Lieutenant Warwick. I'm in the shuttle bay with my security team. Can you join me here, sir?"

"Find something, Lieutenant?"

"Aye Captain, we've made a peculiar discovery; something of interest in a backpack belonging to Leia. I believe you need to see this."

"Very well. Is geophysicist Veillon in the shuttle bay?"

"Negative, sir. Her colleagues believe she may be in her quarters."

"On my way," Foxwell replied. The captain pivoted toward Beta. "Find Zara Veillon and meet me in the shuttle bay."

* * *

Shuttle Bay

"This is what we've uncovered, Captain," Lieutenant Warwick announced, directing Foxwell toward a workbench. On top of the bench were two small metallic boxes, each with a hinged top and flip latch in front. Both were secured with a small titanium padlock.

Foxwell grabbed the handle of the closest box, lifting it upward several inches before lowering it back on the bench. "It's heavy," he declared as the chief engineer arrived, gazing at the boxes. "My guess is they're both made of lead."

"Your guess is correct, Captain. They *are* lead, with sufficient volume to safely contain a small amount of low yield ionizing material," Chief O'Donovan posited.

Foxwell exchanged glances with O'Donovan and Warwick. "Any attempt to open the boxes?"

"No, Captain," Warwick replied. "We're awaiting the arrival of Beta and the geophysicist."

* * *

"It's definitely rilidium," newly appointed Chief Geologist Zara Veillon declared, standing in front of the workbench. She and all personnel had donned radiation suits before using a laser torch to remove the padlocks. The contents of both boxes had been removed and placed on the bench, identified and tested for radiation levels. "It's safe to remove our ionization suits," she announced, her voice muffled by the hooded portion of her suit. Foxwell, Beta, and the remaining senior department heads carefully removed their protective clothing. They gathered around the Galactic Fleet geophysicist.

"What are we looking at, Dr. Veillon?" Foxwell asked.

"The first box contains a hypospray injector and several vials," she began. "The vials contain rilidium in what apparently is a liquid injectable medium. The other box revealed a small, round tin with a screw thread lid containing approximately half an ounce of processed rilidium ore, ground into a very fine powder. Both are emitting ionization particles, but at safe levels. However, if deeply inhaled, ingested . . . or injected, it's deadly."

Rivera examined the hypospray injector and vials, then the powder. "I agree with the findings of Dr. Veillon, Captain. I can run additional tests on the vials in sickbay, but the fact they're radioactive pretty much confirms what she stated."

"Run the tests, Doctor. I want those results available when Leia is questioned."

Rivera nodded, followed by a hailing signal from the closet companel.

"Engineering, O'Donovan here," the chief engineer responded.

"This is Lieutenant Roberts on the bridge," the on duty conning officer announced. "Please inform the captain we are approaching the exoplanet. *Stargazer* will be in orbit around Luyten b in less than thirty minutes."

Part VII

Stardate: Nov. 28, 2096

"Status, Lieutenant Roberts," Foxwell called out. He and Beta stepped out of the turbo lift onto the bridge, and Beta continued in the direction of her science station.

"Orbital path around Luyten b established; impulse engines disengaged; atmospheric probes launched eight minutes ago," Roberts confirmed.

Beta swiveled her chair and gazed at Foxwell. "Probes and sensor scans confirm the exoplanet is class M, Captain."

Foxwell returned a confirming nod, then stood in front of the main viewing screen. "It looks absolutely stunning from here," he proclaimed. He described the planet's atmosphere as orange, with bands of copper and cyan, high-lighted by random cloud cover. "The surface topography appears balanced—blue with water, a rocky terrain, and a hearty sprinkling of vegetation." Smiling, the captain turned in the direction of the helmsman. "Maintain standard orbit; position hull sensor arrays to surface coordinates provided by Galactic Fleet Command."

"Aye, Captain," the helmsman replied. "Maintaining standard orbit, data accessed and entered; hull sensors locked onto coordinates," he repeated.

Foxwell walked to the science station. "Beta, analyze the sensor data received for the most suitable landing area; we'll be setting the *Stargazer* on the surface for closet access to the rilidium ore deposits. Notify all departments we'll be on the surface in one hour."

"Acknowledged, Captain; department heads alerted." Beta swiveled her chair in the direction of the sensor viewer.

Foxwell walked back to the command chair, standing next to the arm containing the companel. He tapped the engineering key.

"Engineering, O'Donovan here."

"POD, notify Dr. Veillon and the chief mining engineer to prepare for a familiarization survey. Initial mining and geology surveyors will be organized into two teams of four personnel. You, Beta, Chief Security Officer Warwick, and I will accompany the surveying parties. All personnel will meet in the shuttle bay within the first hour of setting down on the exoplanet. Contact Lieutenant Warwick and Chief Geologist Zara Veillon and make them aware."

"Aye, Captain; Beta just informed me we'll be on the planet's surface within the hour."

* * *

Foxwell sat in his command chair. He tapped the starship's PA system key. "All personnel—this is the captain—standby and brace for atmospheric entry."

Beta swiveled her seat in the direction of the command chair. "Captain, suitable landing area located approximately two kilometers from primary site of rilidium ore deposits."

"Acknowledged—transfer data to the navigational system."

"Transfer completed," Beta replied.

"Helmsman, let's take her down. Initiate landing sequence."

"Aye Captain, impulse engines reengaged; all descent and landing systems online."

"Switch to manual control."

"Aye, Captain. Engaging reaction control thrusters; landing pylons extended and locked."

"Commence landing—steady as she goes," Foxwell directed.

Using the joystick, the helmsman carefully piloted the *Stargazer* toward the designated landing area. As he adjusted the diverted thrust characteristics of the RCS engines, the *Stargazer* was maneuvered into position until it hovered directly over the site coordinates provided by Beta.

"Setting her down in five . . . four . . . three . . . two . . . one . . . The *Stargazer* has landed," the helmsman announced. The starship's enormous structure buffeted softly, its supporting pylons gripping the undisturbed soil of the heralded Earthlike planet.

Foxwell stood and walked behind his command chair.

An applause combined with a loud cheer from the bridge crew echoed around the circular platform. Affirming smiles and gazes followed the *Stargazer*'s successful arrival, lifting the spirits of the crew previously dampened by sabotage and murder.

"Good job everyone," the captain announced, beaming proudly. He patted the navigator and helmsman on the shoulder before turning and locking eyes with the communications officer. "Xuriya, notify Galactic Fleet Command: *Stargazer* has touched down on Luyten b."

"Aye, Captain."

Foxwell pivoted and walked to the science station. "Beta, confirm basic weather and atmospheric conditions."

"Temperature outside the *Stargazer* is currently 66 degrees Fahrenheit, humidity 56 percent. Winds are negligible, no precipitation. The troposphere of Luyten b is comprised of 76 percent nitrogen, 22 percent oxygen. The remaining 2 percent is argon, water vapor, and carbon dioxide—almost identical to Earth."

"Forward those stats to all departments, then accompany me to the shuttle bay."

"Acknowledged, Captain."

"Xuriya, you have the bridge until relieved per the duty roster."

* * *

Shuttle Bay

Confirming the presence of all designated personnel, Foxwell led the two groups of surveyors and Galactic Fleet officers to A deck. Newly appointed Chief Geologist Zara Veillon took charge of selecting two surveying teams. Communicators and fusion laser pistols were issued to accompanying Galactic Fleet personnel. Entering the unlock code on the access control panel, the chief engineer proceeded to deploy the *Stargazer*'s access ramp, observing through a portal the ramp's simultaneous unfolding and extension.

"Ramp deployed and positioned on the planet's surface, Captain," the chief engineer reported.

Beta studied the external environmental control screen on the bulkhead next to the starship's dual access plug door. "Atmospheric conditions on the planet's surface are suitable for humanoid life, Captain," she reconfirmed.

"Excellent," Foxwell replied. "Let's get down there and

find out what we're dealing with."

Beta entered the door's unlock code, then enabled the servo-drive mechanism. She tapped the "open door" icon on the interface control panel. The door responded with a low-frequency whirr and sharp hiss. As the door unsealed and cycled through its opening sequence, the pressure inside the starship equalized with the outside environment.

Foxwell stepped forward and peered outward, completing a panoramic visual before stepping out and onto the angled ramp. Desiring a look at objects more distant, he removed the vortex field viewer from his utility belt, scanning left to right several times before reattaching it to his belt.

"First impressions, Captain?" Beta asked.

Foxwell turned and smiled, followed by a thumbs-up. Exiting the *Stargazer*, he led a procession of starship senior officers followed by the Galactic Fleet surveying teams. At the end of the ramp he stopped, the column of personnel stopping behind him. The *Stargazer*'s commanding officer stepped gently onto the surface of Luyten b, the first human from planet Earth to do so. Captain Foxwell turned around and faced his crewmates and surveyors, the line of eager explorers extending all the way back to the starship's reciprocal plug door. He scrolled over the face of every person preparing to step onto the soil of Luyten b. They waited for him to say something.

Foxwell smiled again. "If there is magic on this beautiful planet, it is contained in its soil, its water, its botany, and its atmosphere," he proclaimed.

He gazed at his colleagues. They were quiet, contemplative, remaining stationary on the ramp, immobile as if someone had hit the pause button on a video replay.

"We are here to explore this planet for the element

rilidium," the captain continued, "necessary for starship propulsion and as ordered by Galactic Fleet Command. Every necessary precaution will be taken, not only for the safety of our Galactic Fleet scientists, engineers, and starship personnel, but for the care and safety of this planet's ecological system. I want that clearly understood."

There was no doubting the seriousness of Foxwell's directive. All personnel on the ramp nodded in unison, some quietly uttering acknowledgment. Eagerness to begin exploration was written on the face of every surveyor and starship crewmember.

Convinced his order was understood, Foxwell threw down the welcome mat. "On behalf of planet Earth, Galactic Fleet Command, and the *SS Stargazer*, welcome to Luyten b." He stepped away from the end of the ramp, motioning with his arm for all personnel to join him on the surface of the beautiful, never-before-explored exoplanet.

Foxwell stood aside, smiling, shaking hands, exchanging short pleasantries as each person stepped off the ramp and onto the soil. The geologists and mining engineers were carrying only the field equipment and supplies required for their initial examination and survey. Findings would be conferenced later regarding more extensive or invasive studies.

The captain's communicator chimed its signature beep. "Foxwell here," he responded, stepping away from the ramp.

"Captain, it's Rivera. I need you back onboard."

"Why, what happened?" Foxwell replied, his previous elation now a mixture of concern and confusion.

"It's Leia—she's nowhere to be found."

GALACTIC
FLEET
COMMAND

PART VIII

Stardate: Nov. 28 – Dec 02, 2096

"The medical assistant reported Leia missing from her private cubicle approximately ten minutes ago. I've notified the bridge as well as security," Rivera explained.

"How was she able to walk out of sickbay?" Foxwell asked.

"We believe she donned a set of standard medical PPE garments, to include a mask and headgear—equipment located in lockers in designated cubicles for use by our medical personnel. That would make slipping out of sickbay easy."

Foxwell walked to the nearest companel and tapped the bridge key.

"Bridge, Lieutenant Hewitt here."

Foxwell remembered Hewitt was listed on the duty roster as the conning officer scheduled to relieve Xuriya.

"Lieutenant, this is the captain. Access the interface control panel on A deck. I want you to close and secure the plug access door. Contact Beta and make her aware I've instructed you to do this; let her know she's in charge of the surveying expedition until further notice."

"Aye Captain, right away."

Foxwell tapped the security key on the companel.

"Security—this is Assistant Chief of Security Dawson; state the nature of your contact."

"Lieutenant, this is the captain. Provide a status on the search for Leia Athena as reported by Dr. Rivera."

"I have three teams searching the ship for her," Dawson replied. "Updates are provided as they complete their sweep of each assigned sector; there have been no sightings or other evidence of her whereabouts at this time."

"Lieutenant, proceed to the bridge. I'll join you there shortly," Foxwell ordered.

"Aye, sir."

Rivera turned toward Foxwell. "Captain, before you leave, there's something I need to tell you."

"What is it, Doctor?" Foxwell asked.

Rivera frowned. "As part of his initial search, Dawson dispatched a security team to Leia and her father's stateroom on the hunch she might have taken refuge. She wasn't in either, but they did locate a micro disc in her father's quarters that was brought to sickbay. Professor Adana created this video. I viewed it just before I asked you to return to the ship. I strongly advise you view it as well," Rivera suggested, handing Foxwell the small diskette.

Opening the computer's disc tray by voice command, Foxwell inserted the micro disc. "Close tray," Foxwell repeated, the medical department's monitor illuminating as it displayed a recorded video by Professor Adana.

"Pay close attention, Captain," Rivera urged.

After viewing the ten-minute video, Foxwell sighed, then walked toward an adjoining island in the middle of sickbay; he placed both hands on the edge of the island, extending his arms and looking down at the tabletop. "She's seriously ill . . . isn't she, Doctor?"

"Yes, Captain, she is." Rivera stood next to Foxwell at the island. "According to her father, she suffers from episodes known as brief psychotic disorder. He stated her treating psychiatrist diagnosed the condition approximately six months ago following years of exposure to high amounts of ionizing rilidium radiation."

"I'm confused, Doctor—what's the connection?"

Rivera walked slowly around the front of the island. He turned and faced the captain. "I'm not a geologist or rilidium specialist, but I've read all the medical literature and journals on rilidium poisoning, and how it can affect mind and body. If her father quoted Leia's treating psychiatrist correctly, then what he's saying is that she is the victim of radiation-induced schizophrenia."

Foxwell pushed away from the island. "But she knew the dangers; she knew the rules and procedures regarding safety and the handling protocol to be followed. She had to know in order to avoid overexposure," the captain emphasized.

Dr. Rivera took in a deep breath. "Perhaps her passion for her work clouded her judgment. She struck me as quite ambitious," he continued. "I'm sure you, Beta, and the other senior officers came to the same conclusion. Ambition is a positive trait when channeled appropriately. But there can be a negative side as well, particularly if the motivation behind it is *improperly* channeled. I'm only guessing, but perhaps she was working toward perfection instead of striving for productivity."

Foxwell thought for a moment. "Do you mean in an attempt to seek recognition?"

"Possibly . . . it's as good a hypothesis as any," Rivera replied.

Foxwell was aware his assistant chief of security

awaited his arrival on the bridge. He turned toward his chief medical officer. "Doctor, I know the ship's communication system can be accessed in sickbay. I want you to contact Beta and inform her of Leia's disappearance, that every effort is being made to locate her. Let Beta know I'll attempt to keep her updated."

"There's something else, Captain."

Foxwell looked at Rivera. "What is it, Doctor?"

"The hypospray is missing."

* * *

Exiting the turbo elevator, Foxwell joined Dawson at the security station on the bridge.

"Status, Lieutenant?"

"Just received word one of the security teams believes she may have been spotted in the vicinity of the captain's quarters on D deck. Another possible sighting was reported in the shuttle bay on A deck. If it's the latter, she may be attempting to retrieve something from one of the geology labs set up earlier by the surveying teams," the assistant chief security officer surmised.

"Or attempting to access the rovers—or worse, the shuttle," Foxwell added. "Lieutenant, proceed to A deck; I'll run a security sweep of D deck and meet you in the shuttle bay in fifteen minutes."

"Aye, sir," Dawson acknowledged, entering the turbo elevator and issuing a voice command for the shuttle bay.

Foxwell turned and walked back to the command chair. "Officer of the Deck Hewitt, disable all security codes for the shuttle, rovers, and rover access ramp."

"Aye, Captain."

* * *

"D deck," Foxwell shouted, and the turbo lift began its short two-deck descent.

Exiting the elevator, Foxwell walked cautiously through the deck's corridor, paying close attention to anything out of the ordinary. The pneumatic doors opened as he stepped out of the corridor and into a narrow hallway leading to his stateroom.

He felt a stinging blow to the back of his head, driving him forward and into an adjoining bulkhead; he slid down the compartment wall and onto the deck, face up. Unable to stand or think straight, his vision a blur, Foxwell felt the sensation of being pulled by his arms; he could vaguely make out the outline of what appeared to be a female struggling to drag him through the pneumatic doors of his stateroom.

"Yes, Captain, I arranged for the rilidium circuit boards to fail on our journey to Luyten b," she panted, out of breath after dragging Foxwell into his quarters. Releasing his wrists, she walked around and stood in front of him. "You see, Captain, natural rilidium requires three to five percent enrichment for use in fusion power drives, but I discovered a new, proprietary method of creating one hundred percent enriched rilidium. But my overly cautious and non-imaginative father alleged highly enriched rilidium is violently dangerous, and insisted I abandon my research. He even threatened to expose me if I refused—and to reveal that I was the one who sabotaged the *Stargazer*'s rilidium circuit boards—so naturally I had to eliminate him," she admitted, laughing hysterically.

Foxwell could hear the faint sound of activity as he tried to gather his senses. He tried to push upward, attempting to examine his surroundings. His vision clearing, Leia slowly came into focus.

"Allow us to work with you, Leia. Let us help. Let *me* help you," Foxwell implored, his words barely audible. "It's not too late," he continued, raising his head and extending his hand. He was still too weak to stand or move further.

"You and my father ruined *everything*," she screamed. I could have been the next Hyman Rickover of Galactic Fleet." Leia reached into a small pouch attached to her utility belt, removing a hypospray. She knelt down on the deck next to him. "I administered a small dose of rilidium to myself as a diversion . . . and just to make things interesting," she admitted, "but not before I injected my father with a lethal dose as he slept in his quarters. I'm surprised he made it out into the corridor," she snickered. "Now I'm going to kill you the same way I killed him. It's not a very pleasant way to die, but with the two of you out of the way I'll still have a chance to continue my research."

"You'll never get away with it," Foxwell uttered, still too weak to fight off Leia.

Kneeling beside him, she pushed his head to the side, exposing his neck in preparation to administer the hypospray.

"STOP!" someone shouted from the door opening just outside Foxwell's quarters. There was a blur of activity, followed by the sound of two people struggling in the background. Foxwell lifted his head, catching a glimpse of Xuriya and Leia grappling near his desk. With a short roundhouse kick, Xuriya managed to knock the hypo out of Leia's hand and onto the captain's desk. Leia feigned a grab of the hypospray, picking up a heavy book end and smashing it into the side of Xuriya's head. The communications officer dropped to the floor like a lump of coal.

"So you want to interfere and ruin things too, do you?" Leia seethed, wild-eyed and blinking. "Well, missy, I have just the cure for that." Her eyes filled with rage as she stood over the unconscious Galactic Fleet officer.

Snatching the hypospray off the desk, she knelt next to the unconscious Xuriya, pushing her head to the side to expose her neck.

Just before the hypo touched her skin, Leia suddenly arched her back, her body's muscular and central nervous system contracting forcefully to the sound of a laser pistol firing. She dropped the hypospray, falling on her side and away from Leia. Moaning, she managed to roll over before struggling to push herself up onto all fours. She reached for and grabbed the hypo, focusing her attention again on Xuriya.

"Don't do it, Leia," Foxwell shouted. He struggled to push himself up on his knees, still woozy and unsteady from the prior blow to his head, his fusion laser pistol still pointed at Leia.

She crawled closer to Xuriya.

"Don't do it," Foxwell pleaded again, simultaneously increasing the power setting of the laser pistol to its highest level.

Ignoring the captain's order, Leia again moved toward Xuriya, hypospray in her hand.

Foxwell fired his fusion laser pistol a second time, striking Leia and slamming her against the bulkhead. He staggered to his feet, then his desk, pressing the bridge key on the companel.

"Bridge, Lieutenant Hewitt here."

"This is the captain. Send a medical and security team to my quarters—priority response."

"Acknowledged, Captain. Medical and security team on their way."

* * *

"She's dead," Rivera declared, kneeling next to Leia's body. He turned off the scanner and closed the medical analyzer, then stood. "I'm sorry, Captain."

Foxwell sighed deeply. "What's Xuriya's condition, Doctor?"

"She's got quite a bump on her left temple. I'll need to examine her in medical and run some tests. The medics will use a gurney and accompany her to sickbay. Speaking of which, I need to examine you as well; you've got a nice-sized goose egg on the back of your own head. Oh, and that's an order, Captain."

Foxwell rendered a doleful nod.

* * *

Captain's Quarters, 1600 hours

"Enter," Foxwell uttered, responding to the door chime of his quarters. Beta walked through the open pneumatic doors. The captain was sitting quietly at his desk. The expression on his face was somber, distant.

"May I speak with you, Captain?"

Foxwell looked up at his first officer. "What's on your mind, Beta?"

"The chief engineer just informed me of a priority subspace transmission received regarding delivery of new rilidium circuit boards."

The captain appeared oblivious to Beta's message.

Beta relayed what she was told by the chief medical officer. "I understand Dr. Rivera cleared you to return to duty."

Foxwell nodded. "Xuriya isn't quite as fortunate. She'll

be in sickbay for a few days. She was diagnosed with a grade three concussion."

"The doctor briefed me about what happened after you returned aboard the *Stargazer*. He also offered reassurance Xuriya will make a full recovery," Beta disclosed.

"She saved my life. When Xuriya discovered Leia had disappeared from sickbay, she followed her intuition and proceeded to my quarters."

Beta furrowed her eyebrows. "If I may quote the phrase *a woman's intuition*, Captain, an almost psychic—and sometimes amazing knack—for knowing what others are thinking and feeling, based on an ability to read facial expressions and body language. It would be *reasonable* to assume Xuriya's intuitive feelings first manifested themselves during the evening of the formal dinner."

Indifferent to Beta's explanation, Foxwell sighed. "I wish there was more I could have done to help Leia. It's all such a waste."

Beta placed a consoling hand on Foxwell's shoulder. "Captain, based on everything I've seen and heard, there is nothing more you could have done."

Foxwell sighed with resignation. "Tell me about the survey, Beta. How's that proceeding?"

"Better than expected, Captain. Not only are rilidium ore deposits confirmed in the coordinates provided by the Galactic Fleet geologists, but the information gathered so far appears to indicate the deposits are of a much higher grade than anything previously mined on Earth."

"You mean a natural enrichment?" Foxwell asked.

"Exactly, Captain. If proven correct, it's possible this grade of rilidium will reduce the need to refuel starships by half, and that would include future maintenance replacement of starship rilidium circuit boards. The surveying party has returned to the ship. They are meeting currently to review their findings and to formulate a plan for extracting additional core samples for further testing."

Foxwell managed a half-smile. "It would be a major breakthrough for starship propulsion, and a major plus for Galactic Fleet Command, not to mention the possible applications for civilian use."

"A very *reasonable* assertion," Beta agreed.

* * *

"Of all the planets I've ever known or visited, this is the absolute loveliest," Xuriya declared, smiling and turning her head in the direction of the driver. "Don't you agree?"

Foxwell stopped the two-person rover in front of a cascading waterfall. Located approximately five miles west of the *Stargazer*, it was partially obscured by dense vegetation, forest, and rock formation. It was day four of their touchdown on the planet. Rivera had given the okay for Xuriya to return to light duty. Foxwell felt it was appropriate to personally take Xuriya on a local tour of the never-before-explored Earthlike exoplanet.

"I've never seen anything more beautiful," Xuriya exclaimed.

The magical, Luyten-blue waterfall flowed over the rocks and thundered down into the pool like a gigantic waterspout. When it toppled into the pool, it foamed at the bottom. It smelled fresh and natural, including the leaves and all the natural vegetation. The flowers and small trees surrounding it swayed gently in the wind.

Xuriya smiled. "Thank you for showing me this," she said. They exited the rover and began a short walk around the falls. She held tight to the captain's arm as they continued their excursion around the flowing cascade of water.

"You can thank Beta. She noticed it during an extended scanner sweep of our current position," Foxwell explained.

They sat on the ground in a clearing at the edge of the waterfall's enormous pool. Holding the captain's arm with both hands, she leaned gently against him.

"The Gates of Paradise," she declared happily, gazing misty-eyed at the waterfall.

Foxwell smiled.

THE END

Episode III

The Mars Plague

PROLOGUE

The *Stargazer* has been ordered to proceed to the Red Planet after a deadly plague is deliberately unleashed in the Martian colony, Titan. Every inhabitant is infected, and death is all but certain unless a vaccine can be developed. Their mission: assist the colony's scientists and medical staff to develop an effective vaccine before the virus kills every member of the colony and becomes a threat to Earth. Join the captain and chief medical officer as they battle time and a cunning enemy determined to destroy the colony and Galactic Fleet's most promising new alliance.

GALACTIC
FLEET
COMMAND

PART I

Stardate: Dec. 14, 2096 / 1440 hours

"Approaching Mars orbital parameters, Captain."

"Very well," Foxwell replied, exiting the command chair and glancing at the helmsman. "Disengage fusion drive—engage impulse engines; ahead one-quarter impulse power; initiate orbital sequence."

"Aye, Captain—*Stargazer* approaching Mars orbital insertion; decreasing power to impulse engines. Orbit will occur in five . . . four . . . three . . . two . . . one . . . engines shut down," the helmsman confirmed.

"Acknowledged—maintain standard orbit."

"Aye, Captain."

Walking toward the main viewing screen, Foxwell stopped, rendering a momentary glance at the rust-colored planet. "Orbiting Mars reminds me of that old vintage movie, *The Angry Red Planet*." He turned around, rendering a whimsical smile at his bridge officers. "You never know what you'll find down there," he chuckled.

Beta displayed her usual poker face, furrowing her eyebrows and resuming her scan of the bridge sensors, the remaining bridge crew quietly laughing at the captain's description.

Walking back to his command chair, he stopped and keyed the companel button for sickbay.

"Sickbay, Rivera here."

"Doctor, can I trouble you to report to my ready room?"

"On my way, Captain."

Pivoting in the direction of the science station, Foxwell made eye contact with his first officer. "Beta, please accompany me to the ready room."

Beta stood and followed the captain through the pneumatic doors, both panels opening and closing respectively, the soft whoosh and squeak of the doors echoing in the small compartment.

"Please take a seat," Foxwell requested. "Dr. Rivera will arrive momentarily."

No sooner spoken, the ready room doors opened again, with the *Stargazer*'s chief medical officer appearing in the doorway.

"That didn't take long," the captain commented, making eye contact with Rivera.

"Well, I was just leaving sickbay for my quarters, so your request that I proceed to the bridge was convenient timing. Now, what's this meeting all about?"

"Have a seat, Doctor," Foxwell directed with a motion of his hand.

Rivera walked around the small conference table, pulling out a seat next to Beta.

"As you're both aware, a subspace message received from Galactic Fleet Command two days ago directed the *Stargazer* to set a course for Mars and await further orders," Foxwell began. "I received another subspace message an hour before we entered Mars orbit directing the three of us meet in the ready room at 1500 hours. A priority-one subspace transmission from Admiral Perry is scheduled to begin at 1515 hours for mission specifics and instructions. It is now 1514 hours."

Silent but curious, Beta and Rivera remained seated. Foxwell reached up toward the overhead, pulling down a portable monitor in preparation to view the live Galactic Fleet transmission.

"Let's see what the admiral has in store for us," the captain declared, activating the monitor and making the necessary adjustments for viewing. Foxwell walked around and stood several feet behind his seated officers.

"Greetings Captain Foxwell, Commander Beta, Dr. Rivera. On behalf of Galactic Fleet Command, it is imperative the three of you be present for this briefing regarding a recent order directing *Stargazer* to set course for the red planet. Provisional Governor Jetson Duelow recently informed Galactic Fleet of an outbreak of a plague-like contagion that has spread rapidly throughout the Mars colony, Titan. Their medical facilities have been overwhelmed by a virus of unknown origin. With me is Admiral Ellis Mitchell, Medical Chief of Staff, Galactic Fleet Command. Please pay careful attention to what he has to say."

Admiral Mitchell continued with the briefing. "Thank you, Admiral. As Admiral Perry stated, testing has confirmed every human and Vulcan on Mars is positive for the virus; that includes the entire complement of health care professionals. This particular pathogen, appropriately named *Ares Viral Contagion*, is one hundred percent lethal once symptoms appear. Vulcan inhabitants are equally susceptible to infection but have generally fared better in the early stages due to their unique physiology."

"What is the mode of transmission, and what are the initial symptoms of the disease?" Rivera asked.

"It has been established the lungs are a ready inlet to

the contagion, spreading mainly from person to person, typically through respiratory droplets as a result of coughing, sneezing, or talking. Initial symptoms mimic those of a previous Earth pandemic, Covid-19, then progress rapidly to include respiratory collapse, and ultimately systemic organ failure. However, in the course of treating the disease, it has been determined that two drugs—actonadryl and doxporin vitracide—have been used with limited success in slowing viral replication and immune system overreaction. Several research and medical teams have arrived from Earth and Vulcan and are working with our Mars colony medical researchers and scientists. That's why the *Stargazer* is here. We understand Dr. Rivera has a background in microbiology and immunology."

Foxwell and Rivera exchanged glances. "Then you're ordering the *Stargazer*'s chief medical officer to proceed to the colony and join the current research teams?" Foxwell postulated.

Admiral Mitchell remained silent, glancing at his colleague.

"Galactic Fleet will not order Dr. Rivera to proceed to the Mars colony and join the effort to search for a vaccine or a cure," Admiral Perry continued. "His decision is entirely voluntary."

"And if he chooses *not* to volunteer?" Beta asked.

"In that case, Dr. Rivera will work with assigned medical and scientific research teams in an orbital research and advisory capacity, to be available as required. *Stargazer* will remain in orbit and provide advisory, security, and logistical support until ordered otherwise," Admiral Perry replied.

Foxwell snatched the controller and pressed the mute button. He pivoted and locked eyes with Rivera. "Doctor, you understand you *could* be signing your own death warrant if you agree to be a part of this effort, and a cure or vaccine is not found."

"Once you arrive on the planet, you'll be required to remain until the research is successful, or all Mars colony inhabitants perish," Beta added.

"I'm well aware of the risks involved," Rivera replied. "My MD thesis and dissertation at Galactic Fleet Medical School was management of virus-specific T cells in the lung during respiratory viral infections. I participated in this research in anticipation of neighboring planets possibly harboring infectious microbes and other microscopic pathogens such as this new virus."

Foxwell paused, then nodded and smiled. He knew the chief medical officer's decision even before it was announced.

Rivera turned in the direction of the monitor. Pressing the unmute button on the controller, he stared directly at the screen. "Admiral Perry, Admiral Mitchell—please advise the colony's chief medical officer and staff I'll join them on the ground as soon as arrangements can be made."

GALACTIC
FLEET
COMMAND

PART II

Stardate: Dec 14, 2096

Upon arriving in the shuttle bay at 1800 hours, Rivera and his assistant chief medical officer placed several bags on the deck behind the *Stargazer*'s solo shuttle. Clothing, a minimal amount of medical supplies and lab equipment, stack and carry tray organizers, and logs and journals completed the checklist. Rivera caught a glimpse of the starship's hull number, NC-X1, imprinted on the bottom portion of the rear loading ramp.

Rivera removed a final shoulder bag and set it on the deck next to the others, then turned and faced his colleague. "Per my earlier briefing, you'll be the acting chief medical officer in my absence. I have every confidence in you and the medical staff that the crew of the *Stargazer* will be in good hands until my return. Remember, I'll have an open channel while inside the colony. I'm always available if you need me. Any questions?"

"None, except to tell you I've got this while you're away," the assistant chief medical officer assured Rivera, smiling and extending a warm handshake. "Good luck, Doctor," he added before turning and walking to the shuttle bay elevator.

Rivera returned the smile, watching and waiting until his colleague entered the turbo lift for the return back to sickbay. He turned and pounded on the shuttle's hydraulically controlled rear loading door. A slight whirring sound emanated from the port and starboard hydraulic actuators, and the rear access ramp lowered in response to the shuttle's assigned pilot activating the hatch release in the cockpit.

"Good luck, Doctor," another crew member shouted, standing next to the control room approximately fifty feet behind the shuttle. He would soon seal himself inside the octagonal-shaped control booth in preparation to depressurize the hangar and subsequent opening of the main shuttle bay doors.

Dr. Rivera smiled and waved in response to the man issuing the solo shout out. He accepted it for what it was, no sarcasm intended. Rivera understood his success, his very life, depended on a fortuitous combination of circumstances. And he'd take all the luck he could get. There was no turning back once he reached the surface of Mars and entered the settlement.

With Rivera's bags stowed in the rear of the shuttle, he continued up the angled loading ramp and proceeded forward toward the cockpit. He wanted to greet the pilot whose only job was to deposit the chief medical officer on the surface of Mars next to the colony's primary entry and exit airlock. As understood by Rivera, the shuttle pilot would immediately return to the *Stargazer*.

Well, that's funny, Rivera thought to himself, noticing the silhouettes of two personnel behind the darkened cockpit. "Why am I seeing two pilots?"

"Welcome aboard, Doctor," a familiar voice shouted out as the rear access ramp rose. The pilot stood and moved out of the dark shadow of the cockpit and into the lighted rear cargo hold of the shuttlecraft. Rivera stepped back slowly, his gaze strolling over the face of the unexpected issuer of the greeting. "*Captain*, what in blazes are you doing here?" he asked, utterly stupefied.

"We're both on our way to the Mars colony," Foxwell announced, his tone and expression completely deadpan.

Rivera rendered a puzzled look, then chuckled nervously. "So, let me get this straight—you're taking me there—and dropping me off, is that correct?"

"Yes, I'm taking you there—and no, I will be accompanying you and remaining on the colony," Foxwell clarified. He turned and nodded in the direction of the co-pilot. "Ensign Roberts will set the shuttlecraft down next to the primary airlock. We'll suit up and exit with our gear. Roberts will return with the shuttle back to the *Stargazer*."

"Have you lost your mind?" Rivera shouted. "Do you know what this means?"

"I know *exactly* what it means, Doctor. It means if you and your colleagues are not successful, neither of us will return to the *Stargazer*, except in medically sealed containers for return to Earth and cremation."

Appearing baffled, Rivera shook his head. "I don't understand, Captain. What is it *you* plan to do? And who's in charge of the *Stargazer* while you're away?"

Foxwell turned and locked eyes with Rivera. "Beta will be in command during our absence. She's been thoroughly briefed. We have a mission to complete. Now, strap yourself in." Foxwell returned to the pilot's seat in preparation for shuttle departure.

"This is the dumbest . . ." Rivera mumbled to himself before Foxwell cut him off.

"What's that, Doctor?" Foxwell asked, smiling and shouting over the whirring sound of the shuttle's gyros after flipping the master switch to the on position.

"Nothing," Rivera shouted back. He redirected his complaint to difficulty with the safety restraints shuttle pilots and passengers are required to use. "Why the hell do passengers have to wear a five-point harness? It's like donning an interstellar straitjacket. The only thing missing is a lethal injection IV line and a nod from the warden."

Foxwell and his co-pilot looked at each other and chuckled. Opening a channel to the shuttle bay's control booth, Ensign Roberts instructed the control booth operator to activate the shuttlecraft turntable, slowly rotating the shuttle one hundred eighty degrees to allow for a nose-first departure. After confirming the shuttle's impulse engines were energized and all pre-flight checks completed, Foxwell opened a channel to the command chair on the bridge.

"Bridge, this is shuttlecraft NX-01, do you copy?" Foxwell hailed.

"Aye Captain, bridge acknowledges," Beta responded.

"Shuttle and crew ready for departure."

The first officer keyed the shuttle bay control booth, linking communications with the shuttle bay and the shuttlecraft. "Shuttle Bay Control, this is the bridge—the shuttlecraft reports ready for departure. Proceed to depressurize the shuttle bay and open shuttle bay doors."

"Aye, Commander," the control booth operator responded. "Depressurization and zero gravity confirmed." The shuttle bay doors slowly opened.

As Foxwell engaged the vertical and horizontal thrusters, the shuttlecraft rose steadily then moved forward in the empty void above and around it. Foxwell hailed the bridge. "Shuttlecraft NX-01 exiting the shuttle bay."

"Acknowledged," Beta replied, adding: "From the crew of the *Stargazer* to Captain Foxwell and Dr. Rivera—

our hopes and best wishes go with you for a successful mission."

"Thanks . . . we'll need it," Foxwell replied, viewing the red planet through the cockpit's two-inch-thick quartz windows. Engaging the port and starboard impulse engines, he maneuvered the shuttlecraft into a lower orbit. Craning his neck to the right, Foxwell attempted to check on the condition of Rivera. "How you doing back there, Doctor?"

"Like I'm stuck in quicksand, that's how I'm doing," Rivera complained. "How long will it take to reach the surface?"

"About fifteen minutes," Roberts chimed in.

"It might get a little rough when we make contact with the atmosphere, Doctor. Just a heads up."

Rivera frowned. "Then I should get my money's worth from this medieval torture device I'm wearing," he yelled in a sarcastic tone.

Approaching atmospheric entry coordinates, Foxwell engaged the shuttle's manual control system. "Ensign, activate exterior thermal coolant."

"Aye, Captain. ETC engaged."

Using gravity and drag in unison with the impulse thrusters, Foxwell slowed and maneuvered the shuttlecraft into the Martian atmosphere. A friction-generated, fiery-red plasma bubble enveloped the shuttle. Approximately ten minutes into their descent, the previously smooth flight was now bumpy and unsteady.

"We've reached the troposphere—disengaging ETC."

"Shuttle sensors have located the Martian settlement," Roberts confirmed.

"Yell when you acquire a visual," Foxwell shouted, the shuttlecraft bouncing around like a steel ball in a pinball machine. "Looks like dust storm activity has reduced visibility."

Following the navigational system's recommended angle of descent, Foxwell continued to reduce altitude until the shuttle finally broke through the dusty pea soup. The turbulence ceased.

"There it is, Captain," Roberts shouted.

"Got it," Foxwell called out, maneuvering the shuttle in a wide arc around the Martian colony, visually searching for the flashing beacon on the colony's shuttle pad.

Staring at the instrument panel, Roberts noticed a flashing indicator light on the sensor display. "Sensors are picking up the beacon's signal, Captain."

"I see it," Foxwell confirmed. "It's flashing in unison with the beacon. Almost there," he muttered.

Spiraling downward in a controlled descent, Foxwell aligned the shuttle with the shuttle pad located approximately thirty meters in front of the colony's primary airlock.

"One more pass," Foxwell declared, leveling and reducing speed before coming to a gentle rest on the Martian surface.

After seeing the instrument panel readings were within normal limits, Roberts turned his head. "How you doing back there, Doctor?"

"How am I doing?" Rivera parroted sarcastically. "Like I'm the main ingredient in a shake and bake contest, that's how I'm doing."

Foxwell and Roberts exchanged glances, quietly laughing.

PART III

Stardate: Dec 14, 2096 / 1930 hours

Confirming arrival with provisional colony authorities, Foxwell, Rivera, and Roberts donned environmental suits as they prepared to depressurize the shuttlecraft.

"Doctor, Ensign Roberts—can you read me?" Foxwell asked, checking communications after helping one another secure the polycarbonate helmet to the neck ring on their suits.

Roberts turned in the direction of Foxwell and rendered a thumbs-up.

"Give me a verbal, Ensign," Foxwell ordered.

"I read you loud and clear, Captain."

"Doctor—how about you? Did you hear the communications check between Roberts and myself?"

"That's affirmative."

Foxwell pivoted toward Roberts. "Ensign, prepare to depressurize the shuttle."

"Aye, Captain," Roberts acknowledged, moving forward and occupying the pilot's seat. "Ready when you are," he said, turning in the direction of Foxwell.

"Begin depressurization sequence."

Roberts flipped the depressurization enable switch,

then slowly turned the pressure relief valve. A hissing sound followed, indicating atmosphere and pressure within the shuttlecraft was equalizing with the Martian atmosphere outside. The hissing sound finally stopped when both gauges displayed the same internal and external indicator readings on the shuttle's cockpit monitor. Roberts turned and gazed at Foxwell. "Depressurization complete, Captain."

"Open rear access ramp," Foxwell directed.

"Aye, sir."

With the rear access door fully extended, Roberts exited the command seat and assisted with the removal of bags, equipment, and supplies in the rear cargo area of the shuttle. Moving everything within a few feet of the colony's primary access airlock, Foxwell turned and glanced at Rivera.

"That appears to be everything, Doctor."

Rivera stared somberly at Foxwell. "You sure you want to do this, Captain? It's enough I'm risking my own neck—why in the name of Orion's Belt do you want to risk yours as well?"

Ignoring the question, Foxwell scanned the Martian surface and horizon. The open sky appeared a light blue, its tone and shade eerily transitioning to a faint red as he followed the sky downward toward the horizon. Rust-colored soil blanketed the rocky surface, with numerous canyons, craters, hills, and dry lake beds all visible in the distance. Clouds dotted the sky. The Martian wind created dust whirls that skipped along the hard surface like a breeze that rippled the liquid surface of a pond.

Foxwell turned toward his chief medical officer. "What was it you were saying, Doctor?"

Rivera frowned, then sighed deeply. "Forget it. Is

someone planning to open the airlock before our oxygen supply is depleted?"

"Captain Foxwell, Dr. Rivera, this is Titan Colony Security—we're monitoring your communications. We are preparing to depressurize the airlock. Let us know when you're ready."

Foxwell glanced at his chief medical officer and smiled. "Looks like you just received your answer, Doctor. Titan Colony Security . . . standby," Foxwell replied.

Roberts turned in the direction of Foxwell. "Captain, is there anything else I can help you and Dr. Rivera with?"

"That's a negative, Ensign." Foxwell reached over and patted the shuttle co-pilot on the shoulder. "Appreciate your help, Roberts. You are cleared to return to the *Stargazer*. Have a safe return."

The young officer fidgeted. "Sir, uh, if you don't mind. I'd like to . . ."

Noticing his hesitancy, Foxwell pivoted in the direction of the younger officer. "What is it, Ensign?"

Staring between Foxwell and the chief medical officer, Roberts nervously blurted: "The crew sends best wishes to you and Dr. Rivera for a safe and successful outcome." He paused before continuing. "To be honest, we're dammed worried about the both of you."

Foxwell and Rivera exchanged glances. "Well wishes and support of the crew is appreciated, Ensign," the captain noted, rendering another pat on Roberts's shoulder. Please let everyone know."

"Aye, sir, will do."

Dr. Rivera walked up to Roberts. "You want to know how you can show your appreciation, Ensign?"

"Uh, yes sir—name it," Roberts answered.

"When this mission is complete and you return with

the shuttlecraft for the captain and yours truly, I don't want to feel like I'm on an amusement park ride during the return trip to the *Stargazer*. You think you can make that happen?"

Roberts grinned. "Count on it, Doctor."

* * *

Walking through the airlock's primary access door, Foxwell and Rivera stood by. The plug door closed automatically, sealing itself as the environment of the airlock adjusted itself to an Earthlike sea-level atmosphere: 21 percent oxygen, balance nitrogen at 101.3kPa. Monitors revealed temperature and environmental readings.

"Captain, Dr. Rivera, this is Titan Colony Security. Please lower the gold visor on your helmet."

"Acknowledged," Foxwell replied.

"Standby for decontamination," a computer voice message alerted.

Horizontal and vertical rows of positron charged ultraviolet diodes "swept" the chamber in a series of pulsed waves, covering every square inch of the small cell to include the visitors from the *Stargazer.* Thirty seconds later a steady burst of UV light emanated upward from the floor, a vacuum activating to remove all traces of dust from the spacesuits and boots of the visitors.

"Captain Foxwell and Dr. Rivera, this is Titan Colony Security. Atmosphere and pressure readings inside the chamber are within normal limits and breathable." A panel near the second access door opened followed by a rail extending with an attachable flat tray. "Please remove your spacesuits, leave them on the floor in exchange for the colony-manufactured jumpsuits and footwear provided."

After donning the light blue jumpsuits, Foxwell and

Rivera proceeded through a sealed hatch and into the second chamber. "Close and seal the hatch, place a pair of the dark-lensed goggles attached to the bulkhead over your eyes, then stand on the footprints imbedded in the floor," a computer voice directed.

"Acknowledged," Foxwell confirmed again.

"Extend your arms, look up toward the overhead," the computer voice continued.

After they complied with the instructions, another wave of ultraviolet light illuminated the chamber.

"Decontamination procedures complete," the computer-generated voice affirmed.

"Welcome to Mars, and to our colony, Titan, the first interplanetary settlement in our solar system," a humanoid voice announced. The sealed door of the second chamber opened subsequent to the greeting.

Walking into what appeared to resemble a small auditorium, Foxwell and Rivera were met by a team of medical personnel pushing a small portable tray. Two hyposprays and several vials sat on top. Two security personnel flanked a third unknown party standing to the side of the medical team. They approached the starship captain and his chief medical officer.

"Captain Foxwell, Dr. Rivera," the unidentified man greeted. "I am Provincial Governor Jetson Duelow, the voice that welcomed you just moments ago." Smiling and sporting a full head of immaculately groomed gray hair and matching beard, the diminutive elderly leader of the first Martian colony greeted his new arrivals. "I cannot begin to tell you what your presence here means. We are keenly aware you are risking your lives. You'll have our full cooperation. I've instructed our medical, scientific, and security personnel to fully cooperate and provide whatever support is needed."

"Thank you, Governor," Foxwell responded. "On behalf of Galactic Fleet Command, we'll do everything we can to assist in containing and beating this disease. You have the full resources of the *Stargazer* at your disposal, beginning with Dr. Rivera and myself."

The governor extended his hand, first to the captain. Foxwell appeared reluctant. He quickly glanced at Rivera.

"It's okay, Captain. We were infected the moment we stepped into this chamber in spite of the decontamination procedure just completed—that was a precaution to preclude introducing anything new into the colony."

Foxwell smirked. "I was going to quote the phrase *old habits die hard,* but I don't want to jinx what we're here to do." He reached for and shook the governor's hand, followed by Rivera.

"Speaking of which, you never answered my previous question regarding exactly *why* you're here, Captain?" Rivera threw out again. "Why are you so reluctant to—"

"Sorry to interrupt," a colony physician jumped in, "but we do need to administer the antiviral and anti-cytokine injections before you exit our orientation room." Other medical technicians approached Foxwell and Rivera, unzipping the jumpsuit on their right and left shoulders. Hyposprays were administered into both arms of the *Stargazer's* captain and chief medical officer.

"These injections will impede the progression of the virus of which you are both now infected," a medical assistant reminded Foxwell and Rivera while rezipping their sleeves.

Duelow turned and gazed at Rivera. "Doctor, the medical assistants will gather your equipment, supplies, and personal affects. Quarters will be assigned, after which you'll be taken to our laboratory and introduced to our chief virologist, epidemiologists, and Titan Colony physicians all working around the clock to stop this virus."

Rivera understood the inference. "I'm ready," he acknowledged.

Governor Duelow waited until the *Stargazer*'s senior physician had exited the orientation room. He pivoted in Foxwell's direction. "I understand the security-one priority message transmitted to your private channel was read and understood, Captain?"

"That's affirmative, Governor. The only other *Stargazer* personnel privy to the message contents are my Science Officer and Second-in-Command Beta, Chief Engineer O'Donovan, and Chief Weapons Officer and Head of Security Warwick."

"Dr. Rivera is not aware of the situation . . . as we understand it. Is that correct, Captain?"

Foxwell's face twisted with irritation. "Rivera is only aware that an unknown virus is ravaging the colony; that his job is to work with your team of scientists and medical professionals." He paused. "He's also aware, as I am, that we'll both die, along with you and every human and Vulcan in this colony, if their combined efforts are not successful. Does that answer your question, Governor?"

Duelow exhaled a despairing sigh. "It does, Captain."

PART IV

"Pleased to meet you, Chief," Foxwell said, shaking hands after being introduced by the colony's governor. Chief of Security Dalton Gareth was taller than average, over six and a half feet, built like a rock with wide shoulders and a tapered abdomen beneath a jumpsuit similar to those worn by his titan colleagues. Closing the door of his large, rectangular-shaped office, he invited the Galactic Fleet officer and the Titan Colony governor to sit by waving his hand in the direction of two visitor chairs in front of his desk. "I've heard a lot about you—and the accomplishments of the *Stargazer*."

"Thank you, Chief," Foxwell replied. "It's kind of you to say. Just to clarify, however, all accolades belong to the brave men and women who crew the *Stargazer*. Without question she's manned by the best people in Galactic Fleet."

"No doubt, Captain," Gareth replied with sincerity, smiling as he sat at his desk. "Considering the risks involved, we are grateful beyond words for your presence, as well as Dr. Rivera. His knowledge and assistance could mean the breakthrough our scientists and researchers are seeking."

Foxwell shifted anxiously in his seat. "Dr. Rivera will

do his part, I can assure you. Having said that, let's the three of us get down to brass tacks. A private conference with Galactic Fleet Intelligence just prior to departing the *Stargazer* with Rivera alluded to the possibility that *Ares Viral Contagion* may have been intentionally manufactured and released by an enemy agent from the Eridani star system."

Governor Duelow swiveled his chair to face Foxwell. "Captain, the Martian colony Titan has been in operation since the early 2040s subsequent to the first crewed mission to Mars in 2034. Nothing like this has occurred in almost six decades of operation. Our scientists and researchers do not believe the virus originated on Mars or was brought here by any of its normal rotational inhabitants. Our scientists and lab personnel analyze surface rock and soil samples as well as core sample extractions taken hundreds of feet below the surface. We also analyze and test ice crystal, fog, frost, and water samples on a regular basis as well as samples of the Martian atmosphere. To date, no pathogens indigenous to Mars have been discovered. And we do not experiment or attempt to artificially create viruses or pathogens of any kind."

"Noted, Governor. However, it was you who forwarded the allegations of contagion to Galactic Fleet Command," Foxwell pointed out, "based on what you believed to be solid evidence." A pause. "May I see that evidence?" he asked.

Governor Duelow looked in the direction of his chief of security, then nodded. Gareth stood. "Follow me, Captain."

Walking to the end of his office and toward a row of weapon safes, he entered a code on the first safe's biometric circular keypad. He swung the door open, moved past the stowed weapons, miscellaneous accessories, and mainte-nance manuals to a second row of adjacent shelves. Gareth removed a cardboard box and turned around, placing it on a table behind him. "You wanted to see evidence, Captain. Take a look inside."

Foxwell removed the top of the box, holding it momentarily as he stared at the contents inside. With an incredulous expression, he slowly placed the top down on the table. Reaching inside, he grabbed a familiar object, removing the item and slowly raising it upward, his attention locked on the device he held firmly in his hand.

"Do you know what that is, Captain?" Governor Duelow asked.

Continuing to stare at the apparatus in his hand, Foxwell answered. "I do. It's a handheld *phaser*—clearly of Eridani origin. I've seen them before. Several were captured during the battle of the Epsilon Eridani star system in 2092. They are phased array pulse energy devices. These weapons fire particles known as nadions. At its lowest setting, it disrupts a life form's nervous system, rendering it unconscious or causing it to become incapacitated. At its highest setting, it is enough to dematerialize the targeted object. Galactic Fleet scientists and engineers are still analyzing and studying these phasers, attempting to reverse-engineer in an effort to duplicate the technology."

Chief of Security Gareth turned and gazed at Foxwell. "Your analysis is unerring, Captain. It is also the conclusion of Titan Colony Security and Galactic Fleet Command after we jointly studied the weapon via a video conference."

"How did you happen upon it?" Foxwell asked.

"The phaser was discovered in our hangar bay around 2300 hours during a routine patrol by a member of our security team. The officer discovered it stuffed in a dead junction box attached to a supporting beam next to the transporter platform used by our Vulcan colleagues."

"Interesting," Foxwell muttered.

"The Vulcan starship *Soval* beamed a team of ten scientists and two crew support personnel approximately three weeks ago to assist Titan's staff of medical researchers and scientists. The *Soval* departed immediately for return to Vulcan."

Foxwell walked and pondered quietly around the security office. "Smuggled into the colony most likely via transporter from the Vulcan starship along with the virus, either by an Eridani agent surgically altered to resemble a Vulcan, or perhaps knowingly by a Vulcan official or crew member sympathetic to their grievances with Earth," he postulated.

"The virus made its appearance approximately a week before the phaser was discovered," Governor Duelow explained. "Our scientists carefully examined and tested its surface components, comparing the results against those of infected inhabitants for the virus's genetic material using nucleic acid and antigen testing, which detects the presence of viral proteins that spur the production of antibodies—the immune system's response to invaders."

"What were the results of the comparison?" Foxwell asked.

"The analyzed samples allowed for a full sequence of their genome, or genetic material using the most advanced methods. Based on information contained in our database, it proved conclusively the virus is of Eridani origin," Duelow asserted.

Foxwell turned, gazing at Duelow. "That would have been the result of testing blood and tissue samples taken from wounded Eridani prisoners captured during the short war of 2092."

"That is correct, Captain."

"Have you narrowed it down to individual DNA?" Foxwell asked.

"We have, Captain," Gareth replied. "Touch DNA testing was conducted by obtaining skin cells transferred to the phaser by the Eridani agent. Fortunately, the security officer who discovered it made that process a little easier by securing the weapon without contaminating it."

"Have you compared the results to the DNA of all Vulcan inhabitants and recent arrivals?" Foxwell asked.

"Yes," Duelow answered. "Virus testing and treatment protocol required blood and other fluid samples from every human and Vulcan in the colony. As part of this, we discreetly conducted separate DNA testing. This remained confidential per orders from Galactic Fleet. As a precaution, they ordered us to await your arrival before attempting to take the primary suspect into custody."

"Who is it?" Foxwell asked.

"A Vulcan crew member by the name of T'kor," Gareth said.

Foxwell rubbed his chin pensively. "That would mean the real T'kor is dead; probably murdered on Vulcan by a surgically altered Eridani, or a Vulcan sympathizer—carried out before the *Soval* departed for Mars."

Duelow nodded slightly. "Your hypothesis appears logical."

Noting the irony embedded in the governor's reply, he turned and faced the colony's governor and chief of security. "Where is T'kor presently?" Foxwell asked.

Gareth walked back to his desk. "Computer, what is the current location of Vulcan inhabitant T'kor?"

"T'kor's last known location was in the transporter room," the computer's audible voice answered.

"When did he arrive?" Gareth asked.

"Less than one minute ago," the computer voice replied.

Alarmed, Foxwell walked hurriedly toward Gareth's desk before shouting: "Disable the transporter."

Working a control interface linked to the transporter room, Gareth suddenly stopped. He craned his head in Foxwell's direction. "Too late, Captain," he yelled out. "Someone just beamed off the red planet."

Part V

Stardate: Dec 14, 2096

"Foxwell to *Stargazer*."

"*Stargazer*, Beta here."

"Beta, the colony's transporter just completed an activation cycle. Have sensors picked up any anomalies in the last sixty seconds?"

"That's affirmative, Captain. A matter stream was detected at approximately thirty thousand kilometers, just prior to de-cloaking of an Eridani warbird at the same distance and heading. We have the warbird onscreen, high magnification."

Foxwell paced anxiously around the security office. "If memory serves me, that would be consistent with their transporter's maximum range."

"That's affirmative, Captain, not to mention they are in direct violation of Galactic Fleet Directive 1990.105 prohibiting non-Earth vessels of any kind from entering our solar system without specific prior approval or a formally concluded and ratified treaty."

"Acknowledged. We believe an Eridani saboteur surgically altered to resemble a Vulcan just transported to the warbird," Foxwell explained. "Evidence discovered appears to corroborate he may be responsible for contaminating the colony with the virus and is now fleeing."

Beta furrowed her eyebrows. "That would be a *reasonable* assumption."

Turning around, the helmsman shouted: "Commander, confirming warbird movement—she may be preparing to depart."

Beta stood and positioned herself behind the navigator. "What is their heading, Ensign?"

"Bearing 310 Mark 15." He quickly turned and craned his head in the first officer's direction—"*the Eridani star system*, Commander."

Overhearing the conversation, Foxwell exhaled a long breath. Pursing his lips, he angrily tapped his fingers on the control interface in the security chief's office.

"Well, Captain?" Chief of Security Gareth prodded. "What do you intend to do?"

"I recommend you immediately contact Galactic Fleet Command, Captain," Governor Duelow suggested.

Ignoring both colony officials, Foxwell raised his communicator to his lips. "Beta, on my authority, lay in a pursuit course; overtake and disable the Eridani warbird should they fail to respond to your hails to stop and turn over the party that beamed himself to their ship. Deploy tachyon subspace transmitters during pursuit as a means of maintaining immediate communications. Use the magnetic grappler and tow their vessel back to Mars. A computer image of the Vulcan imposter has been forwarded."

"Acknowledged, Captain." Orders were given to break orbit and pursue the Eridani starship, now hurtling toward their solar system at more than ten times the speed of light.

"Xuriya, open a channel to the warbird," Beta ordered.

"Aye, Commander, hailing frequencies open."

"This is Commander Beta of the *SS Stargazer* of Galactic Fleet Command representing planet Earth. Transporter computer logs on the Martian colony and sensor readings aboard the *Stargazer* confirm one humanoid transported to your vessel from the planet moments before your departure. This individual is wanted for return to the colony for questioning regarding a viral disease outbreak. You are ordered to bring your starship to a full and complete stop and assist in delivering the party in question to the *Stargazer* for return to the planet Mars."

Staring at the main viewing screen, the helmsman shouted, "Commander, the Eridani warbird is slowing; they have raised their shields."

"They're powering up weapons systems," the navigator cautioned.

Beta stood. She shot a quick glance at the helmsman. "Disengage fusion drive—come to a full stop."

"Full stop, Commander."

"What is our current distance?"

"One hundred thousand kilometers."

"Let me know the moment they deviate from their present course."

"Aye, Commander," both replied in tandem.

Beta sat down again at the command chair. She keyed the *Stargazer*'s PA system. "Weapons officer, report to the bridge."

"Acknowledged—on my way," Warwick responded.

Beta stood again. "Apparently my message was received—and they didn't like it."

Alternating his attention between the main viewing screen and the sensor displays on the control panel, the helmsman quickly craned his neck in the direction of the first officer. "Commander," he yelled out, "the warbird has fired two plasma energy pods from her aft silos. They are heading directly for us."

Unfazed, Beta gazed at the main viewing screen. "We're beyond the effective range of their plasma weapons, Ensign. The energy pods will dissipate well before they reach us. That was their answer to our demand for return of the party who beamed aboard—and a warning not to continue our pursuit."

Arriving on the bridge, Warwick assumed his station at the tactical weapons console. After quickly scanning the interface control panels, he spun his chair in the direction of the *Stargazer*'s first officer. "Weapons station manned and ready, Commander."

Beta returned to the command chair and keyed the starship's PA system. "This is Commander Beta. All hands— CONDITION RED. I say again—CONDITION RED."

"The warbird is moving again, Commander," the navigator reported.

"Same heading as before. They are now moving at light speed and accelerating."

Xuriya turned and gazed at the first officer. "All departments report manned and ready, Commander."

Beta spun the command chair in the direction of the weapons station. "Lieutenant, energize all weapons systems—polarize the hull plating."

"All weapons energized and ready. Hull polarized at one hundred percent," he replied.

Beta stood and positioned herself behind the helmsman. "Ensign—engage fusion drive engines—all ahead, light factor 1. Increase light speed incrementally; close to within fifty thousand kilometers and hold—maintain stationary velocity."

"Aye, Commander."

Beta turned around and walked toward the communications station. "Xuriya, contact the chief engineer and the assistant chief medical officer. Tell them to report to the bridge. Upon arrival, direct both to the ready room along with yourself and Lieutenant Warwick. The navigator and helmsman will have the conn during the briefing."

"Acknowledged."

* * *

"Making that decision unilaterally is a huge gamble, Captain," Governor Duelow grumbled, walking toward Gareth's desk.

"I believe the evidence is sufficiently compelling to justify my actions, Governor," Foxwell argued. "I assume full responsibility."

Gareth reached for and keyed his companel. "Yeoman, report to the colony security office."

"Aye, sir. On my way."

Gareth stood. "We'll prepare and forward a priority-one subspace message for the purpose of briefing Galactic Fleet Command. You're welcome to review the message before it's transmitted, Captain."

"I would like a brief meeting with my chief medical officer," Foxwell requested, disregarding Gareth's remark.

"Yes, by all means," Governor Duelow replied. "In the meantime, I'll personally escort you to your assigned quarters." He turned and looked at Gareth. "Chief, make arrangements for Dr. Rivera to meet with the captain in his quarters within the hour."

Gareth nodded.

* * *

"I've called you here to bring you up to date on our current situation," Beta announced as she began the meeting. Briefing the *Stargazer*'s senior officers regarding the decision and subsequent order to pursue the fleeing starship, Beta recalled her previous encounter with the humanoid species during the battle of the Eridani star system in 2092. "The Eridanis consider themselves a warrior race. They are technologically advanced and fiercely territorial. They are hostile to Earth and Vulcan. Tactically, their starships are the equivalent of our own, with the added ability to protect their hull by the use of invisible sectional shielding."

Warwick nodded. "Like our polarized hull, it would take repeated hits to weaken their shields to the point of failure."

"That is correct," Beta confirmed. "Our task is to disable their vessel and tow the warbird back to Mars should they ignore repeated demands to stop and deliver the party in question." Beta looked around the ready room. "Any questions?"

The assistant chief medical officer exchanged glances with Beta. "The medical department is ready, along with all first aid and triage stations," he advised.

"Thank you, Doctor." Turning in the direction of the chief engineer, Beta furrowed her eyebrows. "Chief O'Donovan?"

"Engineering is ready, Commander," O'Donovan replied.

"Excellent. This meeting is concluded. Please return to your departments and brief your subordinates." Beta walked out of the ready room and returned to the command chair.

The navigator swiveled his chair around. "Commander, sensors are picking up faint activity coming from the warbird—attempting to identify."

Beta keyed the *Stargazer*'s PA system. "All hands will remain at their battle stations—maintain CONDITION RED."

GALACTIC
FLEET
COMMAND

PART VI

Stardate: Dec. 15, 2096

"Enter," Foxwell uttered in response to the door chime.

Walking into the captain's assigned quarters, the *Stargazer*'s chief medical officer sauntered in the direction of the queen-size bunk. Foxwell was lying on his back, his hands behind his head, staring upward at the overhead.

"Don't blame you for napping, Captain," Rivera said. "We could all use some rest. It's been a long day."

Foxwell sat up, then stood. "Rest will have to wait." He yawned. "So, tell me Doctor, what's the situation in the lab regarding the virus?"

Rivera sighed. "Well, we've only been here a few hours. The scientists from Earth and Vulcan have confirmed it to be an unknown but extremely virulent SARS virus, transmitted by contact with infectious material such as respiratory droplets or bodily fluids. It's characterized by fever, headache, body aches, a dry cough, hypoxia, and usually pneumonia. It's at that point systemic toxemia occurs followed by multiple organ failure . . . and death. To date eleven colonists have died, two Vulcans and nine humans. Two of the deceased were scientists."

"Any progress on a vaccine?"

"Yes. According to the chief virologist, a vaccine should be ready for testing within forty-eight hours. There are plenty of inhabitants eager to volunteer."

"How long will the two injections we received protect us?" Foxwell asked.

"It depends on individual physiology. The colonists who died received those same injections, keeping the virus at bay for seven to nine days. Like rabies, once symptoms occur, no amount of vaccine will work."

Foxwell nodded. "Thanks for the update, Doctor. I'll let you get back to the lab."

"Hold on a minute," Rivera protested. "What's the status regarding *Stargazer*? Have you heard from Beta?"

Caught off guard by Rivera's question, Foxwell paused. "As a matter of fact, I have," he replied, rendering a wry smile.

"And?"

Placing a reassuring hand on the shoulder of the *Stargazer*'s chief medical officer, Foxwell walked the doctor toward the pneumatic doors of his quarters. "Beta said to tell you everything in sickbay is fine. The senior medical officer you left in charge has everything under control—nothing to worry about."

Rivera smiled.

* * *

Beta stood and walked around the bridge flight control console. She stared briefly at the main viewing screen, her bionic eye catching a slight shift in the visual spectrum of the warbird. She executed an about-face, exchanging glances with the flight control officers. "Provide a status, helmsman."

"Sensors confirm the warbird is activating its cloaking device," the helmsman responded.

Viewing the main sensors at the science station, the chief weapons officer turned in the direction of the first officer. "Commander, last sensor reading before the warbird engaged its cloaking device confirmed she is proceeding in the direction of a comet."

Beta's eyes widened. "Acknowledged." She turned and stared again at the main viewing screen. "We'll target their starship as its wake through the comet's tail reveals its location. It will be our only chance to disable their vessel. Time of warbird contact with the comet's tail, Lieutenant?"

"Two minutes, thirty seconds, Commander," Warwick replied, returning to the weapons station.

Beta pivoted and walked to the communications station. "Xuriya, open a channel to the warbird, all frequencies."

"Aye, Commander—hailing frequencies open."

Repeating her previous message to come to a stop and return the party beamed aboard, Beta ordered the chief weapons officer to engage the *Stargazer*'s cloaking device.

"Cloaking device engaged," Warwick confirmed.

"Acknowledged," Beta replied. Now concealed, the first officer maneuvered the starship around the warbird, positioning the *Stargazer* for an optimal firing position.

"A wake should appear behind the plasma vented by their nacelles as soon as they enter the comet's tail. That should tell us exactly where the warbird is," the helmsman speculated.

Beta turned her head toward the weapons officer. "Plot their exact point of entry, Lieutenant."

"Computed—their port side will be completely exposed and targeted."

"Time of contact with the comet's tail?"

"Eighteen seconds."

"Let's make ourselves visible, Lieutenant," Beta directed, scurrying back to the command chair. "Prepare to fire laser canons on my order—maximum power. I want their shields totally disabled."

"Cloaking device disengaged—forward laser cannons ready."

"Steady . . . steady as she goes," Beta calmly cajoled the navigator and helmsman, her eyes fixated on the main viewing screen.

Made visible against the brightness of the comet, the shape and outline of the cloaked Eridani vessel projected a perfect silhouette against the lighter background of the comet's bluish ion tail.

"FIRE!" Beta shouted.

The *Stargazer's* laser cannons scored multiple hits running the entire length of the warbird's protective shields.

"Cease fire, Lieutenant," Beta shouted again. She swiveled the command chair, aligning it with the communications station. "Keep all hailing frequencies open."

"Aye, Commander," Xuriya replied.

"Caught them totally by surprise." Warwick turned and smiled. "Sensors indicate their shield strength now at forty-eight percent."

"They're not making any attempt to return fire—or run," the helmsman reported.

"Their weapons and propulsion systems may have sustained serious damage, even with the shielding," the navigator chimed in.

Redirecting her attention back to communications, Beta stood. "Xuriya, any response to my last message?"

"Negative, Commander."

Beta turned her chair and gazed at Warwick. "Weapons status, Lieutenant?"

"Forward laser cannons remain locked onto the warbird's port side. One more volley should do it."

Beta swiveled the command chair back around and gazed at the main viewing screen.

"FIRE!" she yelled.

The *Stargazer*'s laser cannons raked the port side of the warbird a second time, their shields straining to deflect and diffuse the concentrated energy beams.

"Sensors confirm their shields have collapsed," Warwick bellowed.

"Cease fire, Lieutenant."

Xuriya stood and pivoted toward the command chair. Holding her earpiece firmly, she hollered, "The warbird is hailing us, Commander."

"On screen," Beta ordered.

Routing the warbird's optical communication signal to the main viewing screen, it became obvious damage to the Eridani vessel had scrambled the video portion of the signal. Audio was barely coherent.

"This is Captain Lera Braji, commanding the Eridani starship *Kyozist*. We protest in the strongest terms possible your unprovoked attack on our vessel, as well as your demand we turn over a member of our crew."

Beta stood within feet of the main viewing screen, her arms folded confidently across her chest. "This is Commander Beta of the SS *Stargazer*. There will be no discussion," she began. "You will make immediate arrangements to remand custody of the crew member in question to the *Stargazer* as previously requested. Failure to comply will result in the *Kyozist* being towed back to the planet Mars. With the exception of life support systems, your vessel will be disabled and kept in indefinite orbit around the red planet."

Several minutes elapsed with no response from the warbird.

Beta turned around. "Xuriya, mute the audio."

"Audio disabled, Commander."

"Navigator, helmsman, do sensors confirm any weapons, propulsion, or shield activity on the *Kyozist*?"

"Negative, Commander," they replied in tandem, then the navigator added: "They must have sustained more damage than expected."

"Or they're playing possum—waiting for an opportunity," the helmsman added.

The first officer pursed her lips. "I *know* the Eridanis. They will *never* agree to our demands to voluntarily surrender their vessel or hand over a member of their crew."

Pivoting in the direction of the weapons station, Beta exchanged glances with Warwick. "Lieutenant, target the nacelles on the *Kyozist*—just enough damage to render them inoperable in the unlikely event they're still functional."

"Acknowledged, Commander. Forward laser cannons locked on both nacelles."

"Fire on my command," Beta directed.

Beta turned and looked at Xuriya. "Restore audio, Lieutenant."

"Audio enabled."

"This is Commander Beta directing my message to Captain Braji of the *Kyozist*. You have fifteen seconds to reply to my previous message. What is your answer?"

Fifteen seconds later—no response.

Beta wheeled around and locked eyes with Warwick.

"FIRE!"

Part VII

GALACTIC FLEET COMMAND

Stardate: Dec. 15, 2096

"Cease fire," Beta ordered. "Status of their nacelles, Lieutenant?"

"Inoperable, Commander."

Pivoting in the direction of the command chair, Xuriya shouted out, "They're hailing us."

"On screen, Lieutenant."

The video portion of the transmission remained scrambled. Audio was sporadic, but still discernible.

"This is Captain Braji. I agree under protest to your demand, Commander," he angrily replied. "Please provide instructions regarding method of transfer."

"Via transporter, Captain, directly to our sickbay," Beta instructed. "You will don the crewmember in a pre-inflated, positive-pressure biohazard contamination suit or its equivalent prior to transport. We will provide the exact coordinates. You have exactly twenty minutes to complete the transport, beginning—now."

"Very well, Commander," Captain Braji responded, his tone notably reluctant.

Craning her head, Beta glanced in the direction of the communications station. "Xuriya, contact sickbay and brief the assistant chief medical officer regarding a pending transport of a possible infected Eridani crewmember. They are to take all necessary biohazard precautions to include arrangements with security for quarantine of our Eridani guest."

"Aye, Commander."

"Also, provide sickbay coordinates to the *Kyozist*."

"Acknowledged."

"Mr. Warwick," Beta continued, "you will dispatch a properly suited biohazard security team to sickbay to assist the medical personnel regarding handling and quarantine of the party in question."

"Understood, Commander."

* * *

Having escorted Rivera to the door of his quarters minutes earlier, Foxwell walked back to the stateroom's guest station. He reached for his communicator on the adjacent credenza to contact the *Stargazer*, to be followed by an update with Provincial Governor Duelow and Chief of Security Gareth. The door chime on the automatic doors sounded for a second time. His first thought was that it was Rivera.

"Enter," he responded.

The automatic doors opened with their usual swish and squeak. Standing in the hall just outside the stateroom was the chief of security. He was a large and powerfully built man, his presence filling the entire open double doorway.

Catching the captain off guard by his unannounced presence, Foxwell exchanged glances with Gareth. "I was just on my way to your office," he explained. "Standby while I contact the *Stargazer*. Afterward, I'll accompany you back to the security office and we'll update Governor Duelow."

"That won't be necessary, Captain," Gareth blurted, the double doors closing after he entered the stateroom. He reached behind his back, revealing a dark object. It was the Eridani phaser. "Toss the communicator on the desk—then move away from it," the chief of security ordered, pointing the phaser at the starship captain.

Incredulous, Foxwell threw the communicator on top of the guest station. "All right, I'll play along," he pretended, turning and moving stealthily toward Gareth. "So, tell me Chief, what's this all about?"

"It's about an agreement with the Eridanis. They infect the colony with a lethal virus, making it appear the Vulcans are responsible. The virus is so contagious and deadly it strains relations between Earth and Vulcan to the breaking point . . . which in turn strengthens the Eradani star system by default, shifting the balance of power in their quadrant of the galaxy back to them."

"What's in it for you?" Foxwell asked.

"After a vaccine is developed in the Titan's lab, the chief virologist will take credit for its creation. I'll be happy to ride on his coattails and enjoy the fruits of his success. That will open plenty of doors for me."

"So, he's in on this as well?"

"He's family—my older brother."

"And Governor Duelow?"

"Let's just say he's indisposed at the moment," the security chief sneered.

"You seem to forget the *Stargazer* will soon return to Mars," Foxwell reminded Gareth.

"On the contrary, Captain, the *Stargazer* will soon be nothing but space junk. Captain Braji has already initiated the auto-destruct system aboard the *Kyozist*. It's set to explode the moment he beams T'kor to your starship. The close proximity of the *Kyozist* will ensure the *Stargazer's* complete destruction."

Alarmed, Foxwell strained to maintain his demeanor. He knew the *Stargazer's* hull would have to de-polarize in order to complete the transport of the warbird's crew member. "Part B of you and the chief virologist's plan to cover your tracks, I presume?"

"Almost, Captain. You see, you're only moments away from having an accident with this phaser," Gareth continued, a wicked smile appearing. "My report will detail an incident between you and Governor Duelow in which you were both engaged in a struggle for the phaser after an argument, at which time the weapon fired, vaporizing both of you."

Foxwell nodded. "Sounds like a plan—the problem is it won't work."

Gareth responded in a mocking tone. "Now it's your turn to explain. Here we both stand. I'm holding the phaser, seconds away from killing you. But I'm curious—how's it not going to work?"

"To begin with—the phaser. It's inoperable."

Gareth laughed again. "You're wrong, Captain. I test-fired it before I left the security office. It worked perfectly on Duelow."

Foxwell's face now contorted with rage. "You're telling me you killed Governor Duelow?"

The security chief doled out an evil grin. "Yes, with the simple squeeze of the firing trigger—poof, he simply vanished, disintegrated. And now it's your turn." He pulled the phaser's firing trigger—nothing. His attention drawn to the inoperable energy weapon, he pulled the trigger in rapid succession several more times, and each time the phaser failed to fire.

"I told ya," Foxwell sneered. He lunged at Gareth, knocking the phaser out of his hand. The security chief grabbed Foxwell under his armpits, lifting the starship captain off his feet, tossing him like a ragdoll onto the guest station. Uninjured, Foxwell hopped onto a credenza. Leaping sideways at Gareth, he locked his legs at the knees around the huge man's head and neck, his weight and body rotation combining to pull Gareth's torso down and forward, his forehead striking the deck of the stateroom before he flipped completely over. Releasing his leg lock, Foxwell quickly stood, watching and waiting as a dazed Gareth turned over, attempting to push himself up on his feet. Making it to his knees, Foxwell delivered a spinning kick to the side of Gareth's head. He fell face forward on the vinyl-coated stateroom floor.

Winded, Foxwell ambled toward the bed. He grabbed the communicator, flipping open the antenna grille. "*Stargazer*," he shouted.

"*Stargazer*, Beta here."

Speaking with unmistakable urgency, he ordered his first officer to abort the mission. "Beta, the warbird's captain has initiated the auto self-destruct. Initiate emergency departure—NOW," Foxwell ordered.

"Acknowledged, Captain."

Beta hurried toward the flight control console. Ignoring the navigator and helmsman, she leaned over the control panel, raising a fiery-red switch guard, exposing the emergency escape actuator. As she pressed the panel button, the *Stargazer*'s sensors and navigational system instantly took control of the starship's fusion drive, plotting and initiating an immediate light speed escape and withdrawal maneuver based on the coordinates of the *Kyozist*.

"Aft sensors detect a massive explosion at the previous *Kyozist* coordinates," the weapons officer hollered.

Beta took in a deep breath. "As I expected, Lieutenant," she affirmed, returning to the command chair.

A hailing signal emanated from the command chair's companel. "Beta, here."

"Commander, this is the assistant chief medical officer. We are in receipt of one Eridani crew member. He was not bio-suited as you previously instructed. Coordinates provided to the *Kyozist* allowed for transport to a bio-containment area assembled in sickbay by security prior to their beaming the Vulcan imposter to the *Stargazer*."

Exhaling a sigh of relief, Beta pushed herself up from the command chair. "Are you telling me there is no danger of contamination?"

"Affirmative, Commander. A force field was set up by security and activated the moment our guest arrived, containing both the Vulcan imposter and the virus. A bioscan sensor located in the area of containment has confirmed he is positive for the virus."

"Acknowledged—on my way."

Walking around the flight control console, Beta turned and looked at the navigator and helmsman. "Deactivate emergency escape. Set a new course for return to Mars—light factor 2."

"New heading 130, mark 345," the navigator replied.

"Light factor 2," the helmsman said.

The first officer craned her neck toward the tactical station. "Lieutenant Warwick, please accompany me to sickbay. Xuriya, you have the bridge."

"Aye, Commander."

* * *

Captain Foxwell stepped back, observing as Assistant Chief of Security Summers and two other security officers helped the unsteady Gareth to his feet. Restrained with a double set of handcuffs, he was assisted out of Foxwell's quarters, a colony medic in tow.

"He'll be confined to the brig while we conduct a preliminary investigation," Lieutenant Summers declared. "Ultimately, he'll be transferred to Earth to stand trial, along with the chief virologist."

"You have his brother in custody?" Foxwell asked.

"He was escorted from the lab and placed in a holding cell," Summers confirmed.

Summers reached down to the floor and retrieved the phaser. A curious expression appeared. "Why were you so sure this weapon would not fire when Gareth pulled the trigger?"

Foxwell cocked his head. "I'm one of a few people who are aware the Eridani phaser is equipped with a safety interlock in the form of a code processor for safing its power functions. I was betting that T'kor set the safety interlock to fire only once and then deactivate as a means of extending the life of the power cell before he hid the weapon in the empty junction box where it was discovered. When Gareth admitted he used the weapon to kill Governor Duelow, I knew the phaser would not fire a second time."

"That was a life-gambling bet, Captain. Either you have the luck of the devil—or there's something else you're not telling me," Summers exclaimed.

Foxwell smiled. Appreciative of his candor, he chose not to respond to the officer's remark. "I need to contact my ship," he informed Summers. Retrieving his communicator, he flipped open the antenna grille, the handheld device emitting a confirming chirp. His only thoughts were that of his crew. *Are they safe and on their way back to the red planet?* He brought the communicator toward his lips.

"Foxwell to *Stargazer*," he called.

A momentary pause. "*Stargazer*, Beta here," came the reply.

Foxwell heaved a sigh of relief.

GALACTIC
FLEET
COMMAND

PART VIII

Stardate: Dec 15, 2096

"*Stargazer* is on a return trajectory to Mars, Captain," Beta assured Foxwell. "No damage or casualties sustained as a result of Captain Braji's decision to initiate self-destruct. Estimated time of arrival is four hours, thirty-two minutes."

"And T'kor?" Foxwell asked.

"T'kor was beamed to a Bio-level 4 containment area in sickbay just prior to the explosion which destroyed the *Kyozist*. Warwick and I are en route to confer with the assistant chief medical officer and the Eridanian," Beta replied.

"Acknowledged. Keep me informed—Foxwell out."

* * *

Making his way to the colony laboratory, Foxwell ran into his chief medical officer in a corridor leading to the captain's stateroom. Rivera was exhausted—and angry.

"I was just on my way to your quarters, Captain," Rivera began, irate. "I suppose you would like a progress report on a vaccine?"

Foxwell sensed the doctor's fury. "I have a feeling

there's something else you want to tell me. Go ahead—spit it out."

"A short while ago, and without warning, Titan Colony Security hauled the chief virologist away. They went on to brief the laboratory staff regarding the conspiracy as well as Governor Duelow's death. To say the information was a shock is a total understatement."

Foxwell attempted to soft-pedal the issue. "Now that you know the entire story, Doctor, you can provide me with an update on the vaccine."

Rivera's face twisted in wrath at the captain's seemingly flip response. "My only question is: Why wasn't I informed of this from the beginning?"

Foxwell sighed. "As far as Galactic Fleet Command is concerned, your decision to volunteer to assist the colony's physicians and scientists was predicated on your complete focus regarding development of a vaccine. It was on orders from Galactic Fleet that you not have any knowledge or involvement regarding its origin or my investigation. This was done to prevent distraction, to maintain a clear purpose, along with your physician and scientist colleagues."

An exhausted Rivera leaned against the corridor's bulkhead. "Captain," he began somberly, "that might have been a moot issue had a vaccine been developed."

Bewildered, Foxwell stared at his chief medical officer. "What do you mean? You told me a vaccine would be ready for testing within forty-eight hours."

"It would have," Rivera responded, "until the chief virologist got wind of his brother's arrest. Right before security raided the lab it's believed Gareth's brother deleted key virus-related data from the laboratory's computer hard drive—data that cannot be retrieved according to their IT people."

* * *

"He's unconscious," the assistant chief medical officer informed Beta and Warwick.

Beta gave an obvious sigh. "I came to that conclusion when I saw him lying on the floor through the isolation room observation window," she noted. "Is there anything you can do for him?"

"Medical scanners in his isolation compartment confirm T'kor is positive for the virus—and highly symptomatic," the acting chief medical officer divulged. "There are no physical injuries. He was transported without the biohazard contamination suit you instructed Captain Braji to place him in. We can't get to him without risking contaminating the crew."

"What's the alternative?" Warwick asked.

"Without further supportive treatment, his condition will deteriorate. He'll lapse into a coma and then organ failure," the doctor declared.

"It would be *reasonable* to assume it was intentional on their part," Beta speculated. "The Eridanian way of settling the score by means of infecting the crew of the *Stargazer* as payment for their destruction. What they didn't count on was our preparedness." The first officer exchanged glances with the acting chief medical officer and Warwick. "Job well done," she applauded.

* * *

"Get some sleep, Doctor," Foxwell told Rivera. "The *Stargazer* will arrive in approximately four hours. We'll conference with Beta and your assistant chief medical officer. If he's able to do so, perhaps we can glean additional information from T'kor now that he's in custody and isolation in sickbay."

Rivera shook his head. "No, Captain. I would prefer to continue using my own research data I have on micro discs I brought with me. I deferred to the colony's chief virologist because it appeared his work was near completion, and that he was taking us in the right direction. I have my own theory regarding a vaccine."

Foxwell smiled. He respected Rivera's tenacity. "Very well, but only until the *Stargazer* arrives, then I want you to get some rest."

"Agreed." The bone-tired physician turned and walked back to the lab.

* * *

Heading in the direction of the colony's security office, Foxwell detached the communicator from his utility belt.

"Foxwell to *Stargazer*."

"*Stargazer*, Beta here."

"Beta, provide me with an update regarding arrival—and status of T'kor."

"Time of arrival is three hours, forty-eight minutes, Captain. T'kor is unconscious and isolated in sickbay. The medical staff is unable to safely access the Eridanian due to a high probability of contamination of the crew. It is recommended T'kor be transported to sickbay on Titan using the colony's transporter as soon as we're within transporter range."

"Acknowledged. Contact and advise when the *Stargazer* is within range—Foxwell out," he responded, closing the communicator's antenna.

Arriving at the colony's security office, he asked to see

the detained chief virologist.

"That's fine with me," acting Chief of Security Summers replied. "Gareth and his brother are confined in separate sections here in the security wing." He led Foxwell through a set of double doors and down a corridor to a cell block consisting of three individual cells. Sitting on a bunk behind the one-inch thick steel bars, the chief virologist had a steely but resigned look on his face.

"I'll give you some privacy," Summers offered. He turned around and walked away.

Alone with the confined microbiologist, Foxwell returned the scientist's icy stare. "Would you be willing to talk?"

The middle-aged scientist slowly stood, then snorted indignantly. "I've got nothing to say." He turned and walked away.

"You might want to reconsider," Foxwell suggested. "I have no doubt you and Gareth are facing life without parole—which means banishment from Earth; perhaps the penal colony on one of the Martian moons, Phobos or Deimos. You on one moon, your brother on the other. That you would be sentenced to life on a Martian moon— there's a certain poetic justice, don't you think?" Foxwell snickered.

Standing in front of a bulkhead, his back to the starship captain, the chief virologist shook his head and sighed. He was smart enough to know his options were limited, if non-existent. The penal colonies on the Martian moons were an absolute reality. Remaining quiet, he craned his head in Foxwell's direction.

"You have something to say, Doctor?"

"Can I speak with Gareth?" he asked in a subdued tone.

Foxwell nodded. "I'm sure I can arrange a meeting with your brother."

* * *

"Maintain standard orbit," Beta directed the navigator and helmsman.

"Aye, Commander," both replied in tandem.

First Officer Beta exited the command chair and proceeded to the communications station. "Xuriya, contact the captain and transfer the link to the ready room. You have the conn."

"Acknowledged—link established."

Leaning over the companel in the ready room, Beta confirmed the *Stargazer* had arrived and was in orbit around the red planet. "Waiting for instructions regarding transport of the Eridanian, Captain."

Foxwell cocked his head to the side. "It was decided T'kor would be transported when the *Stargazer* was within transporter range," he reminded his first officer. "What happened?"

"He's still unconscious, Captain. I believed it prudent to wait until we were in orbit; my knowledge of transporter technology confirms it will allow for a matter stream of greater intensity, placing less stress on his already weakened condition."

Foxwell nodded. "Makes sense," he said. "I'll make arrangements for his immediate transport directly to the colony's medical facility. Be ready to forward sickbay's coordinates when requested. Contact me should T'kor disclose any information before beaming him to the colony."

"Acknowledged."

* * *

"Good news, Captain. The chief virologist provided the location of a backup micro disc in his quarters," acting Chief of Security Summers revealed. "The disc contains all the information deleted in the laboratory's computer database."

"Is Rivera aware of this?"

"Our IT people are uploading the information as we speak. Dr. Rivera has informed me a vaccine will be ready within hours."

"Excellent. The *Stargazer* has returned and is in orbit. T'kor is in custodial isolation and needs to be transported to the colony's medical facility, ASAP. His condition appears to be critical, but stable."

"His transport will be completed within the hour," Summers informed Foxwell. "I'll place the medical staff on notice and arrange for a Vulcan transporter technician to coordinate with your sickbay."

"I'm hoping the medical staff can further stabilize T'kor long enough that we can get a few answers out of him," Foxwell uttered.

* * *

Titan's chief medical officer and several assistants gathered around T'kor. Lying on a medical diagnostic bed after transport to the colony's emergency room, T'kor was wrapped with a dupioni thermal blanket, a level three medical-grade mask covering his face. Medical facility staff appeared to work feverishly to stabilize the profoundly ill Eridanian. The bio-function monitor above his bed displayed the faintest life support biometrics.

"Stand aside," a voice in the background shouted.

Startled by the unexpected command, the chief medical officer and his assistants turned around. Standing several feet behind, Summers was present and holding the Eridani phaser. He continued to shout, alternately pointing and waving the deadly energy weapon in tandem with his commands to move away from the patient.

"What's this all about?" the chief medical officer barked.

"Just move away from T'kor," Summers repeated.

The chief medical officer and his assistants slowly moved back.

With a vile smirk, Summers aimed and fired the phaser at the figure on the diagnostic bed, vaporizing its occupant.

The colony's acting chief of security craned his neck at the sound of footsteps several feet behind him. "Give me the phaser, Lieutenant," a familiar voice ordered.

Summers quickly turned. It was Foxwell.

"Stay back," he yelled, aiming the phaser at Foxwell's torso.

"We know all about your involvement regarding the conspiracy to contaminate the colony and bring the virus to Earth," Foxwell revealed. "Yes, the Eridanian plot to drive a wedge between Vulcan and Earth, the personal fortune awaiting you based on development of an effective vaccine. Killing T'kor would not have covered up what we already know."

"What are you talking about?" Summers shouted. "You don't know a thing."

"That's where you're wrong," Foxwell revealed. "T'kor admitted guilt before he died on the *Stargazer*. We have his confession on videotape."

"W-what?" a befuddled Summers gasped. He craned his head in the direction of the diagnostic bed.

"That was a mannequin you vaporized—one of the medical department's anatomical dummies. Now give me the phaser, Lieutenant—that's an order," Foxwell shouted, walking toward the now-discredited security chief.

"Stay where you are," Summers threatened. He flailed around, raising and pointing the phaser at the starship captain.

Stopping, Foxwell extended his hand toward the weapon. "Give me the phaser," he repeated.

"I swear I'll kill you," Summers snarled, moving his index finger from the side of the phaser to its trigger button.

"Arrgh!" His body stiffened in response to the beam of a directed energy pulse. He uttered a faint, choking gasp before toppling over backward onto the deck.

Moving closer to the now-unconscious Summers, Beta looked up at Foxwell. "Are you okay, Captain?" she asked, a fusion laser pistol in her hand.

Foxwell sighed. "Another two seconds and that would've been a moot issue."

"Summers believed he had made arrangements to beam T'kor to sickbay, but he was already dead," Beta explained. "He told us before he died about the conspiracy involving himself, Summers, Gareth, and his scientist brother. He correctly believed Summers would kill him after arrival. It was *me* the Vulcan transporter technician beamed to the colony's sickbay. Fortunately, Summers was not there when I arrived."

"That's why we placed the dummy on the diagnostic bed," Foxwell added. "We knew he'd want to kill T'kor before he could implicate him in the conspiracy. He had access to the phaser and its firing security code."

"I set my fusion laser pistol on its highest stun setting," Beta pointed out. "He'll be unconscious for quite a while."

"He'll have plenty of time to recover in his own jail until we transport him back to Earth to stand trial along with Gareth, and the colony's chief virologist," Foxwell vowed.

PART IX

Stardate: Dec. 16, 2096

"Dr. Rivera would like to see you and your first officer," a lab assistant informed Foxwell. The white-coated assistant had just walked through the auto-controlled double doors connecting the emergency room to the colony's main sickbay corridor.

"Is he in the lab?" Foxwell asked.

"Yes," the lab assistant answered. "Follow me, please."

Foxwell and Beta accompanied the assistant back to the colony's laboratory, entering through the hermetically sealed doors. Rivera was seen talking with several other scientists and physicians at the far end of the lab.

Approaching the *Stargazer*'s chief medical officer, Foxwell blurted, "Excuse the interruption Doctor, but we were told you wanted to see us."

"I do," he answered, a weary but elated smile appearing.

"Good news?" Beta asked.

"Better than good news," Rivera replied. "Not only have we developed a vaccine, but in the process I'm almost certain I have discovered a *cure* for the virus."

"That's fantastic," Foxwell exclaimed. "The best we were hoping for was an effective vaccine."

"That was my position as well," Rivera conceded. The *Stargazer*'s chief medical officer glanced at Beta. "Well, well . . . aren't we curious," he needled. "I can make out that expression a mile away."

Furrowing her eyebrows, Beta replied, "I am the *Stargazer*'s science officer, Doctor. It would be totally *unreasonable* if I were not curious about your discovery regarding a cure."

Exchanging his smile for a playful but serious expression, Rivera locked eyes with the Galactic Fleet cyborg. "Tell you what I'll do. Your arrival on the colony has exposed you to the virus. If you agree to volunteer to be the first patient to receive the vaccine, I'll fill you in on how I developed a curative treatment for the *Ares Viral Contagion*. What do you say?"

Beta looked around, exchanging glances with Foxwell.

"Don't look at me," Foxwell exclaimed, throwing his hands up in the air.

Beta shifted her gaze back to the doctor. "A *reasonable* proposal—agreed."

Rivera grinned. "Step this way," he said, coaxing the *Stargazer*'s science officer into a large cubicle just a few feet away. "I need you to lean forward against the table," he instructed.

Several small refrigerators lined a wall of the partitioned-off enclosure. Opening the closest medical cooler and removing a vaccine-ready syringe, Rivera said, "You'll need to expose your left or right buttock, Commander. I cannot administer the injection into your bionic arm."

"It's not available in a hypospray?"

"When the vaccine is produced in quantity on Earth, it will be. Right now it's administered as an old-fashioned intra-muscular injection, just like in earlier times."

Rivera took careful aim and jabbed the needle into Beta's right ventrogluteal muscle before pressing the plunger on the syringe until it was empty.

"Wow, that looked like it went all the way to the bone," Foxwell declared. "Looked more like you were throwing a dart than giving an injection."

Rivera grinned. "There, it's all over. That didn't hurt—did it?" he asked in a disingenuous tone, hoping she would express at the very least a minimal amount of discomfort.

"A rhetorical question, Doctor," Beta replied as she readjusted her uniform. "It felt like an injection, nothing more," she added, her tone and expression deadpan.

Foxwell smirked.

"Wipe that silly grin off your face, Captain—you're next," Rivera said.

* * *

Vaccinations were administered to all colonists not displaying symptoms of the virus; curative injections and IVs along with palliative care was provided to those who were actively ill or showing beginning symptoms of the disease.

"We'll have to vaccinate all personnel aboard the *Stargazer*, Captain," Rivera advised. "Our return will expose the entire ship's company to the virus. I recommend we not return to Earth or receive any new personnel aboard the *Stargazer* for a minimum of ninety days while the medical department monitors the health of the crew."

"A *reasonable* precaution," Beta chimed in.

"Those same requirements will apply to the Martian colony as well," Foxwell stated. "No one leaves or arrives for a minimum of ninety days." Foxwell directed Rivera to forward information regarding the vaccine and curative treatment to his acting chief assistant aboard the starship. "Instruct him to disseminate that information to all departments and to prepare a vaccination schedule for the crew."

"Consider it done."

"You'll need to assume the duties as the acting provisional governor during this period, Captain," Beta noted.

Foxwell nodded. "I'll forward a recommendation to Galactic Fleet Command that the *Stargazer* remain in our solar system for training and orbital surveillance of our closest neighboring planets. We can quickly return to Mars for our vaccinated crews' use of their recreational facilities, and to allow them the feel of solid ground."

"Acknowledged." She turned and exchanged glances with Rivera. "Now, Doctor, please brief me regarding the cure you developed."

"Oh, uh, yes, Commander," Rivera mumbled. He guided her out of the cubicle and into the lab's working area, briefing her on the technology. "It's called DRACO, an acronym for double-stranded RNA-activated caspase oligomerizers," he explained. "It's based on antiviral technology developed approximately eighty years ago."

"I'm vaguely familiar with that technology," Beta affirmed. "Continue please." Her level of interest piqued.

"Basically," Rivera continued, "when one end of DRACO binds to dsRNA, it signals the other end of DRACO to initiate apoptosis, killing cells before a virus has a chance to replicate."

Beta nodded in response to Rivera's explanation. "Interesting," she said. "Can this same science be applied to other viruses as well?"

"I'm convinced it can be . . . absolutely."

Walking farther away and out of earshot, Foxwell

grinned. He removed his communicator from his utility belt, flipping the antenna open.

"Foxwell to *Stargazer*."

"*Stargazer*, Chief Engineer O'Donovan here."

Foxwell smiled at the sound of O'Donovan's voice. "I see Beta left you in command."

"Aye, Captain, that she did."

"*Stargazer* and crew status?"

"All departments secure and operational—all personnel present and accounted for. No crew members admitted to sickbay or confined to the brig," the chief engineer happily replied.

"Excellent," Foxwell responded before informing the chief engineer that both a cure and a vaccine had been created.

"That's outstanding news, Captain." He smiled in response. "Not that I or any member of the crew were ever in doubt, but we were all awfully worried about you and Dr. Rivera," he relayed in his thick, Irish accent. He paused for a moment before continuing: "Is there anything I can do for you before you return?"

Foxwell gave an appreciative smile. "As a matter of fact, you can. Make arrangements for Ensign Roberts to return in the shuttle with four security officers. Inform the security detail they'll be vaccinated and briefed regarding their assignment upon arrival."

"Acknowledged. Will you be returning, Captain?"

"I will, along with a very tired chief medical officer and vaccinated first officer."

"I'm looking forward to your return—all three of you."

* * *

Aboard the shuttle for departure, two hours later

"Wait a minute. Why is *she* piloting the shuttle?" Rivera asked, pointing toward Beta. "It was Roberts who brought you and me to the colony, and Roberts who returned in the shuttle. Why isn't *he* piloting the shuttle back to the *Stargazer*?"

Foxwell craned his neck in Rivera's direction. "You seem to forget, Doctor, Beta's first assignment was with Shuttle Fleet Command Center in Houston at the beginning of her career with Galactic Fleet," he explained. "She was a shuttlecraft *test* pilot. You won't believe what she can do behind the controls."

Taking that as an ominous warning, Rivera checked his five-point restraint.

"Don't worry, Doctor—I made certain you were strapped in *tight* when we boarded." Foxwell grinned.

Looking in the direction of the pilot's seat, Beta turned her head and locked eyes with the *Stargazer*'s chief medical officer. It was the first time he had ever seen her display any emotion via a facial expression. She was sporting a wicked grin.

"Shuttle pre-flight checks complete," Beta shouted. "Prepare for departure."

Rivera gripped the armrests and closed his eyes.

"Ay, caramba," he muttered.

THE END

THE END

EPISODE IV

THE GREY CONSPIRACY

PROLOGUE

Ordered to proceed to the Zeta Reticuli star system, the purported home of the Greys, the *Stargazer* is tasked with investigating a reported increase in abduction activity taking place on Earth. Their mission: to locate and neutralize the ability of the Greys to continue their illegal kidnappings and alleged gruesome experiments. Determined to pursue and stop the Greys after two crew members are abducted, Captain Foxwell and his away team come face to face with a ghastly discovery, and evidence of a conspiracy that threatens to change the course of Earth and human history forever.

GALACTIC
FLEET
COMMAND

PART I

Stardate: April 03, 2097 / 1040 hours

"FIRE!"

Captain Foxwell swiveled the command chair away from the weapons officer and back to the main viewing screen, his attention now fixated on the two energy torpedoes advancing toward their intended target.

"Lay it out for me, Lieutenant," he yelled.

"Torpedoes are locked and approaching their target at sub-light speed . . . five thousand kilometers and closing," Warwick shouted from the weapons console.

"Impact imminent," Beta announced, her attention focused on the sensors at her science station.

The resulting explosion and fireball were accompanied by a simultaneous release of energy, the result of a subsequent exothermic reaction. The unidentified and targeted alien vessel broke apart, wreckage expanding in a random pattern.

"Sensor readings confirm a debris field," Beta shouted. "No other vessels or objects detected."

Foxwell glanced at the companel on the command chair before keying the *Stargazer*'s PA system. "This is the captain. All departments secure from CONDITION RED,

I repeat, secure from **CONDITION RED**." He stood and walked in the direction of his first officer. "Beta, make arrangements for all senior officers to report to my ready room for a briefing in fifteen minutes. The navigator and helmsman will take the conn."

Beta swiveled her science station chair in Foxwell's direction. "Acknowledged."

* * *

Captain's Ready Room

"Identification and origin of the attacking vessel are unknown, Captain," Beta answered in response to Foxwell's question. "The *Stargazer*'s computer library is devoid of any information subsequent to data provided by our sensors."

"A targeted debris retrieval operation might provide some answers," Warwick suggested.

The chief engineer sighed, then shook his head. "The risk of biological or radiation contamination makes that option too risky," he cautioned.

Dr. Rivera swiveled his chair in the direction of the captain. "I concur," he affirmed. "We don't know a thing about who they are or where they're from."

"We don't even know *why* they attacked," Xuriya chimed in.

Foxwell looked around the conference table and nodded. "Our recent experience with the pathogen on Mars rules out retrieval and inspection of any kind." A pause. "Enough said about that." He turned in the direction of his communications officer. "Xuriya, for the benefit of all present, quote the new mission orders received from Galactic Fleet Command two days ago."

Xuriya returned a confirming glance. "Aye, sir." Standing with her personnel access display device in hand, she held it up and read out loud: "'Stardate: April 01, 2097—To: Captain Jon L. Foxwell. The *Stargazer* will cease and desist current operations and immediately proceed to the Zeta Reticuli star system. You will establish orbit around its star, Zeta Reticuli 2, and await further orders. Confirm via subspace transmission when orbit is established. End of transmission.'"

Foxwell looked around the crowded room. "Any questions or comments?"

"We're just beyond the star's orbital parameters, Captain," the weapons officer pointed out. "The sooner we establish orbit, the sooner we'll find out the reason we're here."

"A *reasonable* presumption," Beta chimed in.

"Anyone else?" Foxwell inquired.

Silence.

"This meeting is concluded," Foxwell declared. "Return to your departments, brief your personnel, and prepare for orbit around Zeta Reticuli 2." Training his eyes on his first officer, he whispered, "Remain here."

Beta confirmed with a nod.

The department heads rose from their seats, then exited the cramped room in single file, the automatic doors shutting with their usual swoosh.

Beta turned in the direction of Foxwell. "You wish to speak with me further, Captain?"

"Yes," he said in a contemplative tone, pacing around the ready room and rubbing his chin. He stopped, then pivoted in the direction of his first officer. "This entire incident is damn peculiar. *Was* it an attack?"

"A *reasonable* assumption, Captain. A plasma energy

beam of unknown composition *was* fired in our direction. Absent additional evidence or information to the contrary, that in itself would appear to lend credence to your question," Beta surmised. "Do you plan to submit a report to Galactic Fleet Command regarding the incident?"

Heaving an exasperated sigh, Foxwell replied, "That's the normal protocol."

Beta understood the inference. She raised a brow. "What do you have in mind, Captain?"

"Clarification," he retorted. Darting past his science officer, he uttered, "Let's get back to the bridge."

Following the captain out of the ready room, Beta resumed her usual duties at the science station, and Foxwell returned to his command chair.

"Navigator, helmsman . . . initiate orbital insertion protocol."

"Aye, sir," they replied in tandem.

Foxwell swiveled his command chair in the direction of his communications officer. "Xuriya, forward a subspace message to Galactic Fleet Command; advise the *Stargazer* is in synchronous orbit around Zeta Reticuli 2."

"Aye, sir."

Standing, he approached the main viewing screen, staring in astonished amazement at the blazing ball of plasma as the *Stargazer* inched closer to the giant sphere of super-heated ionized gases.

Sensing the message was incomplete, Xuriya tactfully interrupted, "Will that complete the message, Captain?"

Shaking off his fixation with the celestial orb before him, Foxwell wheeled around.

"Finish with this sentence: 'Awaiting further orders.'"

PART II

Stardate: April 03, 2097

Ensign Roberts's Quarters

"That was the lamest joke ever," Ensign Sarah Lindsey laughed, mocking the corny story told by Roberts during their previous mission to the planet Vorcia. "I can't believe you even brought it up."

Smiling, Roberts scooted closer to his girlfriend, threading his arm between her neck and his bed's second pillow. He draped his hand over her shoulder and wrapped his other arm around her slender waist, pulling her close. "Well, it was *you* who was reminiscing about how we met . . . and that joke *was* part of it," he added for emphasis.

"It was still lame."

"I thought you were intrigued," he replied.

"And I thought you were a nerd."

"I prefer the term 'intellectual badass.'"

Sarah cackled. "*Shut up,*" she teased. "By the way, how did you manage to get your own quarters? All the rest of us peasants below the rank of lieutenant are required to share quarters."

"Lest you forget, I am the BULL ensign," Roberts

answered. "I'm the senior ensign onboard the *Stargazer*, and as such, entitled to my own quarters."

"You're FULL of bull, mister," she chortled. Caressing his chin between her thumb and fingers, she gave a gentle shake, then quickly kissed him.

Embracing, they suddenly drew back, startled by a faint glow of light emanating from the office section of Roberts's quarters. The sound of movement pulled them from their romantic daze to full alertness. Roberts immediately sat up, threw his bed sheet off, then swung his torso around. Reaching into the nightstand drawer, he grabbed his fusion laser pistol.

Rising to a sitting position, Lindsey held fast to the sheet in front of her. "What the hell is—"

Roberts craned his head in Lindsey's direction, tapping his lips with his index finger. He turned his head again in the direction of the unknown illumination. Rising from the bed, he was soon joined by Lindsey, now robed and standing next to him, clinging to his arm. They crept in the direction of the connected work area. Entering the office through the opening in the dividing wall, they stopped, both staring in shock and amazement at the source of the light. Roberts lowered his laser pistol.

"Are you seeing what I'm seeing?" she asked in astonishment.

"We've heard and read so many stories and descriptions. They're exactly as described," he replied, bewildered.

"How did they get aboard?" she asked, perplexed.

As Roberts exchanged glances with Lindsey, his laser pistol dropped to the floor. The sound of a hollow thud followed, echoing in the now-empty quarters.

* * *

"Captain, a priority-one subspace message just arrived from Galactic Fleet Command," Xuriya quietly announced. "Admiral Perry awaits your private audience."

Foxwell craned his head in her direction. "Forward it to my ready room."

"Aye, sir," she replied, swiveling her chair back to the communications console.

Exiting the command chair, Foxwell strolled in the direction of the science station. "Beta, please accompany me to my ready room. Xuriya, you have the conn."

"Aye, Captain."

The automatic doors closed behind Foxwell and his first officer as they stood next to the conference table. Glancing upward at the ready room control system, Foxwell pulled down one of several portable monitors before activating the display screen to begin the Galactic Fleet video conference. A computer-generated voice announced: "This is a priority-one subspace message from Admiral Perry, Galactic Fleet Command, to Captain Jon L. Foxwell of the *SS Stargazer*."

His image appearing, Admiral Perry sat at the head of a large conference table with several other senior Galactic Fleet officers in attendance. "Greetings, Captain Foxwell and Commander Beta," he began impassively, a blank expression on his face. "Please have a seat."

"Thank you, Admiral. It's always a pleasure speaking with you. Commander Beta and I appreciate your confidence and counsel."

Admiral Perry rendered a half-smile in response. "Captain, your previous subspace transmission confirmed the *Stargazer* is in orbit around Zeta Reticuli 2."

"That's affirmative, Admiral, per orders from Galactic

Fleet Command two days ago."

"And what is *Stargazer*'s current status?"

"Fully operational and in synchronous orbit. I've ordered the hull to remain in a twenty-five percent polarized state for added shielding against the heat and radiation of the yellow dwarf star."

Admiral Perry paused. He glanced around the meeting room, taking note of his colleagues sitting at the conference table. They were all wearing anticipatory expressions. He turned again in the direction of the monitor. "Do you have anything else to add, Captain?"

Foxwell furrowed his brow. Wary and mindful of the question, he took in a deep breath. "Yes, Admiral. The *Stargazer* was attacked by an unknown alien vessel just prior to orbital insertion."

"And the status of the alien vessel?"

Foxwell and Beta exchanged glances. Admiral Perry's sudden question regarding the destroyed vessel raised a red flag in the mind of the wily starship captain. Foxwell turned and faced the monitor.

"Admiral, with all due respect, my gut tells me you know the answer."

"Answer the question, Captain. That's an order."

"The *Stargazer* was attacked without warning. I ordered what I believed was an appropriate response," Foxwell replied sternly.

"Why wasn't that in your report?"

"Perhaps to facilitate a more transparent discussion," Foxwell answered. "May I ask why I wasn't informed of the presence of the alien vessel?"

Admiral Perry exhaled an exasperated sigh. "Hear me out, Captain. The *Stargazer* was ordered to the Zeta Reticuli star system to investigate increasing reports of alleged human abductions here on Earth by the Greys. Initial investigation appears to support those allegations. Earth sightings of UFOs/UAPs have increased, along with cattle and another animal mutilations. The ship you destroyed was an auto-piloted AI decoy, specifically designed to sense and preclude abduction activity. The decoy was placed into orbit around Zeta Reticuli 2 several days ago by the Vulcans at our request in anticipation of the *Stargazer*'s arrival."

Seeking clarification, Foxwell asked, "Abduction activity? You mean abduction of *Stargazer* personnel?"

"That is correct, Captain. Destroying the decoy has rendered that capability ineffective. The energy emission directed at the *Stargazer* was specifically engineered to fully polarize the hull plating. It was not hostile fire. Unfortunately, a programming error occurred which prevented the transmission of a message notifying the *Stargazer* of its intentions prior to the plasma discharge. Per the Vulcans, the Greys have the ability to penetrate solid matter, to include anything they wish to bring or depart with, but not a starship hull polarized at maximum power. Your entire crew is now susceptible to abduction by the Greys."

Turning in the direction of Foxwell, Beta muttered, "Captain, I recommend you immediately order the *Stargazer* to CONDITION YELLOW and increase polarization to one hundred percent."

Foxwell nodded. He moved toward the nearest companel and keyed the captain's chair. "Bridge . . . this is the captain."

"Bridge . . . Xuriya here."

"Xuriya, go to CONDITION YELLOW. Increase hull polarization to maximum level."

"Aye, Captain." A momentary pause. "CONDITION YELLOW in effect . . . hull polarized at one hundred percent."

Foxwell spun around and returned to the video monitor. "What are your orders, Admiral?"

Admiral Perry stood and proceeded around the conference table, stopping next to his senior tactical officer. "Admiral Kelsing," he called out. "Will you please enlighten Captain Foxwell regarding his new mission orders?"

Admiral Kelsing craned his head and smiled. "My pleasure, Admiral Perry." Adjusting his conference table video monitor and referring to a star chart, Kelsing began: "Captain, you will break orbit around Zeta Reticuli 2 at the conclusion of this briefing. You will assemble an away team and proceed at light factor 2, bearing 045 mark 17 toward the constellation Cetus. There you will rendezvous with the Vulcan starship *T'Vahl*, currently in synchronous orbit around its star, Tau Ceti."

Foxwell pulled a surprised face. "Did I hear you say . . . a Vulcan starship?"

Kelsing turned and faced the monitor. "Yes, Captain, you did," the admiral clarified. "Captain Strojok of the *T'Vahl* will open a hailing frequency and make initial contact when the *Stargazer* is within thirty thousand kilometers. You and your away team will follow his instructions from there. Any questions?"

Foxwell shook his head. "No questions, Admiral. Your orders are clear."

"Good luck, Captain," Admiral Perry chimed in.

Foxwell's display screen turned dark.

Silent, Foxwell thoughtfully eyed the blank screen, returning the monitor to its stowed position. Taking in a deep breath, he pivoted in the direction of his first officer. "What is our time of arrival to the constellation Cetus?"

Referring to a star chart monitor, Beta entered the information provided by Admiral Kelsing. "Tau Ceti is a solitary

G-class star in the constellation Cetus. At light factor 2, it will take approximately twelve hours."

Foxwell nodded. "Remain here and conduct a database search for all information regarding the Greys, then schedule a meeting of all department heads."

"Acknowledged."

The companel emitted a hail.

"Ready room, Foxwell here."

"Captain, this is Chief of Security Warwick. My apologies for the interruption, but it's urgent I speak with you. My assistant chief and I are on the bridge, just outside the ready room."

Foxwell exchanged a quick glance with Beta, then turned and voiced his reply into the companel. "Enter."

The hiss of the automatic doors followed their entry into the ready room. Foxwell spun around. "What is it, Chief?"

"It's regarding Ensign Roberts and Lindsey," Warwick answered, a concerned expression on his face.

Foxwell exchanged a worried look. "What about them? Has something happened?"

Warwick sighed. "They're nowhere to be found, Captain."

"What do you mean they're nowhere to be found?" Beta cut in. "We're on a starship . . . where would they go?"

"Neither showed up for their duty shift," the assistant chief of security replied. "Their immediate superiors contacted security. We checked their quarters, then conducted a ship-wide search—nothing."

"And the remaining crew?"

"All other crew members are present and accounted for," Warwick assured the captain.

Foxwell turned and ambled toward a viewing portal

on the opposite side of the ready room. Staring through the portal at the hot ball of glowing gas the *Stargazer* was orbiting, he quickly spun around.

"The Greys have them."

PART III

Stardate: April 04, 2097

Where the hell am I? Lindsey thought, slowly awakening and finding herself on what appeared to be a medical examination table. Her arms were secured at the wrist, her legs secured at the ankle, a thick belt tightened snugly around her waistline. She looked anxiously around the large, dark compartment with a ceiling that appeared to extend upward into indefinite darkness.

"Hello!" she yelled, her voice echoing. "Is someone here?"

Lindsey struggled with the restraints securing her to the gurney. Shifting around to the extent her restraints would allow, she caught sight of a diminutive figure approaching. She immediately recognized the strange creature to be the same or identical as the two beings encountered earlier in Roberts's stateroom. Slender and approximately four and a half feet in height, they were silvery gray in appearance, with a large hairless head, almond-shaped eyes, and slits for a nose and mouth.

"Do not be afraid. You will not be harmed." The words formed in her mind, becoming clearer and more pronounced as the being moved closer.

Mesmerized by the alien's dark oval eyes, she felt a strange mixture of trepidation and calmness. "Where am I? Why am I here? Where have you taken my friend?" Lindsey asked out loud.

The alien being was soon joined by two other Greys. "Your friend is safe and unharmed. You will be reunited soon. Please remain calm."

* * *

"Captain, we're being hailed by the *T'Vahl*," Xuriya announced, spinning around in her seat.

Foxwell stood. "On screen."

"T'nar pak sorat y'rani," Captain Strojok coolly announced, his deadpan expression and presence filling the viewing screen.

Foxwell wheeled around, an expectant gaze directed at his communications officer.

"It's Vulcan, Captain. It's a generic form of greeting in their language," Xuriya translated.

"That's why I turned in your direction, Lieutenant. I'm aware you have a rudimentary knowledge of the Vulcan language."

Beta left her science station and joined Foxwell, both walking closer to the main viewer. "Thank you for the greeting, Captain Storjok," Foxwell began. "We were expecting your hail."

With a stiff and unwavering demeanor, Strojok continued. "I am aware of your preliminary briefing with Galactic Fleet Command regarding your mission. You and your away team will gather in the shuttle bay at 1600 hours. Our transporter personnel will beam the entire party aboard the *T'Vahl* for further orientation and briefing. I look forward to meeting you in person, Captain," Strojok concluded. The main viewing screen went dark.

Foxwell smirked. "Talk about getting to the point . . . that was textbook," he blurted, somewhat baffled and still focused on the blank viewing screen.

"Vulcans don't usually mince words," Beta noted. "At least not until they become more acquainted."

Foxwell turned around, his face contorted in frustration. "Yeah, yeah, I know all about Vulcan psychology; how they're compelled to conduct themselves by way of the discipline of logic; how they're sometimes viewed as being cold and arrogant in their dealings with humans, et cetera," he muttered.

"All true," Beta noted. "But they haven't been wrong in any of our previous collaborations. Perhaps it would—"

"We've got two missing crew members," Foxwell snapped, cutting her off. "Whatever else we are ordered to do, Lindsey and Roberts are *my* priority. Is that understood?"

"Affirmative," Beta quickly replied, looking baffled.

Sighing, Foxwell rendered an apologetic smile. "Beta, your briefings are always very informative. What time have you scheduled the conference regarding the Greys?"

"1500 hours."

* * *

The Greys removed Lindsey's uniform. Beginning her exam in a supine position, they plucked strands of her hair, took clippings of her nails, and scrapings of her skin. The samples were inserted into clear glass tubes. Using a straw-sized silvery probe, they examined her eyes, ears, nose, and mouth, the results displayed on a separate video monitor. Electrodes were connected to her head, upper torso, and limbs, with wires leading to what appeared to be a separate, three-dimensional monitor, its display completely unfamiliar.

After spraying her abdomen with a cold, clear fluid, the leader painlessly inserted a large needle through her navel. They placed her feet into stirrups at the end of the table, preparing her for what appeared to be a gynecological exam. When she resisted, the leader placed the tip of his index finger on her forehead, inducing a deeper, submissive trance.

The alien beings collected samples of saliva, blood, urine, and a small amount of lymphatic tissue and uterine fluid. Satisfied the examination was thorough and complete, they removed the abdominal needle and electrodes, followed by unlocking her restraints. After they helped Lindsey don her uniform, she was assisted into a sitting position on the examining table.

Feeling confused and disoriented, the young ensign looked around the cold and unfamiliar room. "Why are you doing this?" she asked.

"Would you like us to take you to your friend?" the leader asked, his question transmitted by thought.

Despondent and feeling helpless, she tearfully whispered, "I would, yes."

* * *

Captain's Ready Room, 1500 hours

Department heads seated, the captain and first officer entered the ready room. "Senior Officers," Foxwell began, "your presence here today is for dissemination of additional information regarding new mission orders per our previous meeting. Beta has completed the necessary research and will conduct the briefing. Please give her your undivided attention." He turned in the direction of his science officer and nodded, then took a step back and leaned against a bare bulkhead, his arms folded.

Reaching up, Beta grabbed and pulled down a monitor, adjusting the screen until a star map appeared. Stepping away with the monitor's remote in hand, she began the briefing: "Zeta Reticuli is a binary star system consisting of Zeta Reticuli 1 and its larger cousin, Zeta Reticuli 2, both located in the southern constellation of Reticulum in the Milky Way Galaxy. Distance from Earth is 39.3 light years. Both stars share nearly identical characteristics with our Earth's sun. A planet orbiting Zeta Reticuli 2 was discovered in September 1996. Over time, three additional planets have been discovered, the fourth planet confirmed to be in their star's habitable zone, and purportedly the home of the Greys."

"What is our mission regarding these beings?" Chief of Security Warwick asked.

Foxwell moved away from the bulkhead. "You're getting a little ahead of yourself, Lieutenant," he interjected. "However, in answer to your question, it is my intention to form an away team; we will beam aboard the Vulcan starship *T'Vahl*, where another briefing by the Vulcans will be mission specific." Foxwell turned and gazed at his science officer. "Please continue."

Scrolling over the faces of the *Stargazer*'s senior officers, Beta resumed her briefing. "As stated previously, the fourth orbiting planet is known as Zeta 2 Reticulum 4. Research and persistent allegations over past decades are that the Greys most frequently described in alien encounters and abductions derive from this fourth planet. They are described as humanoid creatures, with smooth, gray-colored skin, large heads, and dark, almond-shaped eyes. Subsequent examination of several Greys Earth authorities have taken into custody dating back to 1947 have led to their reclassification as an Extraterrestrial Biological Entity, or EBE. Basically, they are humanoid robots rather than life forms, specifically engineered for long-distance travel through space and time. We have no information regarding who created them."

Exchanging glances, the *Stargazer*'s senior officers fidgeted uneasily in their chairs. An agitated Rivera raised a hand, chopping at the air in an effort to be recognized.

"You want to say something . . . or ask a question, Doctor?"

Rivera pushed his chair back and stood. After a quick gaze at his colleagues, he turned and looked at Beta. "We all have a rudimentary knowledge of the Greys, Commander, dating back to when we were kids. We're aware of the stories regarding abductions, implants, animal mutilations, shadowing and buzzing of our military installations and nuclear facilities, and general surveillance of Earth, although it's alleged their activity is not limited to only our planet. And for the record, let me make it clear I am not minimizing the danger regarding the abduction of Roberts and Lindsey. Their location and safe return are of utmost priority."

Foxwell stepped forward. "Get to the point, Doctor."

Clearing his throat, Dr. Rivera continued. "The point is, we've tolerated their intrusion into human affairs for more than a century. Now all of a sudden, there's a renewed urgency regarding these creatures and what they're doing, otherwise the *Stargazer* would not have been ordered to Zeta Reticuli. I'm fairly certain I speak for all the senior officers when I say we're anxious to know what that urgency is."

The ready room intercom flashed a hailing signal.

Walking toward the companel, Foxwell uttered, "This is the captain."

"Sorry for the interruption, Captain," the navigator broke in. "The helmsman and I thought you'd like to know we're now on a parallel course with the *T'Vahl* . . . Both vessels proceeding at one-quarter impulse power."

"Very well, Ensign. Maintain present course and speed."

"Aye, sir."

Foxwell turned and locked eyes with Rivera. "You know what I know, Doctor. As stated previously, more information will be forthcoming after we beam aboard the *T'Vahl*. For the record, the only urgency I'm presently concerned with is the safe return of Lindsey and Roberts."

Rivera sighed. "Amen to that."

GALACTIC
FLEET
COMMAND

PART IV

Holding each other in a comforting embrace, the traumatized *Stargazer* crew members sought to console one another.

"Are you okay, Sarah?" Roberts asked. He stepped back, resting his hands on her shoulders as he anxiously scanned her face.

Teary eyed, Lindsey returned his sweeping glance with an identical look-over. "Where are we? What do they want with us?" she muttered, so traumatized she could barely speak.

They looked around, taking in every detail from the cold metallic floor to the drab gray ceiling and walls. The soft lighting combined to create a dreary atmosphere and feeling that something traumatic had occurred, with only vague traces of memory struggling to surface.

"I don't know . . . maybe their ship, maybe on their world," Roberts guessed, scanning the barren and empty compartment. Spotting what appeared to be a small service hatch on the opposite side of the large and foreboding hollow they occupied, he placed his hand under her elbow, guiding her in the direction of the narrow egress in the bulkhead.

"Why did they leave us here? Where did they go?" she whimpered.

He met her gaze with his own. He could tell by the expression on her face she was frightened. "We're not hanging around to find out," Roberts replied in a reassuring tone. Leading her to the small opening, he stooped down and cautiously peered out. Pushing away and standing upright, he turned toward Lindsey. "There's a passageway extending in both directions. We'll go this way," he decided, pointing left.

Taking hold of Sarah's hand, he stooped down and leaned forward, allowing his six-foot frame to more easily fit through the opening as Lindsey followed. They traversed cautiously down the narrow passageway—barely six feet high and three feet wide, softly illuminated by what appeared to be a lengthy run of fiber optic lighting—approximately twenty yards before arriving at another small hatch, this one fitted with a sealed door. Two indicator lights—one green and illuminated, the other red but off—were visible on the bulkhead several inches above and to the right of the hatch, with a small, silvery knob underneath each light. Roberts surmised the illuminated green light confirmed the door was locked and sealed, with a possible pressure or temperature difference on the opposite side. "Looks like we've run head-on into the proverbial fork in the road," he quipped.

Lindsey looked around nervously. She was in no mood to appreciate any witty remarks. "What do we do now?"

"We take it," Roberts sighed. Feeling a wave of apprehension, he glanced upward, gazing at the lights and shiny smooth button under each, hesitating momentarily before pushing the pearly colored nub underneath the darkened red light.

* * *

Pacing around the ready room, Foxwell stopped, then wheeled around. "The following personnel will comprise the away team: myself, Beta, Dr. Rivera, and Lieutenant Warwick. Lieutenant, you will select two additional security personnel."

"Aye, sir."

Turning in the direction of Chief Engineer O'Donovan, he continued, "Chief, you will remain aboard and assume command."

"Aye, Captain."

Looking over his chosen away-team members, Foxwell continued. "All of you will arm yourselves with fusion laser pistols and proceed to the hangar bay. Doctor, you will bring a standard away-team emergency medkit. Anything else will have to be provided by the Vulcans based on mission destination and specifics, considering they are responsible for the final briefing." Foxwell looked around. "Any questions?"

Silence.

"We'll meet in the hangar bay no later than 1550 hours . . . dismissed."

After returning to the bridge accompanied by Beta and Chief Engineer O'Donovan, Foxwell stood next to the helmsman and navigator. He exchanged glances with both before asking, "Any further communications from the *T'Vahl*?"

"Other than their initial acknowledgment, just a standard message confirming both starships are traversing on a parallel course at one-quarter impulse power," the navigator replied.

"Both vessels are within visual range," the helmsman added.

"Onscreen . . . starboard sensors," Foxwell ordered.

Foxwell gazed in amazement at the Vulcan starship. It was a cone-shaped design with "wings" on either side of the forward hull. There were three engine pods, each separated 120 degrees. Foxwell recognized the *T'Vahl* to be a multi-purpose science and surveillance vessel, lightly armed and capable of warp speed. The rich copper hue provided a compelling contrast against the darkened background of intergalactic space. "Interesting color," he commented.

"That it is," the chief engineer agreed, standing alongside the captain and staring into the viewer.

Foxwell turned and faced O'Donovan. "The *Stargazer* is yours, Chief."

"Aye, Captain," he acknowledged. "I'll take good care of her."

Offering a reassuring smile, Foxwell patted the shoulder of his chief engineer as he continued in the direction of the science station. "Beta," he muttered softly, a subtle reminder it was time to make their way to the hangar bay.

"Ready, Captain," she replied. Entering the last of several commands into the science station's interface control panel, she stood and followed Foxwell into the bridge turbo lift. Engaging the elevator master switch, Foxwell leaned toward the built-in companel. "Hangar bay," he uttered, and the turbo lift began its trek through a vertical and horizontal system of turboshafts connecting key sections of the *Stargazer*.

* * *

As Roberts removed the palm of his hand from the button, the red light illuminated. A soft hissing sound followed. "As I suspected," he mumbled, noticing the green indicator light was now off.

"What do you mean?" Lindsey asked, anxiously craning her head in different directions. She couldn't shake the feeling they were being watched.

"A slight pressure difference . . . but why, I don't know."

Following the seal breach, the door loosened and partially cracked open. Moving his hand from the knob to the door, Roberts gave it a slight push, the door slowly rotating outward. Sensing the hatch was an egress to a larger room, he cautiously poked his head inside the softly lighted room. What he saw shocked him to the core. He quickly pulled back into the passageway.

Caught off guard by Roberts's reaction, Lindsey placed her cupped hands over her nose and mouth.

He took a quick breath and turned around, his back making contact with the bulkhead before sliding slowly downward to a sitting position on the deck. Exchanging a curious expression for one of intense startlement, he slowly exhaled.

"What is it?" Lindsey shouted, dropping her hands and looking Roberts in the eyes.

Roberts searched his own memory. "Remember all the hype regarding the Greys and their purported agenda? I mean *all* of it . . . since childhood."

Lindsey gave a puzzled look. "You mean . . . about abductions?"

"I mean everything we've ever stumbled across regarding these beings . . . from childhood until our own encounter and abduction."

She flashed Roberts a frenzied look. "Vaguely . . . I mean . . . I don't know."

Roberts sat back and exhaled deeply. "Then have a look . . . see for yourself," he told her, tilting his head toward the small hatch.

Feeling overwhelmed, Lindsey moved painstakingly toward the glossy metallic door, stooping down and pushing it farther open. She extended her head through the door opening just enough to view the inside of the chamber, then immediately recoiled, pulling the door back against the hatch frame. Jolted, she turned around, her face ashen.

Roberts stood. Placing a reassuring hand on Lindsey's cheek, he gently turned her face toward his, their eyes meeting. "Everything rumored about the Greys is true," he asserted. "That room . . . that chamber . . . everything in there proves it."

Still reeling in shock, Lindsey's eyes drifted back in the direction of the closed hatch.

"Dear God in Heaven," she mumbled.

GALACTIC
FLEET
COMMAND

PART V

Stardate: April 04, 2097

As they exited the turbo lift, Foxwell and Beta spotted the other members of the away team. Noticing all were armed with laser pistols, Foxwell turned and gazed at his first officer. "You and I will carry fusion laser rifles."

Beta shifted in the direction of the shuttle, secured to the deck by several tie-down chains. "The shuttlecraft has two rifles in the rear compartment bulkhead," she reminded the captain.

Walking to the rear of the shuttle, Foxwell unlocked and lifted the keypad cover. As he entered the code, the rear shuttle ramp opened and extended. Up the ramp and into the rear of the shuttlecraft, he opened a camouflaged bulkhead cover and removed the two laser rifles. He tossed one to Beta.

"Six personnel are present, Captain," she noted. "Are you forming two teams?"

Foxwell quickly surveyed the team members. "Affirmative . . . Listen up," he said in a loud voice. "I'll lead team one. Warwick and Security Officer McKenzie are with me. Team two will be led by Beta—Rivera and Security Officer O'Malley are with her."

Removing the communicator from his utility belt in response to an audible beep, he flipped it open. "Foxwell here, go ahead."

"O'Donovan on the bridge, Captain. We just received a hail from the *T'Vahl*. I'm assuming it's regarding transport of the away team."

"Affirmative, Chief . . . tie their signal into my communicator."

The chief engineer reached over and touched the transfer icon on the command chair's interface companel. "Aye, Captain, you're tied in."

"Acknowledged." Changing frequencies on his communicator, he responded to the hail from the Vulcan starship. "This is Captain Foxwell."

"Greetings, Captain," the familiar voice of Strojok crackled through. "I presume you and your away team are ready to beam aboard?"

"That's affirmative," Foxwell replied, irritated by Strojok's terse demeanor. "Six present in the hangar bay and ready to beam aboard your vessel."

"Very well . . . standby." The Vulcan captain turned and nodded at the *T'Vahl*'s operation's officer. Standing in front of the transporter console, the Vulcan officer energized the transporter system. Establishing a lock on the six Galactic Fleet personnel and monitoring the transporter's various functions, he placed his fingers on the panel's three touch-sensitive light bars. As he moved his fingers upward on the interface control panel, the transporter began the process of dematerializing all six *Stargazer* away-team members into energy patterns. Within seconds they were all reconverted into matter, rematerializing inside the transporter room of the Vulcan starship. They fidgeted slightly, their eyes wandering about as they adjusted to their new surroundings.

"Welcome aboard the *T'Vahl*," Strojok greeted, a stony expression etched across his face. He was dressed in the traditional uniform of a Vulcan starship captain: high-collared jacket and trousers, a distinctive V-shape design covering his chest and stomach with a trapezoidal crest in the center. His captain's rank insignia was displayed on the collar.

Stepping forward, Foxwell walked up to the Vulcan captain. "I'm Jon Foxwell, commanding officer of the *SS Stargazer*, reporting aboard as ordered by Galactic Fleet Command. It's my understanding we're here for an additional briefing regarding the Greys."

"That is correct, Captain," Stojok replied. "Please allow me to introduce sub-commander Utek, First Officer and Science Officer." He turned and extended his arm as she walked into the transporter room from an adjoining passageway.

"Commander," Foxwell uttered in polite acknowledgment. Utek donned the same uniform as her captain, but without the trim or visible rank. He took note of her petite size and closely cropped hair. She was alluringly attractive.

"Commander Utek will lead you and your away team to the briefing room. I will join you and your colleagues momentarily. Is there anything I can do for you or your crew prior to the start of the briefing?"

"Thank you, Captain, but no," Foxwell replied in a haughty tone. Directing his away team to follow the Vulcan first officer, she led them into a passageway and toward the bow of the vessel. They glanced curiously over the interior of the *T'Vahl*, never having been aboard a Vulcan starship. Utek led them through a hatch and into the auxiliary control room, where a pair of twin turbo lifts were encased in the supporting bulkhead. She slowed, then stopped, turning around to confirm the presence of the six *Stargazer* personnel. "We will take the elevators," Utek announced, her tone and demeanor as apathetic and cold as her captain's. "Like your starship, our ready room is accessible from the bridge."

Foxwell chimed in. "Team one . . . step inside," he directed, pointing to one of the turbo lifts.

Following suit, Beta echoed the same order: "Team two . . . inside the other lift."

Arriving on the bridge, the *Stargazer* away teams exited the elevators and followed Utek into the briefing room; the copper-colored and textured ceiling and bulkheads matched the exterior hue of the Vulcan starship. The *T'Vahl*'s briefing room was noticeably larger, the illumination softer than the interior of the *Stargazer.*

"Interesting," Beta noted, looking around the room, glancing upward at the ceiling. "The lighting throughout their vessel appears to proportionally imitate the amount of light Vulcan receives from its sun."

"Apparently so," Foxwell replied, engaged in his own visual inspection of the dusky compartment.

Foxwell stopped and turned in Utek's direction. "Who will be conducting the briefing?"

"Captain Strojok and I," she answered coolly. "He will arrive momentarily. Please situate your away-team around the conference table while I prepare for the briefing."

Quickly eyeing his crew members, Foxwell directed the *Stargazer* personnel to take a seat. He turned in Beta's direction. "You and I will stand."

Acknowledging with a nod, she slung her laser rifle over her shoulder, stepping away from the table and crossing her arms.

Moments later the briefing room's sensor-controlled

doors opened. The seated away-team members rose in a polite show of military custom as the Vulcan captain entered the ready room, accompanied by his operations officer. "Please remain seated," he requested, extending his hand outward. He turned his head in Foxwell's direction. "Any questions before we begin, Captain?"

"None," Foxwell blurted. "However, to avoid being redundant or repetitive," he continued, "be advised we have conducted our own briefing regarding the Greys, their known history regarding visitations to Earth, their activities, and the planet we believe they inhabit."

"Very well," Strojok replied. "Sub-commander Utek will—"

"One more thing," Foxwell interrupted, exchanging glances with Strojok and Utek. "Two of my crew were abducted less than twenty-four hours ago. Whatever purpose this mission is tasked with accomplishing, it is my intention to locate and retrieve those two missing officers."

Strojok furrowed his thick eyebrows. "Captain, we—"

Foxwell pivoted and locked eyes with Strojok. "It's not up for debate, nor will I tolerate any interference," he replied forcefully.

Appearing unfazed by Foxwell's sudden outburst, Stojok calmly exhaled, then pressed his lips together. "Captain, we were unaware of this event. Rest assured you have my full support regarding the safe and successful rescue of your missing crew members."

"As long as that is understood, you'll have *my* full cooperation," Foxwell pledged.

"Your concern is logical," Strojok replied. "Now, let us proceed with the briefing." Craning his head, he turned his attention toward Utek. "Sub-Commander, you may proceed."

With a confirming nod, Utek walked up to the conference table. Holding a remote, she raised her arm until a noticeable click was heard. Seconds later, a transparent display screen appeared above the table. On screen was a colorized star map of the Zeta Reticuli star system.

"Interesting," Beta quietly uttered, staring intently at the display hologram.

Using the same remote, the *T'Vahl*'s first officer adjusted the display to highlight Zeta 2 Reticuli. "This is a yellow dwarf-class G2 star located less than a light year away from its binary neighbor, Zeta Reticuli 1," she began. Four planets and their orbital paths gradually illuminated around the G2 star. "The fourth planet, named Zeta 2 Reticulum 4 by Earth astronomers is our target planet," she continued. "It is within the habitable life zone of Zeta 2 Reticuli and has been positively confirmed by Vulcan astronomers to be the home world of the Greys."

Uncrossing her arms, Beta walked closer to the display. She turned and gazed intently at Utek. "Earth scientists have been *reasonably* certain of the existence of these four planets, to include habitation of the Greys on Zeta 2 Reticulum 4," she chimed in. "It appears your research has settled that question."

"Confirmed as well by our Intelligence Bureau; it is the only logical conclusion," Utek replied.

Foxwell stepped forward, annoyed. "Commander Utek, Captain Strojok," he began, "we appreciate the information. The only conclusion I've come to is that the suspected address for the Greys has now been officially confirmed by the post office on both our worlds." A pause. "If you don't mind, can we get on with the mission aspect of the briefing?"

Utek and Strojok exchanged glances. "I believe Captain

Foxwell is being sarcastic," Strojok blurted.

"As I understand it, for humans it is a way of expressing themselves based on emotion," Utek confirmed.

"Such as when they are annoyed or irritated," Stojok added.

Utek tilted her head. "Illogical."

Foxwell placed his hands on his hips. He looked down at the smooth copper-toned deck and shook his head, then craned his neck at the sound of a chuckle. It was his weapons officer. "Do you find this amusing, Mr. Warwick?"

Quickly changing his expression, Warwick cleared his throat. "Uh, uhm, no sir," he replied.

Beta turned and looked at Foxwell. "Captain, may I suggest—"

"Settle down, everyone," Foxwell bellowed. He pivoted in the direction of Strojok. "With all due respect, Captain, what is the game plan?"

The Vulcan captain glanced at Utek, then nodded.

"Intelligence and sensor probes have confirmed the presence of an unknown number of developing humanoid life forms deep underground on Zeta Reticulum 4," Utek continued. "Information gathered and analyzed by our scientists has led us to conclude that the Greys are engaging in transgenic experimentation."

Foxwell looked at Beta with a baffled expression. "Transgenic experimentation? Explain."

"Concerning humans and the Greys, transgenesis is the process of introducing one or more DNA sequences by artificial means into a fertilized egg or developing embryo," Beta described. "It becomes integrated into the chromosomes. When a hybrid grows to adulthood, it is believed the humanoid can transmit their DNA to its offspring."

Foxwell pulled a face, then glanced full circle around

the conference room. "So, what you're telling me is: The Greys are operating a genetic reproduction factory whose sole purpose is to produce alien-human hybrids."

"In a word . . . yes, Captain," Utek answered.

Strojok stepped forward, his eyes falling on Foxwell. "Transgenesis is the means by which the Greys create optimal bodies native to a specific planetary ecosystem. By crossing humans with themselves, a new species is developed bearing a physical body which is predominantly human, and with a consciousness that is predominantly Grey alien."

Dr. Rivera rose from his chair and loped around the conference table, standing next to Foxwell and Beta. "My apologies for the interruption, Captain, but I could not sit idle any longer." He turned to Strojok and Utek with a quizzical glance. "You stated earlier that your scientists have concluded transgenic experimentation is occurring." Hesitating for a moment, he asked: "Can you provide any proof?"

"Affirmative," Utek replied. She turned and bobbed her head at the *T'Vahl*'s operations officer.

Returning a confirming nod, the operations officer stepped back and opened the ready room door panels. "Bring in the specimen," he shouted.

Two Vulcan science officers, both wearing light gray coats with padded shoulders, wheeled a medical stretcher into the ready room. The gurney's occupant was fully covered with a stretched polyester sheet that resembled aluminum foil.

"Remove the covering," Utek ordered.

The Vulcan science officers stood on opposite sides of the wheeled gurney. As they carefully rolled the silvery sheet from top to bottom, an adult humanoid species with superficial properties both human and Grey alien came into full view.

Standing, the *Stargazer* crew members moved away from the conference room table and joined Foxwell and Beta. Staring in disbelief, they all gawked in morbid fascination at the entity resting on the mobile trolley.

Utek turned and locked eyes with Rivera. "Is this sufficient proof, Doctor?"

PART VI

GALACTIC
FLEET
COMMAND

Stardate: April 04, 2097

"What are we going to do?" Lindsey asked, eyeing her colleague.

Roberts responded with a sympathetic grimace. "Listen, we both need to get a grip. The good news is neither of us are injured. The bad news is we're involuntary guests of these alien creatures, and it probably has something to do with what we've just seen. I agree they're observing us, so why don't we just play along for the time being? They know we're not going anywhere."

Slowly regaining her composure, Lindsey took a deep breath. "Other than administering a non-consensual invasive medical exam, the Greys haven't been hostile in any other sense, nor have they issued any threats . . . so far."

Roberts nodded. "I received the same exam . . . the male version."

"There's no question the primary focus was on our reproductive system," Lindsey said.

Roberts face was solemn. "Yes, the primary function of the reproductive system is to ensure survival of the species."

"Species?" Her voice echoed in the narrow passageway. Both turned in the direction of the closed hatch.

"They wanted us to find that room."

Lindsey's expression sobered. "But why?"

"That's exactly what's we're going to find out."

* * *

Clutching Rivera's forearm, Foxwell gently pulled his chief medical officer away from the gurney and behind the conference room table. "So, tell me Doctor, what are we looking at?" he whispered, aghast at what he had just seen.

Rivera's eyes drifted toward the overhead. "Well, it's dead . . . that much I can tell you," he said in a sarcastic tone.

"I'm not a doctor and I could have told you that; try again . . . and that's an order," Foxwell barked, his expression sulky.

Rivera sighed deeply. "Based on everything I've seen and read about regarding the Greys . . . that poor soul lying on the stretcher is a hybrid."

"Hybrid? Elaborate further, Doctor," Foxwell pressed.

"Damn it Captain, it's a genetically manipulated product of alien and human DNA. Does that answer your question?"

Aware of the squabbling, the Vulcan captain, his first officer, and the *Stargazer* away team turned their attention toward Rivera and Foxwell.

"Dr. Rivera is correct," Utek voiced loudly.

Foxwell turned and walked toward the gurney, his away-team members clearing a path. Determined to obtain clarification, he stopped in front of Strojok and Utek. "You stated earlier that transgenesis is the means by which the Greys are creating optimal bodies native to a specific planetary ecosystem. Whose ecosystem are you referring to?"

Utek and the Vulcan captain exchanged a look. "We believe it to be the Earth's ecosystem, to include the ability to adapt to climate change as a result of a continued increase in atmospheric greenhouse gases," Stojok postulated.

"A problem Earth is still struggling to resolve," Utek chimed in.

Foxwell put on a serious face. It required little imagination to believe there was in fact something more sinister regarding the motives of the Greys. "And by what means is this to be accomplished?" he asked, skeptical.

"It is believed their plan is to infiltrate the planet in greater numbers over the next several decades," Strojok explained. "First-generation hybrids still have physical features distinctive to aliens, and have generally been kept in the background, used for experimentation, interaction with human abductees, and DNA collection. Second and subsequent generation hybrids have almost indistinguishable physical features from those of humans, making infiltration of Earth, particularly key government and other authoritative positions, easier to accomplish. With a consciousness that is predominantly Grey alien, and allowing for time and sufficient numbers, it is the collective opinion of Vulcan scientists and our intelligence community that the alien hybrids will in fact, accomplish this through assimilation."

"Assimilation?" Beta echoed, joining the captain as they sought further clarification regarding the rationale of the Greys.

"Yes . . . assimilation," Utek confirmed. "The process whereby the new Grey alien offspring will be absorbed into the dominant cultures of Earth society."

"We've all seen and heard enough," Foxwell replied in a contemptuous tone. Exchanging glances with Strojok and Utek, he demanded they continue with their briefing.

"It's obvious our mission is to put an end to these abductions and hybrid experiments. I've assembled an away team as ordered," he continued. A pause. "So . . . what are the mission specifics?" he demanded, raising the tone of his voice.

Utek walked toward the transparent display. Manipulating the remote, the alien home world reappeared. Several pan and zoom adjustments narrowed the focus to a high-resolution image confirming the existence of an underground facility on the planet's northern hemisphere. Using a laser pointer, she highlighted a point of interest on the image. Wearing a blank expression, the Vulcan science officer shifted her attention between the screen and the *Stargazer*'s crew. "This is your objective: You and your away team will be transported underground directly inside the primary Grey alien research facility."

"Understood," Foxwell nodded, studying the image on the display screen. He pivoted back in the direction of the Vulcan captain and first officer. "How deep underground are we talking?"

"Approximately one hundred meters, Captain," Strojok said.

"Nothing our transporter system cannot handle," Utek added.

Foxwell shook his head, then craned his neck in Beta's direction. "They never use contractions, do they?" he whispered.

"On occasion we do," Utek retorted, overhearing Foxwell's comment. "We tend to minimize their usage in order to be more precise regarding what we say. To Vulcans, it is the more preferred form of speech."

Beta fidgeted. "You forgot they have better hearing than humans."

"Whatever," Foxwell muttered. "I'll match your superior reasoning against their logic any day of the week."

"You don't particularly—"

"Shall we continue with the briefing?" Stojok interrupted.

"That's why we're here," Foxwell said. "Let's get on with it."

The Vulcan captain continued. "We have no internal or external images or video of the Greys' research facility. Nevertheless, our scientists and intelligence services have collected and analyzed sufficient data combined with AI to generate an approximate sized, three-dimensional structure of the underground constructed complex. What is on the inside remains unknown."

Soberly, Foxwell nodded. "It stands to reason we all know what's taking place inside that house of horrors . . . and what we're likely to find."

"Agree, Captain," Beta affirmed. The remaining away-team members mumbled their concurrence in the background.

Strojok stepped forward, coming face-to-face with Foxwell. "Your mission, Captain, is to destroy the facility and neutralize the ability of the Greys to conduct further DNA and hybrid experimentation. You and your away team will be provided with timed linear explosive charges. You will secure the explosives to critical weight-bearing supports; at the appropriate time you will detonate these charges in sequence which will initiate a controlled collapse, destroying the facility and all equipment inside."

Foxwell sighed, shaking his head. "I should have brought my engineer."

"You will be accompanied and assisted by Utek and the *T'Vahl*'s senior engineer," Stojok declared.

Foxwell glanced at Utek, then turned his attention back to the Vulcan captain. "Fine with me, but understand this: Beta and I are in command once this operation begins. Now allow me to digress momentarily. What kind of weapons can we expect the Greys to employ should they put up a fight?"

"Data analyzed appears to confirm they use highly focused directed energy weapons," Strojok replied. "Their exact composition is unknown, but logic dictates they operate by generating radiated energy, resulting in damage that degrades, neutralizes, or destroys any adversarial capability."

"Understood," Foxwell acknowledged. He turned and faced his away-team members. "Away team . . . check your weapons." He pivoted toward Rivera, glancing at the medkit strapped over his shoulder. Noticing his chief medical officer was not carrying a laser pistol, he removed his own from its hook and loop fastener attached to his belt, handing it to the doctor.

"Captain, I—"

"That's an order, Doctor . . . take it."

"What's their plan to monitor our progress?" Rivera asked, referring to the Vulcans.

"The microchip embedded in the Galactic Fleet logo on your uniforms will allow our sensors to track your every movement while inside the facility," Strojok replied.

Foxwell gave an approving nod. He turned again, facing his crew. "Any more questions?"

Warwick stepped forward. "Yes, Captain . . . Roberts and Lindsey . . . what about *them*?"

Eyeballing the away team, Foxwell spoke in a commanding voice: "Make no mistake . . . we WILL find them . . . and we WILL bring them home. Is that understood?"

"Aye, Captain," they all mumbled, exchanging glances and nodding in agreement.

"Let's roll."

PART VII

Stardate: April 04, 2097

Entering through the open hatch and into an enormous compartment, Lindsey and Roberts climbed down a short, metallic ladder secured to the bulkhead. The ceiling was a dull whitish steel with silvery shimmering waves, creating a ripple effect. Attached to the opposite bulkhead wall and deck, dozens of transparent cylindrical tanks were visible as far as the dim lighting would allow. Sensor pads ringed the top edge of the covered cauldrons, containing individual embryos and fetuses suspended vertically in a slightly viscous green fluid. A bottom-to-top bubble stream was noticeable, emanating from several rows of button-size holes in the tanks' supporting base.

Approaching the cylinders cautiously, Lindsey gasped in horror. "This is a nightmare come true."

The Galactic Fleet officers were overwhelmed, the consequence of a malevolent but superior intelligence. The suspended inhabitants appeared to be aware of their presence. They looked like little specimens hanging in oversized jars.

"There must be dozens, if not more of these tanks ringing this circular compartment," Roberts speculated, studying the transparent vessels closely and making mental notes. "Look," he pointed out. "These cylinders rest on a three-foot-high enclosed pedestal. It's obvious a life support system is housed within the supporting platform for the purpose of providing oxygen and nutrients."

"Which keeps them alive and allows for growth," Lindsey noted.

"Notice each fetus and embryo is in a different stage of development," Roberts commented, walking back and forth in front of several cylinders.

"You were right," Lindsey suddenly blurted.

Roberts pivoted. "Right? Right about what?"

"About what you said earlier regarding the Greys. They've embarked on a program of hybridization. They're breeding human beings with themselves to create a new species."

Roberts nodded in agreement. "It's obviously been ongoing for decades. Our presence in this star system and this facility is proof they've ramped up their efforts."

"And these life forms," she shouted, pointing to several tanks. "Even at this stage of development, it's also obvious they have both human and alien features."

Sensing movement, Roberts stepped away from his girlfriend and turned in the direction of an approaching figure. He glanced back in her direction. "Don't be alarmed," he whispered, "but it appears we have company."

Approaching the Galactic Fleet officers, two short Greys were followed by a third, taller Grey. The lanky alien was arrayed in what appeared to be a one-piece protective covering resembling a jumpsuit. The smaller Greys seemed to ambulate in robotic fashion, unlike the taller alien's manner of walking which resembled that of an adult human. All three appeared androgynous.

"What do we do?" Lindsey nervously whispered.

"For the moment . . . nothing," Roberts shot back. "Try to remain calm."

"Do not be afraid," the tall Grey announced telepathically. *"What do you think about what you have seen?"*

Roberts swallowed hard, rage burning through him. "What do I think?" he angrily repeated. "I think you're all a bunch of ghoulish fiends . . . that's what I think. Why in God's name are you doing this?"

The larger Grey walked around his two shorter companions. Projecting telepathic thought, he described what was seen as necessary for their survival, stating their genetic structure had deteriorated, and that they were no longer able to reproduce. He went on to say that if they were unable to resolve the problem, their species would soon cease to exist.

"Why are you taller than the other two?" Lindsey asked.

Looking downward at the two smaller beings before him, he replied: *"They're artificial life forms, created in our image to serve and assist. Our original numbers are dwindling, and the help they provide mitigates additional risk to those of us who remain."*

"Why haven't you approached the authorities on our planet for help?" Lindsey asked.

"We did," the taller Grey answered. *"In your year 1954 we met with representatives of the US government; subsequent agreement was reached. It was known as the Greada Treaty."*

"I'm somewhat familiar with the provisions of that treaty," Roberts said, "having studied it while a cadet at Galactic Fleet Academy. It allowed for abduction of humans on a limited basis for the purpose of medical examination and documentation. The treaty stated that there would be no interference in each other's affairs. We would keep your presence on Earth a secret. You would provide advanced technology and would help us in our technological development. You would not make any treaty with any other nation with the stipulation that no humans would be harmed and would have no memory of the abduction and examinations. More importantly, however, nothing in the treaty allowed for crossbreeding humans with your species."

The alien flailed his lanky arms as he replied telepathically. "*Unfortunately*," he continued, "*it soon became apparent from information gleaned as a result of the initial examinations, and in order to ensure survival as a species, that we would require sperm samples from adult human males, and egg cells from adult human females, along with unborn developing human embryos . . . all needed for further experimentation.*"

"You mean illegal experiments with *stolen* human sex cells and embryos to be mutated with alien DNA," Lindsey angrily jumped in.

"Harvested and altered into hybrid lifeforms . . . all without anyone's knowledge or permission," Roberts added.

"*We had no choice.*"

"Bullshit," Lindsey fired back. "Intelligent beings always have a choice. It's obvious neither agreements nor morality factor into your decisions."

The room fell silent. Roberts stepped forward, coming face-to-face with the six-foot-tall alien. "As far as I'm concerned, we're done talking. You will immediately return my colleague and me back to our starship."

"*Please come with me.*"

Lindsey frowned, then glanced at Roberts, checking for his reaction to the alien's request. He nodded. Following the spindly Zeta Reticulan a short distance around the circular compartment comprised of additional acrylic cylinders, he stopped in front of a functioning, occupied tank. The same viscous green fluid that filled the other tanks was clearly visible. A small bubble could be seen in the center of the tank.

Angry and exhausted, Roberts turned and faced the Grey alien. "You abducted Lindsey and me, then subjected both of us to a non-consensual physical examination. I'm telling you again—"

The tall being raised his hand, cutting off Roberts. He turned and pointed to the tiny globule floating in the middle of the tank. *"This is a five-week-old human embryo."*

Roberts's face contorted in anger. "You mean another *stolen* embryo," he barked. "Who's the lucky mom and dad?"

The tall Grey turned slowly and faced his human abductees. Spreading apart two of his long, spindly fingers, he pointed one at Roberts, and the other at Lindsey. *"It's yours,"* he answered telepathically, his cold, almond-shaped eyes devoid of any feeling or empathy.

GALACTIC
FLEET
COMMAND

PART VIII

Stardate: April 04, 2097

"No, no, nooooo," Lindsey screamed, horrified at what the Grey alien had just communicated. The compartment spun; her eyelids fluttered. She fell forward, Roberts catching her as she fainted.

"Yes . . . it's true," the tall Zeta Reticulan replied in cold, telepathic thought.

"Why . . . why?" Roberts shouted, slowly dropping to one knee as he cradled his girlfriend in his arms.

"Our genetic structure has deteriorated, and we are no longer able to reproduce. Our hybrid creations are a living, functional, autonomous species. They carry our DNA as well as yours, yet are incapable of producing offspring. However, recent research has yielded promising new results which we believe will correct that discrepancy. And we need living human embryos in order to move on to the next phase."

"But why Lindsey and me?" Roberts asked again, the emotional shock stunning him as much as a direct hit from a laser pistol. "Neither of us knew," he cried out, shock and numbness overwhelming him.

"While orbiting our sun, a scan of your starship confirmed she was the only female aboard your vessel who was carrying a

living embryo," the alien explained.

"The only vessel we were aware of was an unmanned probe," Roberts retorted.

"Our vessel was concealed—what you humans refer to as cloaked. You were unaware of our presence."

Roberts carefully lowered Lindsey, gently resting her head on the cold, gray deck. He looked up at the Grey alien humanoid, his eyes and face contorted with rage.

"We mean no harm. Unless we improve our genetic structure, our race will soon cease to exist."

"That's a lie," Roberts fired back, slowly rising to his feet. "It's not about saving your species. The game plan from the beginning has been to infiltrate Earth with your human lookalike sons-of-bitches so you can take control of the entire planet. A bloodless coup. All without firing a single weapon. I know all about your devious plan . . . studied it on Earth in primary school and later at Galactic Fleet Academy. The 'saving the species' story is just a ruse for conquering the planet without destroying it. Easier to assimilate a habitable world that can support life with an intact ecosystem and infrastructure."

"Interesting hypothesis."

Roberts responded with a cynical chuckle. "I wrote a thesis while attending Galactic Fleet Academy. Unfortunately, no one took it seriously. And thanks to a continuous disinformation campaign by world governments debunking the notion that Grey aliens are creating hybrids, the civilian population wasn't buying either story. The powers that be didn't want to admit the Greys had violated the Greada Treaty, abducting humans in far greater numbers than was originally agreed to. It was all swept under the rug."

"Fertile hybrids will make assimilation easier," the Grey admitted. *"Any attempt to stop us will result not only in your*

death and that of your friend," he now threatened, glancing down at Lindsey, *"but the invasion and subjugation of your planet and all its inhabitants as well . . . beginning with your starship."*

Regaining consciousness, Lindsey uttered a faint moan. Roberts kneeled again, then whispered softly into her ear. "Try not to move."

Craning his head upward, Roberts displayed a cynical grin. "Well, I've got some bad news for you."

"And what might that be?"

Roberts smirked. "THIS," he yelled, pouncing on the lanky alien, catching him off guard and knocking him to the floor. He wrapped a jujitsu chokehold around the alien's long, scrawny neck.

Still woozy, Lindsey hoisted herself up onto unsteady feet. Moving away from the ensuing struggle, she bumped into the passageway bulkhead, leaning into it for support. She rubbed the palm of her hands against her eyes, attempting to regain her vision.

Struggling with the gawky alien, Roberts shouted: "You've destroyed countless lives and traumatized generations of innocent humans, not to mention all the Earth animals you've mutilated and killed." He tightened his grip on the towering extraterrestrial.

The Grey alien stood, clamping both hands around Roberts's forearms. Possessing strength that at first glance appeared unlikely due to the creature's slender frame, he easily broke his captive's chokehold. The alien suddenly whirled around, flinging Roberts into the bulkhead wall.

"Now I'll show both of you what we do to those who choose not to understand and cooperate." The imposing humanoid creature strode menacingly toward Roberts, lying slumped on the deck of the alien fetus room.

Leaning against the bulkhead and still feeling light-headed, Lindsey bent over, placing her head down and in the path of a recycling air vent. Out of the corner of her eye, she noticed a small object on the metallic deck sliding toward her, finally stopping a few feet away. *Is that a . . . ? Oh my god, it's a laser pistol!* Looking up and visually retracing the path of the laser weapon, she caught a glimpse of four shadowy silhouettes in the background, slowly advancing in her direction. She struggled to remain quiet, not wanting to alert the Grey to the presence of what she knew was a *Stargazer* away team.

Now fully alert, she moved silently toward the pistol before reaching down and grabbing it. Adjusting the weapon to its highest setting, she turned and pointed it in the direction of the Grey. Only a moment before, he stopped and turned in response to the pulsating sound of an object sliding on the deck. Too late. Lindsey aimed the pistol and fired, striking the alien in the upper torso and propelling him into the bulkhead just to the left of Roberts.

"Are you okay, Ensign?" Beta asked, finally reaching the traumatized crew member.

"Thank God you're here," Lindsey cried with relief, glancing at Dr. Rivera and Security Officer O'Malley. She stepped toward Beta, enfolding her in a thankful embrace.

Moments later Beta stepped back, gently resting her hands on Lindsey's shoulders. "Roberts . . . where is he?"

Tears streaming down her face, Lindsey pivoted in her boyfriend's direction. "Over there," she said, pointing, "next to the bulkhead. He's unconscious . . . alongside the Grey."

Beta turned her head, glancing at Rivera. "Doctor, take O'Malley with you and check on the condition of Roberts and the Grey."

Rivera nodded, moving quickly toward the injured

Galactic Fleet officer with O'Malley.

Removing the communicator from her utility belt, Beta flipped the antenna open, the handheld device chirping in response.

"Foxwell . . . go ahead."

"Captain, Beta here. We've located Lindsey and Roberts."

Foxwell breathed a sigh of relief. "What's their condition?"

"Lindsey is here, standing next to me. Dr. Rivera just completed a cursory examination of Roberts and a Grey; both were found unresponsive."

She handed Rivera her communicator, and the chief medical officer reported his findings: "Captain, Lindsey is alert and oriented with no visible external injuries. Suffice to say she's pretty shook up."

"And Roberts?"

"He appears to have suffered a concussion along with several fractured ribs. I'll need to get him back to the *T'Vahl* for further evaluation." Hesitating momentarily, the doctor continued: "And if you're interested . . . the Grey is dead."

"Understood," Foxwell sighed again. "Contact the *T'Vahl* and make arrangements to transport Lindsey and Roberts to their infirmary."

"Acknowledged," Rivera replied, handing the communicator back to Beta.

"What is your current status, Captain?"

Foxwell looked around. "We're on the opposite side of this circular compartment, one deck up. It appears this is a monitoring center of some type."

"Possibly the control station for the fetus room, which is where my team and I are presently," Beta speculated.

A pause. "Did I hear you say . . . fetus room?"

"Yes, Captain . . . a fetus room," Beta repeated. "You need to see this. There are literally dozens of fetuses and embryos encapsulated in transparent acrylic tanks suspended in what appears to be a synthetic type of amniotic fluid. All are alive and tethered to a centralized life support system. It would be *reasonable* to assume they are monitored where you are presently."

Utek turned and locked eyes with Foxwell. "Captain, we need to get down there and facilitate immediate transport of those cylinders to the *T'Vahl*. A temporary life support system is operational in the hangar bay which will keep them alive until we reach Vulcan."

Foxwell paused, then nodded. "Agree, but only after placement of the demolition charges on this deck; upon completion, we'll immediately rendezvous with Beta and her team on the deck below and repeat the process. You and I will assist your engineer regarding placement of the charges. Warwick and security crew member McKenzie will provide security."

Utek paused, returning a blank stare. "As you wish, Captain."

Foxwell sensed a feeling of disapproval. "Is there a problem, Commander?"

Utek hesitated. "No, Captain. It's just that—"

"Take cover!" Foxwell shouted as energy beams of unknown composition illuminated like tracers over and around the uninvited visitors.

"Whoever they are, it's coming from both directions," Utek called out, crouching on the deck and leaning into a bulkhead, clutching a Vulcan phaser.

A group of the shorter Grey EBEs were spotted advancing toward the away team. Making minimum effort to shield themselves, they continued their approach, bypassing makeshift barriers, passageway egresses, and support equipment anchored to the bulkhead.

"Return fire . . . wide beam . . . on stun," Foxwell ordered.

Using their fusion laser pistols, Warwick and McKenzie fired several short bursts. Four EBEs dropped to the deck, with one continuing to advance. Foxwell aimed his fusion laser rifle and fired, dropping the remaining EBE.

Utek and the Vulcan chief engineer swept as much of the dimmed passageway behind them with their phasers as they could see. Ceasing fire, the corridor went eerily silent.

Slowly, Foxwell stood. He looked ahead, then turned, catching sight of Utek and her chief engineer. "Destroy their weapons," he ordered. "They should remain unconscious for at least half an hour."

Foxwell's communicator chirped. "Go ahead," he responded in a hurried tone, flipping open the antenna.

"Captain, Beta here. We could hear the tumult above. Do you require assistance?"

"Negative . . . situation under control." A pause. "Beta . . . change of plans . . . I need for you to use your best judgment; begin placement of the bilitrium charges on as many weight-bearing supports as you can locate. There won't be enough time for the Vulcan engineer to prepare both decks. We'll rendezvous with you as soon as we've completed placement of our cache of charges."

"Acknowledged."

"Oh, and on a related note, be advised we made quick work of a Grey scouting party. My gut tells me *their* version of a SWAT team is or will soon be on the way."

"Understood," Beta replied.

Foxwell and Utek took positions ahead and behind the Vulcan engineer and *Stargazer* security officers as they began the arduous task of attaching the demolition charges to critical support structures. Completing placement of the last explosive, the Galactic Fleet captain transmitted a pre-arranged code to the *T'Vahl*. Moments later, Utek, Foxwell, and his away team rematerialized on the deck below.

"Good to see you, Captain," Beta greeted.

"Likewise. Status report?"

"All bilitrium charges allotted for this deck have been secured to critical support structures."

Foxwell turned in the direction of the Vulcan engineer. "Is the remote detonation system ready?"

"Affirmative, Captain."

Foxwell wheeled around, making eye contact with Utek. "Contact the *T'Vahl* and prepare to transport the amniotic tanks to the hangar bay."

Remaining silent, Utek turned and walked slowly in the opposite direction, stopping as a small contingent of tall Greys materialized in front of her. Armed with what appeared to be unfamiliar energy weapons, a second group of tall Greys took form on the opposite side, boxing in the entire away team. Utek casually completed an about-face, then locked eyes with Foxwell.

"You will surrender your weapons, Captain."

PART IX

Stardate: April 04, 2097

Returning a surprised stare, Foxwell blurted out, "What is this . . . a joke?"

"Vulcans . . . never . . . joke," Utek replied sternly, her brows furrowed. "Order your away team to hand over their weapons . . . NOW," she demanded. The tall Greys moved closer.

"Not without an explanation," Foxwell fired back. "Away team, maintain your position. Do NOT lower your weapons," he yelled out, maintaining eye contact with the Vulcan science officer.

"*Illogical,* Captain. We outnumber you two to one."

Feigning a nervous chuckle, Foxwell said, "I admit I don't know as much about Vulcans as I probably should, but one thing I do know is . . . none of you have a sense of humor."

Utek maintained the same blank expression. "Nor do we bluff."

"Which is why you'd better have a good explanation."

Moving behind the Galactic Fleet captain, Utek walked slowly until she reemerged in front of him. "What you know and have been told about the Greys is true," she began.

Foxwell cocked his head to the side. "What do you mean? Explain."

"It is correct the Greys are in a reproductive bind on their home world. And it is true human abductions have increased; they view humans as temporary incubators, abducting select members of the human race for removal of sex cells, embryos, and fetuses . . . for the purpose of hybridization."

Beta cautiously approached the Vulcan commander. "Why humans . . . and why the increase in the number of abductions?"

"The growing number of abductees is linked to continuation of the Greys as a surviving entity as well as an increase in atmospheric greenhouse gases on Earth. However you wish to view it, hybridization has become necessary for the long-term survival of both species," Utek answered.

Beta turned in Foxwell's direction. "Captain, I—"

Raising his hand, the starship captain gazed at Utek.

"May I continue?" she requested.

Foxwell leaned forward, his curiosity aroused. While dubious of Vulcan motives and beliefs, he was aware of their reputation for honesty, with exceptions such as survival, or to maximize a positive outcome or minimize harm. *Could this be one of those exceptions?* he thought. He decided to give Utek the benefit of the doubt . . . for the moment. "Go ahead," he told her.

Utek slowly paced. "Earth authorities and the majority of its inhabitants are aware surface temperatures continue to rise due to climate change. Climate accords and geo-engineering projects have failed to resolve the effects of global warming. The Greys are producing hybrids that can better withstand the rigors of a warmer Earth."

"And by coincidence, the Greys as well," Beta

interrupted, "by preserving the part of their DNA that's carried by the temperature-tolerant hybrids."

"My scientific colleagues and I understand the plight of the Greys and humans," Utek continued. "It is only *logical* that we support efforts to resolve the issues that threaten both species."

Foxwell pulled a face. "The Greys save themselves and the human race, and gradually take over the Earth through assimilation. How convenient," he scoffed.

Unfazed by Foxwell's sarcasm, Utek continued her explanation. "As a result of their violation of the Greada Treaty, the Greys are aware they have lost all credibility. They believe an explanation from a representative of the Vulcan Science Council would be more plausible."

"Is this part of a greater Vulcan conspiracy?" Foxwell pointedly asked.

"It is not, Captain," Utek assured. "Only the Greys and a handful of my colleagues with the Vulcan Science Academy are aware of these findings. The argument is twofold: The Greys can no longer successfully procreate, and Earth is warming exponentially and dangerously, calling into question its future habitability."

Unmoved by Utek's explanation, Beta craned her head in Foxwell's direction. "Captain, I'm completely onboard with Galactic Fleet's edict that we destroy this facility. What is occurring here is a clear violation of the Greada Treaty of 1954 . . . notwithstanding everything else we've uncovered."

Utek pivoted in Beta's direction. "You overlook the fact that you are in no position to do anything." Casting a glimpse at Foxwell, she reminded him, "You and your away team are trapped. We . . . not you, are in the driver's seat . . . as humans are so fond of saying."

"You mean you *were* in the driver's seat," a voice

shouted in the background.

Laser fire erupted from both ends of the circular compartment. On both sides of the cornered away team, the tall Greys dropped to the deck in unison with wide beam bursts of laser fire, revealing Ensign Lindsey on one end and Dr. Rivera on the opposite side. Startled, Utek spun around. With her back to Foxwell, he moved toward her. Lowering his laser rifle, he delivered a knife hand strike to her carotid artery. No effect. She immediately wheeled around, countering with a Vulcan nerve pinch to the base of Foxwell's neck. Falling unconscious to the deck, she stepped back and aimed her phaser at his upper torso.

"Utek," someone shouted. Using her powerful bionic legs, Beta propelled herself toward the Vulcan officer, hurling her into the adjacent bulkhead and knocking the phaser out of her hand. During the ensuing struggle, Utek broke free. She reached down and grabbed Foxwell's dropped laser rifle. Raising the weapon above her head, she intended to use it as a club to strike Beta with a fatal blow.

Phaser fire broke out, followed by a coruscating, sparkling whirlpool of color and light. Utek was beginning to dematerialize, her own molecules being drawn into the vortex around her. Her body disappeared . . . she was gone.

Foxwell fell back on the cold metallic deck, having arched himself upright just enough to fire the Vulcan commander's dropped phaser.

Beta stood and walked quickly toward her semi-conscious commanding officer. "Captain, are you all right?" She reached down and helped Foxwell to his feet just as Rivera and Lindsey arrived.

"Doctor . . . what are you . . ." he mumbled, slurring his words. "What the hell are you doing here? I ordered you to report back to the *T'Vahl* with Lindsey and Roberts."

"I arranged for Roberts to be transported to sickbay aboard the *T'Vahl*," Rivera explained, "with specific medical instructions for his care. Lindsey pleaded with me to remain behind and take cover, and to provide additional backup if needed. That's when we noticed Utek demanding you and the away team drop your weapons along with the tall Greys materializing behind her. We set our laser pistols on stun, and quietly approached from both ends. As soon as I heard Lindsey shout, we both fired simultaneously."

Foxwell exhaled a long breath. "Well, that's one out of two," he muttered.

Rivera twisted his head slightly, a confused look appearing. "Say again, Captain?"

"My laser pistol . . . I ordered you to take it before we were transported over here."

Nodding, a slight smiled crossed Rivera's lips. "There *is* another reason Lindsey wanted to remain behind, Captain."

"Go ahead, I'm all ears," Foxwell replied, his face twisted in a painful contortion as he massaged the trapezius nerve bundle in his neck.

Lindsey quickly briefed the captain regarding the living embryo belonging to her and Roberts, confirmed by the *Stargazer*'s chief medical officer.

"It's doubtful their embryo has been hybridized," Rivera continued. "The Greys only took possession of it several hours ago as part of Lindsey's examination."

"That would be a *reasonable* assumption," Beta chimed in.

Foxwell nodded. "Thank the stars for that." Expressing a sympathetic gaze, he assured Lindsey the cylindrical tank containing the living embryo belonging to her and Roberts would receive the highest priority.

"Working with the Vulcan medical staff, I believe we

can safely return their embryo back to her uterus, allowing it to develop full term," Rivera assured.

"And what say you?" Foxwell asked, turning in Lindsey's direction.

Lindsey's expression was soulful. "Neither of us knew, Captain . . . until this terrible ordeal occurred. It's absolutely what we both want."

Foxwell turned and gazed at Rivera. "Out of all the tanks, it's the only living specimen whose identity is known. Make sure that it's properly tagged."

"Already taken care of."

Motioning to Utek's chief engineer with a quick wave of his hand, Foxwell ordered him to make contact with the *T'Vahl*. "Confirm coordinates with your transporter room, then beam the unconscious Greys to the planet's surface, minus their weapons. Following their transport, I want all functional cylinders transported to the *T'Vahl*'s hangar bay. Do this immediately. We need to be out of here before whoever is in charge of these napping humanoids figure out what's happened."

"Understood," the Vulcan engineer replied, moving away from Foxwell and confirming his communication link with the *T'Vahl*. "Transporter room, confirm my position and lock onto all Greys in the immediate vicinity. Beam to the planet's surface . . . without their weapons."

"Acknowledged," the transporter officer replied.

"Beta."

"Yes, Captain?"

"Set the remote detonator's timer for one minute after the last cylinder is transported. I will give the order for those of us who remain to be beamed back to the *T'Vahl* during that sixty-second interval."

"Understood."

Foxwell looked around. Shouting, he ordered: "Away team . . . remain close by and stay alert until we're beamed back aboard the *T'Vahl*."

"Aye, Captain," they mumbled and nodded.

Moments after transporting the unconscious Greys to the planet's surface, the process of beaming the developing hybrids began, to include the embryo belonging to Lindsey and Roberts. In rapid succession, every cylindrical tank containing a live embryo or fetus dematerialized. Converted into sub-atomically de-bonded matter, the particles were streamed into individual pattern buffers where they remained briefly before rematerializing and arriving at their destination aboard the Vulcan starship.

The Vulcan engineer returned and approached Foxwell. "Transport of all functional tanks complete, Captain. The *T'Vahl* acknowledges the transports were successful."

"Excellent," came the reply, followed by a pause. "Uhm, I don't believe your name was ever conveyed to me," Foxwell said.

"Vulyk," the Vulcan chief engineer answered.

"Got it. And thanks again . . . Vulyk." Foxwell gave an appreciative half-smile.

Quickly approaching Foxwell and the Vulcan engineer, Beta announced: "Detonator set for sixty seconds, Captain."

"Very well," Foxwell said, reaching for his communicator. He flipped the antenna open.

"*T'Vahl*, Strojok here."

"Captain, this is Foxwell. Prepare to beam the away team back to the *T'Vahl* . . . on my order."

"Acknowledged," Strojok replied. "I am present in the transporter room. Be advised sensors are detecting a large presence of humanoids moving in two directions toward your position. Estimated time of arrival . . . one minute. Give the command to beam aboard when ready."

"Understood," Foxwell responded. Looking around, Foxwell shouted once more to the away team: "Everyone, listen up . . . Prepare to beam back to the *T'Vahl*."

Pivoting in Beta's direction, Foxwell issued the order: "Start the timer."

"Timer enabled . . . sixty seconds and counting," she yelled.

Raising the volume of his voice, Foxwell looked around again. "Away team, standby to beam aboard the *T'Vahl*." Bringing the communicator to his lips, Foxwell yelled: "Beam us aboard . . . NOW."

Back onboard the *T'Vahl*, the transporter officer craned his head in Strojok's direction. "Captain, I'm having difficulty acquiring a lock on the away team . . . some kind of interference."

"Increase transporter signal strength. Can you identify the source?"

Working the backlit touch panels, the transporter officer craned his head in Strojok's direction. "Affirmative, Captain. Sensors confirm transmission of kelbonite waves from the planet's surface."

Strojok nodded in acknowledgment. "Very interesting," he mumbled, furrowing his thick eyebrows. "Kelbonite results in a scattering of the transporter's annular confinement beam, resulting in sensor interference and preventing a transporter lock. Fortunately, it does not prevent weapons targeting."

"Captain, do you—"

"Origin?" he thundered, cutting off the transporter officer. "We have less than thirty seconds to beam the away team back to the *T'Vahl*."

"Ship's main sensors have identified a specific sector in

the northern hemisphere."

"Acknowledged," Strojok mumbled. "Forward the exact coordinates to the main fire control computer on the bridge. Inform the weapons officer to prepare to fire quadium torpedoes on my command."

A pause. "Weapons Officer concurs, Captain. Fire control system locked onto target coordinates."

"FIRE!"

Another pause. "Captain, the bridge confirms the target has been destroyed."

Strojok yelled out: "Transporter status?"

"I have a lock . . . transport in progress."

A hailing signal from the bridge.

"Strojok here . . . go ahead."

"Captain, this is conning officer. Sensors confirm a series of explosions throughout the facility below the planet's surface."

"Acknowledged. A search and destroy mission on the part of the Greys would now be a logical response. Remain alert."

"Understood, Captain."

Hunched over the control panel, the transporter officer suddenly stood upright. "Captain, the *Stargazer* away team has been successfully transported to the hangar bay."

"Excellent. Contact the *Stargazer* immediately. On my authority, order the conning officer to engage their cloaking device . . . then engage ours."

"Acknowledged, Captain." Pivoting in Strojok's direction, he added, "All personnel accounted for . . . with the exception of . . . Commander Utek."

"Explanation?"

The transporter officer returned a blank stare. "None."

* * *

Stardate: April 05, 2097

T'Vahl *Ready Room: Strojok, Foxwell, and Beta present*

Briefing and counter-briefing complete, Foxwell sought to clarify Strojok's knowledge or collaboration subsequent to admission of the conspiracy by Utek.

"I can assure you, Captain," Strojok began, pacing uneasily around his ready room, "I was completely unaware of Utek's involvement in this scheme. I will complete my report and forward it to the Vulcan authorities and Galactic Fleet Command. You are welcome to review the report before it is submitted."

Foxwell rendered a confirming nod. "Losing one's life is never a win," he replied sorrowfully, referring to the death of Utek, "but I'm still puzzled as to a more precise motivation behind her actions."

"There will be a thorough investigation upon our return to Vulcan, to include detaining and questioning the other scientists involved," Strojok assured. He turned and gazed at the Galactic Fleet officers. "Utek was a model officer, dedicated to her career and the rightness and purity of logic. Her devotion was admirable."

Beta exhaled a thoughtful sigh. "But her actions were not logical, not in this instance."

"I would have to agree," Foxwell added.

"Perhaps your science officer would care to elaborate," Strojok prompted, his facial expression morphing into one of curiosity. "It is my understanding her brain is comprised of a—"

"Half of my brain," Beta cut in, clarifying.

"Beta neutronic labyrinth emulator," Strojok slowly continued, "capable of superior reasoning. Reason versus logic. Perhaps her explanation will be persuasive. I am eager to hear it . . . or her theory."

"With all due respect, Captain, my first officer is under no obligation to defend or clarify her opinions or findings, nor is she required to satisfy your curiosity. This isn't a formal hearing or inquiry. She is also my science officer. I trust her knowledge and judgment explicitly."

Beta pivoted in Foxwell's direction. "Captain, your continued confidence in me is inspiring; nevertheless, I feel compelled to respond."

"And that's *why* you're my first officer," Foxwell said. "However, let's save that exchange for another time." He turned and faced Strojok. "What's the status of the cylinders and the developing hybrids?"

Strojok glanced at Foxwell, his expression deadpan. "The initial report confirmed the cylinders and their occupants were received undamaged and unharmed, respectively. The process of coupling the cylinders to a central life support system is complete."

"Excellent news," Foxwell replied, with Beta nodding in agreement.

"Perhaps you and your first officer would care to accompany me back to the hangar bay?" Strojok proposed.

Smiling, Foxwell nodded and politely extended his arm. "Lead the way."

PART X

Stardate: April 05, 2097

"Permission requested to remain aboard the *T'Vahl*," Ensign Lindsey pleaded, standing in the hangar bay next to Foxwell and Dr. Rivera.

"Captain . . . if I may?" Rivera chimed in.

"Go ahead, Doctor."

"After further evaluation, it is again my medical opinion as well as that of the Vulcan medical staff that the embryo belonging to Lindsey and Roberts has not been hybridized."

Foxwell took in a deep breath. "Continue."

"And it is our joint medical opinion that the embryo can be successfully returned to Lindsey, which will allow it to develop full term inside her womb. The Vulcans assure me they can successfully perform this procedure here on the *T'Vahl*. I would like to remain onboard and assist."

"And what about Roberts? What is his current medical status?"

"Roberts is recovering in the infirmary. He is sedated and resting comfortably. He should be well enough to transport directly to sickbay aboard the *Stargazer* no later than tomorrow."

"What is the condition of the remaining embryos and fetuses?"

Rivera let out a deep sigh. "Preliminary examination appears to confirm all have been hybridized. The job of the nursery was to provide care and nourishment until removal from the tanks at full term. After that, your guess is as good as mine."

Overhearing the conversation, Strojok stepped forward. "Captain, Galactic Fleet Command has acknowledged our report regarding the successful mission. I just received word both the *Stargazer* and the *T'Vahl* have been directed to return to Earth, not Vulcan as originally ordered. The cylinders are to be transported upon arrival to an appropriate support facility for continued monitoring and evaluation."

"No doubt DNA profiling will be part of that process," Beta interjected. "The authorities will seek to match every embryo and fetus to the human mother and father."

"I can only imagine how that will play out," Foxwell mused.

"You and me both," Rivera added.

"Our mission is complete. It's time to return with the away team back to the *Stargazer* . . . with the exception of Ensign Lindsey and Dr. Rivera." Foxwell pivoted in their direction. "Permission granted to remain onboard the *T'Vahl*. It appears there's a baby in the making that needs to be returned to its rightful mother . . . and father."

A radiant smile appearing, Lindsey turned and threw her arms around Foxwell, embracing him with an appreciative and heartfelt hug.

Returning her embrace, he then stepped back, locking eyes with the misty-eyed expectant mother. "Why don't you go to the infirmary and tell the father-to-be the news. I'm sure he would appreciate it, even if he's sedated."

"Thank you, Captain, I'll do that," she beamed, happily wheeling around as she headed for the *T'Vahl*'s sickbay.

A hailing signal was heard in the hangar bay. The Vulcan captain walked toward the companel. "Strojok here."

"Captain, this is the bridge. Sensors have identified three Grey alien vessels nearing our position. They do not appear to be aware of our presence."

"Acknowledged . . . standby." Strojok turned in Foxwell's direction. "They are looking for us, Captain."

"And I'm sure they know we're cloaked," Foxwell said. "If they have any technology that will allow them to detect us in spite of our invisibility, then it's time to set a return course back to Earth."

"Agree." Turning back to the companel, Strojok issued new navigation orders: "Bridge, lay in a course for return to Earth. We will proceed alongside the *Stargazer* at their speed."

"Acknowledged," the conning officer replied.

Opening a secure hailing frequency, Foxwell contacted the bridge of the *Stargazer*.

"Bridge, O'Donovan here."

"POD, this is Foxwell."

"Captain," the chief engineer enthusiastically greeted. "How's the—"

"Never mind that now. Lay in a course for return to Earth . . . light factor 2. We'll be returning on a parallel trajectory with the *T'Vahl*."

"Aye, sir. Sensors have picked up a triad of Grey alien vessels. Looks like they're flying blind out there."

"And that's why we're leaving . . . before they find us. Prepare to engage fusion light drive."

"Aye sir . . . fusion light drive enabled. Return course to

Earth entered. Ready when you are, Captain."

"Engage."

Strojok adjusted the companel settings to communicate with his conning officer on the bridge. "Set a parallel course and speed to match that of the *Stargazer*," he ordered. "Maintain a visual distance of one hundred kilometers. Engage warp engines . . . now."

Foxwell turned toward the Vulcan captain. "I want to thank you for your assistance and support . . . for everything. And a personal thanks to your medical staff for the excellent care provided Ensign Roberts . . . and for that which will soon be provided to Ensign Lindsey."

Strojok remained impassive. "I believe the correct human response is, 'You're welcome,'" he replied, using the contraction. "We will beam you and your away team back to the *Stargazer* as soon as both starships can safely decloak," he assured, adding, "may our collaboration and successful mission help strengthen the growing ties between our two worlds."

Foxwell smiled and nodded in agreement. "As we say on Earth: 'I'll drink to that.'" Clearing his throat, Foxwell continued: "On a separate note, and with all due respect, there is another subject of the utmost importance I wish to discuss with you."

Strojok acknowledged with a curious look. "And what would that be?"

Staring into the eyes of the Vulcan captain, Foxwell did not mince words: "We need Vulcan's help developing warp technology."

Strojok furrowed his thick eyebrows.

"Yes . . . warp technology," Foxwell repeated. "Please know I fully support building mutual trust, understanding, and collaboration through cultural, scientific, and educational programs, et cetera, to include cultivating popular support for the wider relationship between our worlds."

"I am listening . . . continue."

"Then hear this: Although I disagreed with Utek in reference to her motives, I believe part of it was a sincere, but misguided effort to save both the Grey and human species. She had come to the wrongful conclusion that forcefully crossbreeding humans and Greys would solve the conundrum plaguing both species."

Strojok sighed deeply. "It was a gross miscalculation of logic on her part." He turned back in Foxwell's direction. "You mentioned warp technology. Please continue . . . and elaborate."

Foxwell paced slowly around the hangar bay. "Warp technology is not only the future for space travel, but it can also be harnessed to generate limitless clean energy."

Strojok sighed, looking aimlessly around the compartment. "You are correct, Captain. Warp technology has been used on Vulcan for decades to produce all the energy we require. Considering Vulcan is a warmer planet than Earth, it has eliminated the problem of greenhouse emissions, and has benefitted our planet enormously by curtailing a further rise in surface temperatures."

"And I'm certain Utek was aware warp technology could be employed to solve those same issues we've been dealing with for centuries on Earth," Foxwell surmised, "yet she—"

"Utek was opposed to sharing warp technology with humans, along with many others in government and the scientific community," Strojok interrupted.

"That much I know," Foxwell declared. "The question is: Why?"

The older Vulcan captain walked slowly around the hangar. "I am not at liberty to discuss it with you. That is an issue we must leave for the leaders of both our worlds to deal with and resolve."

"It confirms again what I and others have suspected for quite some time," Foxwell revealed. "Vulcan has withheld sharing warp technology with the scientific and engineering community on Earth as an adjunct to complement ongoing research. If the government and people of Vulcan are sincere regarding their desire to deepen our friendship and strengthen ties, I would implore you to take this message to your government, your scientific community, and the people of Vulcan. And I would emphasize this is more imperative than ever, considering Utek's belief that solving the Earth's global warming crisis was her de facto support of a takeover by the Greys through hybridization and assimilation . . . even if it wasn't part of a greater Vulcan conspiracy."

Strojok turned and faced Foxwell. "You have presented a compelling and *logical* argument. I will discuss your proposal with the Vulcan liaison when we return to Earth, with a recommendation that it be brought to the attention of the Vulcan High Council."

"Then our mission has, in fact, been successful, Captain, and I am most grateful."

Strojok raised his right hand, his palm outward. He placed his fingers in a "V" shape, separating the middle and ring fingers, while keeping the others together. His thumb was extended.

"Live long and prosper."

* * *

Stardate: July 01, 2097

SS Stargazer / Hangar Bay / Earth orbit

Attired in full dress uniform, Captain Jon Leonidas Foxwell stood at the podium in front of a wedding party and guests, the groom waiting in front of the podium with the best man and groomsmen. The bride-to-be remained out of sight, finally emerging as the hangar bay's audio system played "Canon in D (Pachelbel's Canon)."

Escorted to the podium by Chief Engineer O'Donovan, he then stepped away as Ensign Sarah Lindsey took her place next to her soon-to-be husband. Flaunting a baby bump in a trendy new Galactic Fleet maternity dress, she beamed happily.

"One of the most enjoyable duties of a ship's captain is the privilege of joining two people in holy matrimony," Captain Foxwell began. "Today I have the honor of uniting Sarah Elizabeth Lindsey and James Patrick Roberts in marriage."

Exchanging vows and pledging their love and loyalty to each other followed by the ring exchange, Captain Foxwell joined their hands together, clasping their hands with his, all three reverently bowing their heads, stating: "In accordance with our laws and our many beliefs, you both have committed yourselves to one another and to your Holy Union through the sacred vows that you have taken and by the giving and receiving of these rings. I now pronounce you husband and wife. You may kiss the bride."

The small crowd of onlookers cheered with enthusiasm as they surrounded the happy couple. Captain Foxwell stepped forward and embraced the bride, rendering a congratulatory kiss on her cheek before turning and shaking hands with Ensign Roberts.

Dr. Rivera and Beta stood next to one another among the throng of guests, slowly making their way forward to offer their congratulations; other crew members hastily rearranged the hangar bay in preparation for the reception to follow.

"My understanding is they'll be honeymooning on the Greek island Santorini," Rivera divulged, "and will spend some time island hopping around other parts of the Mediterranean. The captain granted a two-week leave, as well as the use of his beachfront home in Santo Antão in Cape Verde. Santo Antão has a reputation of being the most visually stunning of all the islands. Did you know—"

"I'm aware of that, Doctor," Beta interrupted, "and I'm very pleased to know the happy couple is eager to enjoy a wonderful honeymoon. I wish both the very best." Stopping and pivoting in Rivera's direction, she placed her hand on his arm. "Reminding you I am the *Stargazer*'s science officer, Doctor, would you agree you are somewhat overdue with your report regarding the return of their embryo retrieved from the Greys?"

Rivera sighed. "Well, this is a helluva time to be asking, but I suppose it's partially my fault. You were not present at the time the Vulcan medical staff and I performed the procedure en route back to Earth. Everything went well. The Vulcans possess incredible medical technology. The embryo was literally *beamed* back inside the mother's womb, and all we did was reconnect the plumbing, so to speak. After a few days of recovery and observation onboard the *T'Vahl*, Lindsey was transported directly to sickbay aboard the *Stargazer*. The captain and Ensign Roberts were fully briefed afterward."

"And if it's not too much trouble, Doctor, can you

provide a three month post-procedural prognosis?"

Rivera grinned in embarrassment. "I'm happy to inform you the embryo is now a three-month-old fetus and progressing well, growing and developing normally. During my exam yesterday, she and the baby were doing just fine. Additional testing again confirmed no hybridization occurred."

"Well, then, to borrow a well-known Vulcan phrase—fascinating."

Sufficiently chastised, Rivera nodded in agreement.

"And may I sincerely add . . . it sounds like the most wonderful wedding gift an expectant mother and father could ever wish for," Beta declared.

"Amen to that," Rivera replied.

Continuing to make their way toward the married couple, Rivera stopped again, then wheeled around. "Just out of curiosity," he asked, "what do *you* think of this whole idea of marriage?"

Beta furrowed her eyebrows. "I've never given it much thought considering my career with Galactic Fleet, coupled with the fact I am a cyborg," she said, pivoting and locking eyes with Rivera. "But I am also a woman. The prospect of marriage is . . . intriguing."

Rivera smiled. "I'm sure someday you will find someone who is worthy of the honor you prefer."

"You mean the 'someone will sweep me off my feet' sort of thing?"

"Absolutely."

"Followed perhaps by a proposal of marriage at some point?"

Rivera chuckled. "Of course . . . but with one important caveat."

"Caveat?"

"Yes, the *only* proposal *you*, Beta, would ever agree to be appropriate and acceptable."

"And what would that be?" she asked, curious.

The doctor returned a mischievous grin. "Well, a *reasonable* proposal, what else?"

Clearing her throat, Beta initially appeared nonplussed at Rivera's flip remark.

Turning away, the chief medical officer attempted to curtail his amusement.

"Oh, puh-leeze, Doctor," she finally grumbled, Rivera now howling with laughter.

THE END

EPISODE V

THE B'ALOSIAN PARADIGM

PROLOGUE

En route to Vulcan as part of a student exchange program, the *Stargazer* receives a priority-one message directing Captain Foxwell to embark Gella, a fugitive B'alosian humanoid, and her escort, Chu'lok, a Vulcan diplomat. The *Stargazer* is ordered to change course and proceed to B'alos, an isolated but known planet embroiled in a longstanding civil war in an unchartered section of the galaxy. Gella's pursuer (Deputy Minister Ragel) soon arrives and demands that she be turned over to him for extradition back to their home planet where she is to be tried as a terrorist. Their mutual hatred is ideology based, and despite attempts by Foxwell and others, they are not prepared to reconcile. The distinction is not lost on the *Stargazer*'s senior officers, who, with much trepidation, recall Earth and Vulcan's history of hate and intolerance.

PART I

Captain's Log / Stardate: Sept. 16, 2097

Ordered to the planet Vulcan, the SS Stargazer is transporting twenty-five science and engineering cadets to participate in a new academic and cultural exchange program that will allow Galactic Fleet Academy students the opportunity for interplanetary visitation hosted by a Vulcan partner institution. In return, twenty-five students from the Vulcan Science Academy will board the SS Stargazer for a return voyage to Earth to embark on a reciprocal journey established and administered by Galactic Fleet Academy.

* * *

Returning his Personal Access Display Device to its charging port on the command chair, Foxwell stood and walked toward the navigational command console. "Navigator, what is our estimated time of arrival to Vulcan?"

Scanning the instruments on the console, the navigator craned his head slightly. "At present speed our ETA is approximately one hour, twenty-two minutes, Captain."

"Still too far away to see their world," Foxwell noted, walking closer to the main viewing screen. "Very well . . . steady as she goes."

Swiveling her seat in the captain's direction, the communications officer announced: "Captain, a priority-one subspace message from Galactic Fleet Command has just been received."

"Wonderful," Foxwell responded in a sarcastic tone, completing an about-face and rolling his eyes slightly. "And here I thought I was going to spend a few days on Vulcan touring their science academy, discussing warp technology with the appropriate officials . . . and should time allow, visit the widely heralded Vulcan Fire Plains and the Voroth Sea."

Xuriya displayed an encouraging smile. "Perhaps it's just a routine message, sir . . . or Galactic Fleet inquiring about our arrival time to Vulcan," she speculated.

Foxwell balked. "A priority-one message from Admiral Perry is never routine, Lieutenant, nor sent for the purpose of arrival confirmation." Exchanging glances with his communications officer, he returned an appreciative smile. "Forward the message to my ready room."

"Aye, Captain," she replied, swiveling her chair back in the direction of the communications console.

Continuing toward the science station, Foxwell stood next to his first officer. "Sensor status?"

Beta swung her seat around. "All sensor grids functioning normally, Captain. No abnormal readings or unusual phenomena noted. Barring any unforeseen anomalies, our journey should remain unimpeded."

Foxwell looked around, pausing to rub his chin. Noticing the captain's hesitation, she rotated her chair again in his direction. "Captain, is there something else you—"

"No . . . no," he mumbled. "Thought I'd check sensor readings. It seems unusual to receive a priority-one message when we're so close to our destination. Just my instincts kicking in, I suppose."

"Understood," Beta replied. "Perhaps you'll discover the subject of the message to be the recently approved student exchange program between Earth and Vulcan. It's my understanding Galactic Fleet Command has designated this cultural and educational affair a top priority."

"Could be," Foxwell cautiously surmised. Exchanging his pensive expression with a smile, he pivoted back in the direction of his science officer. "Well, let's find out. Please accompany me to my ready room. Xuriya, you have the conn."

"Aye, sir."

After accompanying the captain into the ready room, Beta adjusted one of several video display units in preparation for consultation with Admiral Perry. She took a seat at the conference table next to Foxwell and activated the monitor. The Galactic Fleet logo emerged, followed by Admiral Perry's appearance. Confirming audio and dressed in his standard admiral's working uniform, he began: "Greetings Captain and Commander."

"Good day to you, Admiral," Foxwell replied. "Always a pleasure to hear from you, sir. How can we be of assistance?"

The admiral took in a deep breath. "Captain, this message is sent with the understanding the *Stargazer* will reach Vulcan in less than two hours. Is that still accurate?"

"Affirmative, Admiral. One hour, eleven minutes to be exact."

"Very well. You are to assume standard orbit at which time all Earth exchange students will be transported by the Vulcan High Command directly to the science academy."

Foxwell glanced at Beta, perplexed. Craning his head back in the direction of the monitor, he said, "Acknowledged,

Admiral; that's our understanding as well per mission orders received prior to our departure from Earth, to be followed by—"

"Captain, the Vulcan exchange students will not board the *Stargazer* as originally planned," the admiral interrupted. "There has been a change in the *Stargazer*'s mission. Following the transport of the Earth exchange students, a Vulcan diplomatic representative will be transported along with a female humanoid to the *Stargazer*'s hangar bay. Upon confirmation they are safely aboard, you are to immediately break orbit and assume a new heading for the planet B'alos."

Beta gazed at Foxwell. "B'alos is a class M terrestrial world in an uncharted area in the northernmost part of the Alpha quadrant, Captain. We know it is inhabited . . . nothing more."

Caught off guard and exasperated by the unexpected change, Foxwell turned and faced the monitor. "What are the new mission orders, Admiral?"

Adjusting the position of his monitor, Admiral Perry turned and stared back at the screen. "Your guests are to be escorted directly to your ready room where they will brief you on the new assignment, Captain. Also, be advised the Vulcan High Council is unanimous in their agreement that the revised mission is of critical importance."

"And Galactic Fleet Command?" Foxwell asked.

"We are in lockstep with their decision," Admiral Perry declared.

* * *

Escorted from the hangar bay by two security personnel, the Vulcan diplomat and his humanoid colleague sensed the *Stargazer*'s turbo elevator had suddenly stopped.

"Guests on the bridge," a security officer announced, the doors opening with their usual swoosh.

Standing several feet away and facing the elevator, Foxwell and Beta prepared to greet their Vulcan counterpart and the unknown guest he was escorting. "Greetings, and welcome aboard the *Stargazer*," the captain formally announced to both, Beta standing next to him. "I'm Captain Foxwell, commanding officer," he politely announced before pivoting in Beta's direction. "This is First Officer and Science Officer Beta."

"And I am Chu'lok," the Vulcan tersely replied, glancing briefly at his humanoid companion. "We are here on orders of the Vulcan High Council for the purpose of briefing you and your first officer on a critical change of mission."

"Yes, uh . . . so we've been told," Foxwell remarked, his tone irritated but resigned.

Displaying the usual stony and impassive expression, the Vulcan diplomat fit the stereotypical human description of coldness and arrogance. Wearing a two-piece rust-colored formal uniform, the jacket sported a high collar with decorative trim, his diplomatic designation visible on the right collar.

"Live long and prosper," Captain Foxwell uttered, raising his right hand and displaying the traditional Vulcan salute in an attempt to lessen the uncomfortable awkwardness that now permeated the bridge. Foxwell's unexpected change in introductory formalities took the bridge crew by surprise. They turned and gawked like a deer in the headlights.

The Vulcan diplomat spontaneously raised his arm. Spreading all five digits of his hand with the middle and ring fingers separated, his thumb extended, he coolly replied: "Peace and long life."

The accompanying humanoid turned and locked eyes with Foxwell.

"Allow me to introduce myself," she said, ignoring Chu'lok's lack of introductory protocol. "I am Gella . . . from the planet B'alos." Her uniform, an off-white one-piece jumpsuit that covered her entire torso to include her hands, was accentuated with ribbing on the upper arms and sides. The only part of her anatomy that was clearly visible was her head, and more prominently, her face, which took on a noticeable, bluish hue. Her hair was a closely cropped pixie cut silvery white. She appeared and behaved like a human from every other aspect.

"Shall we proceed to your ready room, Captain?" Chu'lok suddenly suggested.

Feeling more at ease, Foxwell exhaled a sigh of relief. "Took the words right out of my mouth," he smiled, extending his arm in the direction of his personal office.

PART II

Stardate: Sept. 16, 2097

Planet B'alos

Engulfed in a centuries-old civil war, civilization is on the brink of total collapse. Neither side is agreeable to any peace overtures nor any idea of compromise. And so the war continues, with unrelenting attacks and counterattacks that are interminably and tragically destroying the planet—adding to the growing roster of billions who have already perished.

* * *

B'alosian Ruling Council:

"Sources have confirmed the traitor Gella is aboard a Galactic Fleet battlecruiser of Earth origin, and is presently en route from Vulcan to B'alos," a member of the ruling counsel announced.

"We must dispatch Deputy Minister Ragel immediately," another member urged.

"Yes . . . yes, agree," the remaining council members mumbled, nodding in the affirmative and exchanging glances with one another. "Summon Ragel and prepare for a briefing."

* * *

SS Stargazer / Captain's Ready Room

"Now that the introductory formalities are concluded, perhaps you can enlighten my first officer and me as to our new mission orders," Foxwell politely demanded, glancing back and forth between Chu'lok and Gella.

Sitting in tandem at the oval table in the ready room, the Vulcan and B'alosian exchanged a hurried look. "Shall I?" Gella offered, appearing eager to brief the captain and his first officer seated on the table's opposite side as to the reason for their presence aboard the *Stargazer*.

Chu'lok rendered an approving nod.

"Very well," she said, her demeanor growing more serious. Turning her attention in the direction of the *Stargazer*'s captain and first officer, she began by thanking Foxwell and Beta for their hospitality.

"Our pleasure. Now, let's get on with it. Why are you two here?" Foxwell asked bluntly.

Gella took a deep breath and sighed. "B'alos has been embroiled in a civil war for hundreds of years, Captain. Reactionary forces have sought to destroy us and assume control as the majority ruling party."

Foxwell gave a puzzled look. "Did you say reactionary forces?"

"Us? Who is . . . *us*?" Beta chimed in, curious.

The companel emitted a hailing signal.

"Foxwell here."

"Sorry for the interruption, Captain," Xuriya broke

in, "but sensors have detected the presence of an unknown spacecraft. It appears to be in pursuit of the *Stargazer*."

Foxwell paused, then looked around the room. "On my way." Exchanging glances with Chu'lok and Gella, he voiced a perfunctory explanation. "Please excuse the interruption; we'll continue this discussion at the first opportunity. Please remain in the ready room until further notice." He pivoted in Beta's direction. "Please accompany me to the bridge."

"Aye, Captain."

Exiting the ready room and onto the bridge, Beta returned to the science station and began reviewing data from the ship's sensors. Standing next to the command chair, Foxwell stared at the main viewing screen. "Switch to aft viewer," he ordered.

"Aye sir," the helmsman replied.

"Distance?"

"Eighty thousand kilometers and closing rapidly," the navigator answered. "Still no visual, even at extreme magnification."

Foxwell spun around. "Beta, I need a sensor status."

Focused on the displays, the first officer responded in a loud voice. "Sensors confirm a small, shuttle-size craft, capable of warp speed. It appears to be coated in an unknown material rendering it detectable only to our sensors, which explains no visual contact." She turned and locked eyes with Foxwell. "Whatever it is, they can outrun us, Captain."

Flustered, Foxwell resisted the fleeting notion of his anticipated discussions with the Vulcans about warp technology. *If only we . . .*

"Xuriya," he yelled out, breaking his train of thought. "Hail the alien vessel . . . all channels."

"Aye, sir."

"They're closing fast," the helmsman shouted.

"All hands, CONDITION RED," Foxwell yelled, the alarm sounding throughout the *Stargazer*. He wheeled in the direction of his weapons officer. "Lieutenant, polarize the hull plating; prepare to fire aft energy torpedoes."

"Aye, Captain."

"Any response to our hails?" Foxwell bellowed, glancing at his communications officer.

"No response, sir."

"Weapons officer, status?"

"Hull polarized at one hundred percent," Warwick confirmed. "Aft torpedoes locked and ready to fire. Distance ten thousand kilometers and closing."

Beta swiveled her chair and stood. "Captain," she yelled out. "Sensors confirm pursuit by the alien vessel has ceased. Aft viewer now confirms a faintly visible debris field. The craft has disintegrated."

Foxwell walked back and sat in his chair, staring at the aft viewer. "Helmsman, disengage fusion light drive. Full stop."

"Aye, Captain. Full stop."

Wheeling around, Foxwell redirected his attention back to his science officer. "Explanation?"

"None, Captain. The vessel's forward momentum and deceleration occurred simultaneously with destruction of the alien ship."

The bridge turbo elevator doors opened abruptly with their usual swoosh. "Perhaps I can explain," a loud voice said. A male humanoid approximately six feet tall of medium build exited. He walked defiantly onto the bridge, his hands lightly clasped behind his back. With closely cropped silvery white hair, he was donned in the same identical off-white one-piece jumpsuit Gella was wearing.

His face portrayed an uncanny, reddish tinge.

The weapons officer brandished his fusion laser pistol, pointing it at the uninvited intruder. Caught totally off guard, everyone on the bridge stood and gawked at the sight of the strange humanoid from another world.

"Everyone . . . remain where you are," Foxwell ordered, discreetly tapping a security alert button on the command chair's control panel. "Secure from CONDITION RED," he shouted into the companel. He turned in the direction of the unexpected visitor. "How did you get aboard?"

"I am Deputy Minister Ragel," the alien announced, ignoring the question. "I am chief administrative officer on the Board of Political Traitors from the planet B'alos. You have onboard your ship an escaped prisoner, Gella, from my planet who fled after being arrested and charged with treason. I am here to take custody of the fugitive and return her to B'alos to stand trial."

The turbo elevator doors opened. Four security officers hurried onto the bridge, fusion laser pistols in hand. Foxwell stood and faced the alien intruder. "And I am the commanding officer of this ship. I am the final authority regarding what happens aboard the *Stargazer*." He inched closer, locking eyes with the B'alosian intruder. "There will be no bounty hunting or self-appointed vigilantism on board this ship . . . is that understood?"

Ragel bowed his head, then let out a deep breath, his hands still clasped behind his back. "I absolutely agree, Captain," he replied apologetically, a half-smile crossing his lips. "That's exactly why I have been authorized by the Board of Political Traitors to—"

"Everyone aboard the *Stargazer*, including visitors . . . are under my command," Foxwell interrupted. "You will both be returned to B'alos, each of you to your own people.

Thereafter you can plead your case to the proper authorities on your planet."

Beta pivoted in Ragel's direction. "Neither Vulcan nor Earth have extradition treaties with B'alos," she joined in. "Therefore, your claim and the rights of the accused require due process only to the extent that we return you safely to your home world, without judgment."

With an exasperated sigh, Ragel reluctantly accepted the explanations given by Foxwell and Beta. "Very well," he grumbled. "Then I would like to go on record that I accept your decision, simply because I have no other choice . . . and under protest."

"Duly noted," Foxwell replied.

"May I see Gella, please?" Ragel requested.

Foxwell gave a contemplative look. "I'll allow it on the condition you remember you are a guest aboard the *Stargazer* and are subject to my authority and the rules and regulations of this starship."

The alien humanoid gave a confirming nod. "With your approval, Captain."

Foxwell wheeled around. "Beta and Lieutenant Warwick will accompany us to the ready room. Security team personnel will remain on the bridge. Xuriya, you have the conn."

"Aye, Captain."

PART III

Stardate: Sept. 16, 2097

Ragel's unexpected entrance into the ready room took Gella by surprise. She immediately stood, backing away from the small conference table and against the bulkhead. "What's he doing here?" she demanded.

Foxwell caught the look of genuine startlement flashing across Gella's face. He turned and glanced at Ragel, his placatory tone and gestures now replaced by a sardonic expression.

Chu'lok stood. "Captain, I must protest this intrusion. There was no warning or advance notice of this B'alosian's participation in our meeting." He turned and faced Ragel. "Who are you . . . and why are you here?"

"You know who I am, Vulcan," Ragel voiced in an accusatory tone. He paused for a moment before continuing: "However, for the benefit of everyone present, and as I have already explained to the captain, I am the chief administrative officer on the Board of Political Traitors from the planet B'alos." He quickly glanced at everyone in the ready room, then pointed at Gella. "You are harboring a fugitive from justice. You are protecting this criminal with the explicit knowledge and approval of your government in collusion with Earth authorities."

Beta walked next to Gella and turned around, staring at Ragel. "You stated she is accused of treason. Exactly what treasonous acts has she been charged with committing?"

Ragel revealed Gella was previously arrested and charged with leading a revolt against the ruling order. Gella responded by alleging Ragel's people are responsible for sowing seeds of hate and destruction, persecuting and arresting her people because of our ideas and beliefs. "They lack empathy and the ability to compromise," she charged, "to include unrelenting efforts to thwart and dismiss our ideas and beliefs. We are simply attempting to make our voices heard."

Ragel lurched forward, his face contorted with rage. "If burning, looting, and terrorizing the general populace fits the description of making your voices heard, then you and your people are doing an admiral job . . . you traitorous criminal of order and decency."

Foxwell stood and leaned over the table. "Calm down, mister." He turned and looked at Chu'lok. "What do you know about this?"

The Vulcan diplomat remained seated at the ready room table, craning his head in Foxwell's direction, his face expressionless. "Vulcan is aware of their longstanding civil war. While we abhor the violence and destruction the conflict has inflicted upon the people of B'alos and their planet, their conundrum has nevertheless been confined to their world. Their hostilities are no threat to Vulcan or neighboring planets; therefore, logic dictates it is a matter for the B'alosians to resolve."

Perplexed for a moment, Foxwell remained standing, not quite sure what to say next. Exhaling an exasperated sigh, he asked, "Then why on Earth and Vulcan are you and Gella here?"

"I have been tasked with ensuring that Gella is returned safely to her planet," Chu'lok answered.

"You're telling me that our new mission orders are to return Gella to B'alos?" Foxwell repeated, incredulous.

"That is correct, Captain."

"How did she get to Vulcan . . . and what was the purpose of her visit?"

"The same way Ragel made his appearance on the *Stargazer*," Chu'lok replied. "We took her into custody after violating our planetary sovereignty in a vessel which disintegrated after entering our atmosphere. They have the ability to generate a protective force field which is penetrable only by others of their species."

Foxwell exhaled another disgruntled sigh. "That explains why they were not injured." He turned and looked at the Vulcan diplomat. "Continue."

"Gella asked for asylum as a political refugee. Her request was refused, and a decision was made to return her to B'alos. She then voiced her concern that the B'alosian Ruling Council would send a political officer to Vulcan to take custody before we could deport her. We decided to return Gella before that party arrived."

"Captain, I must protest," Ragel cut in. "This is interference in the internal affairs of my world. I demand—"

Foxwell wheeled around. "You're in no position to demand anything. You have been granted guest status aboard the *Stargazer* despite your illegal embarkation. Consider yourself lucky I haven't confined you to the brig."

Beta exchanged glances with Chu'lok. "What is the ideological nature of their conflict?"

The Vulcan diplomat's piercing eyes swept over Gella and Ragel in response to Beta's question. "Perhaps it would be better if the two parties from B'alos answered that question," he proposed.

Foxwell nodded. "I agree . . . so let's hear it. And I want no interruptions." He turned and exchanged a look with Gella. "Make your argument."

Gella's golden brown gaze swept over everyone in the conference room, stopping when they rolled over the face of Ragel. Returning a pointed finger at her accuser, she began: "His people seek power over others. They are motivated by wealth accumulation, and prefer conformity, hierarchy, and clear-cut rules for everything. Their goal is domination of society by aristocracy. Their views are incompatible with democracy, prosperity, and civilization in general. It is a destructive system of inequality and prejudice that is founded on deception and has no place on B'alos."

Foxwell glanced at Ragel. "Your turn."

Ragel countered by explaining that Gella's people wanted to use government to impose their values: ". . . in the process reduce people and issues to crude identity politics . . . and by hiding radical agenda programs and policies behind an impoverished sense of morality. They have no loyalty, no respect for authority, and no sanctity. When we refuse to acquiesce to their demands, they respond by encouraging and fomenting violence and destruction of property, threats, and acts of terrorism."

Beta walked toward the conference room table. "This conundrum is exactly what Earth politics devolved into in the latter twentieth and the first several decades of the twenty-first century," she explained. "It was known as The Ideological Conflict Hypothesis: Intolerance Among Liberals and Conservatives."

"That is true," Foxwell joined in. "People moved on, matured . . . became wiser. They decided it was in their best interests to be more tolerant. Liberals and conservatives made the mutually beneficial decision intolerance was no longer a viable policy. Society and government transformed and adapted to the point where political parties and partisanship had outlived their usefulness and no longer served productive purposes."

"Vulcan evolved as well," Chu'lok continued. "Logic overcame political infighting, and our propensity for violence due to past differences and inequities slowly dissipated. Our planet is governed by the Vulcan High Council, a group of seven non-political civilian officials, each responsible for a different ministry. Elections are held every ten years, with candidates selected *logically* based on merit."

Beta glanced at the two B'alosioans. "This explains the blue and red hues regarding the color of their skin, as well as their inflexible and uncompromising liberal and conservative beliefs, respectively; novel traits for each side. It's *reasonable* to hypothesize that strictly enforced partisan segregation over centuries somehow resulted in a change in each group's genetic structure, resulting in the slow evolvement of blue- or red-tinted skin. It means the people of B'alos are blue or red at birth depending on which group they are born within. Their liberal and conservative personas and behavior develop as they grow into adulthood within their segregated environments."

Ragel let out a snickering laugh. "Those are all interesting theories and stories," he began. "And thank you for the history lesson involving your two worlds. I applaud your political and societal progression, but I have every intention of completing my mission, and that is to deliver Gella to the prison authorities and to pursue additional charges for escape."

"You mean to a concentration camp," Gella ranted in a frightened tone. "I am to be incarcerated as an enemy of the

state, without regard to legal norms of arrest and imprison-
ment. Their ultimate goal is my elimination, and that of my
people."

Foxwell glanced at Beta and sadly shook his head. "It
appears your hypothesis rings true." He turned and faced
the two B'alosians. "Our mission orders do not specify
anything other than your safe return . . . which is why I
have decided to return you to your own people. You will
be ferried to the planet via our shuttlecraft, accompanied
by Beta, Chief Weapons Officer Warwick, and two security
officers."

Chu'lok stood. "And I am available to meet with the
B'alosian authorities as an unofficial representative of Earth
and Vulcan," the Vulcan diplomat affirmed, "should the
conditions for such a meeting present itself."

Ragel gazed at Chu'lok and sneered. "Rest assured your
logic and assistance is neither necessary nor welcomed."

"My people will never attend or even suggest such a
meeting," Gella emphasized.

"Nevertheless, any interference to return either of you
to your planet and to your own people will be regarded as
a provocative incident," Chu'lok cautioned. "You would be
wise to consider my warning."

"I concur," Foxwell broke in, glancing back and forth
between the two B'alosians. "And I don't want any more
trouble now or on the shuttle when we return you home . . .
from either of you." There was a slight pause before he
added: "Have I made myself perfectly clear?"

Gella slowly stepped forward. "Yes, Captain . . .
understood."

Foxwell turned and locked eyes with Ragel. With a
subdued sigh, he muttered, "You have my word, Captain."

PART IV

Stardate: Sept. 17, 2097

Ordered to escort Gella and Ragel separately and away from each other, security officers maintained a constant presence around the two B'alosians as the *Stargazer* continued on its journey to B'alos. Gella and Ragel attempted to enlist the sympathies of the senior officers and crew while en route to their home world.

Approaching B'alos, Beta analyzed the sensor readings from her station on the bridge. She swiveled her chair in the direction of Foxwell. "Captain, sensors have detected massive destruction of major cities. Fires and secondary explosions continue to erupt all over the planet."

Foxwell stood. "What the hell is going on down there? Do sensors indicate or confirm any interplanetary attack from known or unknown vessels?"

"Negative," Beta replied. "The destruction appears to be solely the result of conflict on B'alos. It's *reasonable* to assume there has been a major escalation of their global civil war."

"What's your best initial assessment?"

Beta pressed her lips together, then sighed. "Total worldwide destruction, Captain, with no indication of any living humanoids remaining on the planet."

Foxwell stood. "Xuriya," he shouted while staring at the main viewing screen. "Open all channels . . . position all communication arrays in the direction of B'alos. Commence standard communications protocol."

"All channels open, Captain; transmitting on all frequencies."

"Maintain a continuous transmission loop."

"Aye, sir."

Foxwell turned in the direction of his chief security officer. "Lieutenant Warwick. What's the status regarding our guests' whereabouts?"

Warwick glanced at the crew locator on his control panel. "Gella is in the crew lounge," he replied. "Ragel is in the security department. Both are under escort."

Foxwell craned his head in the direction of the communications station. "Anything?"

"No response, sir."

Beta returned to her station. She leaned over and reviewed the sensor readings before turning to Foxwell. "Sensors confirm more than a billion dead . . . the remaining population of the planet. It appears both sides have mutually destroyed themselves as a consequence of their ongoing political conflict."

Foxwell ambled slowly in the direction of his security chief. "Have security escort Gella and Ragel to my ready room," he ordered, his tone of voice somber.

"Aye, Captain."

* * *

Captain's Ready Room

Informed by Foxwell of their findings, Gella and Ragel were offered a choice of beginning a new life on Vulcan or Earth, imploring them to give up their mutual hatred of one another, reminding both that same antipathy resulted in the destruction of their planet and genocide of their people.

Ragel turned and stared at Gella, an expression of hostility contorting his face. "You . . . you and your people did this," he raged. "You uncivilized representative of all that's putrid and evil. You and your depraved sympathizers destroyed our planet and killed *my* people."

Gella screamed back at Ragel. "No, it was you . . . you and your people who have wielded all power and control for centuries, you pathological megalomaniac. It was you and your fascist xenophobes who destroyed our world and killed *my* people."

Ragel and Gella lunged at each other, both grasping the other by the neck. An audible and noticeable energy aura appeared around both as they struggled in the small compartment comprising the ready room. A security officer attempted to separate them but was thrown backward by the energy generated by the electromagnetic field.

"Enough!" Foxwell shouted. "Keep this up and you'll accomplish the same thing that has occurred on your planet. You'll kill each other or destroy the *Stargazer*. Neither of you will survive."

Releasing each other, they doubled over, both exhausted from the struggle and ensuing energy drain.

"I appeal to both of you to set aside your hatred," Foxwell implored. "You are the only survivors of a destroyed world. Accept our offer of a new life on Earth or Vulcan."

"Captain Foxwell is correct," Chu'lok joined in. "Accept

the offer extended and return with us to begin a new life. It is the only *logical* alternative."

"I prefer to return to my home world," Gella demanded.

"I too, prefer to return to B'alos," Ragel insisted.

Strolling over to the last living survivors of a worldwide Armageddon, Beta again attempted to persuade Gella and Ragel to reconsider.

"B'alos is a dead world," she reminded them. "There are no living B'alosians remaining. The planet's infrastructure has been totally destroyed. Your decision to return is totally *unreasonable*."

"Totally *illogical*," Chu'lok affirmed. "Long-term survival will be impossible."

Gella and Ragel insisted they be returned to B'alos.

Foxwell shook his head in quiet contemplation and sighed. "There is no recourse but to grant their requests," he acquiesced. Walking quietly around the cramped compartment, the *Stargazer's* captain stopped, looking outside the ready room's only viewing port at the surface below. The starship was close enough to view thousands of fires still raging across the battered globe, the resultant smoke and ash rising through the atmosphere, slowly spreading over its once living green surface and blue oceans like a metastasizing cancer.

The ready room's companel emitted a hailing signal.

"Foxwell here."

"Captain, our trajectory toward B'alos remains unchanged," the navigator cautioned. "If we continue on our present course, the *Stargazer* will breach orbital parameters and enter the planet's atmosphere."

"Prepare to assume standard orbit," Foxwell ordered.

"Aye, sir."

Foxwell spun around and faced everyone in the ready

room. "Although B'alos is now a dead world, neither Gella nor Ragel have committed any crime that would require they be returned to Vulcan or Earth to face charges. And we cannot force them against their will to remain with us."

Beta nodded. "The *reasonable* expectation would be for the only two survivors of B'alos to remain with us . . . but I agree they cannot be forced to do so."

"And I concur," Chu'lok noted. "It is the only *logical* alternative, but I acknowledge they have the right to exercise their own choice . . . even if that choice ultimately proves to be *illogical*."

Foxwell glanced at his first officer. "Make preparations to ferry our guests to a non-battle zone of their choice on the planet's surface. Chief of Security Warwick and two of his officers will accompany you. Gella and Ragel will be restrained in separate seats in the rear of the shuttle. Arrange for a containment field to be activated in a manner which ensures our B'alosian guests remain separated."

"Aye, Captain."

* * *

Standing next to Chu'lok on the bridge and watching the shuttlecraft depart on the main viewer, Foxwell declared all Gella and Ragel have left is their mutual hatred of each other. "There is no question they wish to continue the fight, even if it means the total extinction of their species."

"The last two sapient life forms on a dead planet," Chu'lok noted.

Foxwell watched the main viewer as new fires and secondary explosions continued to erupt on the surface of B'alos. "It's difficult and frightening to believe Earth came close to suffering a similar fate," he confessed to Chu'lok.

"Our planet was on the verge of a global civil war; intolerance and hate had escalated to the point liberals and conservatives had drawn up plans to annihilate each other . . . but cooler heads finally prevailed. A catastrophe was averted. Now we look back and wonder how that even happened. It's required reading at the academy."

"And I confess past events were very similar on Vulcan," Chu'lok acknowledged. "We were once an extremely violent and emotional people. War, paranoia, and homicidal rage was common, to the point our violent nature threatened our own extinction as well. It was only through a culture of strict discipline, study, and meditation that we evolved and replaced emotion with a mastery of logic in nearly every aspect of our existence."

Foxwell sighed deeply. "It's a tragedy that what worked for Vulcan and Earth was never given a chance on B'alos. All those misguided people had was their mutual intolerance and hatred, and they couldn't evolve beyond it."

Xuriya swiveled her chair in the direction of Foxwell and Chu'lok. "Captain, Commander Beta reports she has returned Gella and Ragel to the planet's surface. There were no issues. The shuttlecraft is on a return course to the *Stargazer*."

"Very well," Foxwell replied, returning to the command chair. "Helmsman and navigator—prepare to set a course for Vulcan as soon as the shuttle and its crew have safely returned to the hangar bay."

"Aye, Captain," they replied in unison.

Foxwell gazed quickly around the bridge before returning his attention back to the Vulcan diplomat. "We have a group of Vulcan exchange students who are eager to begin their journey to Earth," he announced, a tired look in his eyes.

The bridge crew looked around at each other. They were again perplexed by Foxwell's use of a certain adjective within his pronouncement.

Chu'lok portrayed a contemplative expression. "Did you say . . . eager?"

THE END